#2
E B
3.97
3/71

WITHDRAWN

Books
by Jerome Weidman

NOVELS
I Can Get It for You Wholesale
What's in It for Me?
I'll Never Go There Any More
The Lights Around the Shore
Too Early to Tell
The Price Is Right
The Hand of the Hunter
Give Me Your Love
The Third Angel
Your Daughter Iris
The Enemy Camp
Before You Go
The Sound of Bow Bells
Word of Mouth
Other People's Money
The Center of the Action
Fourth Street East

SHORT STORIES
The Horse That Could Whistle "Dixie"
The Captain's Tiger
A Dime a Throw
Nine Stories
My Father Sits in the Dark
The Death of Dickie Draper

ESSAYS AND TRAVEL
Letter of Credit
Traveler's Cheque
Back Talk

PLAYS
Fiorello!
Tenderloin
I Can Get It for You Wholesale
Asterisk: A Comedy of Terrors
Ivory Tower (with James Yaffe)

Fourth
Street
East

Fourth Street East

A Novel of How It Was

by
Jerome Weidman

Random House
New York

Weidman

Copyright © 1970 by Jerome Weidman

All rights reserved under International
and Pan-American Copyright Conventions.
Published in the United States by
Random House, Inc., New York, and simultaneously
in Canada by Random House of Canada Limited, Toronto.

Library of Congress Catalog Card Number: 75-117698

Manufactured in the United States of America
by The Book Press, Brattleboro, Vermont

9 8 7 6 5 4 3 2

FIRST EDITION

For Peggy
and Our Sons
Jeff and John

Contents

Fourth
Street
East

1

The Head
of the Family

One thing I have learned. The only people who ever get rich on compound interest are bankers. The rest of us have to figure out a quicker way to do it. My father never did.

There are those who say my father never figured out anything. He was certainly not a brilliant man. I have heard him called stupid. Perhaps he was. If so, he was decent and stupid. I found myself thinking about this on a Sunday morning two weeks ago. That was the day they buried him.

Forty-eight hours earlier, after finishing his breakfast, my father dropped dead of a heart attack. Dropped is the literally accurate word. My mother, who was facing him across the table, says he stood up, then fell down. There was no noticeable pause between these two abrupt movements. The doctor tells me death was so sudden that he is certain my father could not have had a moment of pain. I hope the doctor is right. My father deserved that. He had just passed his eighty-second birthday. To my knowledge, not one of those eighty-two was ever celebrated.

Of the first thirty, I know only what I have heard. I was born when my father was twenty-eight, and during my first two or three years I seem to have been aware of only one parent: my mother. This is not surprising. Nobody ever called her stupid.

During my third or fourth year my mind began to record the impression that there was a third person around the house. Years later, long after I had accepted the fact that I lived with two adults, I began to hear things about my father's early years.

I heard them from relatives who came to call, usually on my mother. From neighbors who dropped in, always to see my mother. From shopkeepers in the neighborhood to whom I was sent, by my mother, for the breakfast rolls, or the salt-peter she needed for putting up a new batch of corned beef. None of these things I heard was said directly to me. They were scraps of sound that passed over my head. Some were accompanied by laughter. I did not realize then that to many of our relatives my father was a joke. Some of these sounds, especially the ones I heard in Deutsch's grocery or Mr. Lesser's drug store, had an edge that made for uncomfortable listening. I did not realize then that to many of our neighbors my father was an object of contempt.

Some of these scraps of sound vanished after they passed over my head. I cannot remember what they contained. Many stuck with me. I was unaware of this. They kept piling up without my knowledge, like bits of cigarette tobacco in the corners of a pocket. Sunday morning, two weeks ago, standing beside a freshly dug grave, the accumulated scraps of almost half a century suddenly began to fall into a pattern. Now that he was dead, I could see my father clearly.

Joseph Tadeus Isaac Kramer was born in either 1885 or

1886. The uncertainty about the date is due to the fact that neither my father nor I was ever able to locate his birth certificate. He did not recall that it was the practice to keep such records in the corner of Europe where he was born. It is possible that his birth was never officially recorded anywhere.

On his U.S. citizenship papers, however, which bear the date 1914, the year of his birth is given as 1886. Even if my father, pressed by the authorities to help them fill in a blank space on a form, had given them no more than a guess based on his best recollection, the chances are that such a guess would have been fairly accurate in 1914, when my father felt he was only twenty-nine years old. My mother felt differently.

There was no doubt about the year of her birth. The receipt for the steerage passage in the Dutch ship that had brought her to this country indicates clearly that Anna Zwirn was born in 1885. Thus, if my father's 1914 guess about the year of his birth was correct, Joseph Tadeus Isaac Kramer was one year younger than his wife. My mother did not like that.

Another thing she did not like was the complexity of my father's family tree.

His father had owned and operated a roadside inn near a town called Woloshonowa in either Austria or Poland. The uncertainty was irritating but understandable. The boundary line between the two countries at this point was changed frequently, not always as a result of the outcome of a war. My father's father—I find it difficult to think of him as my grandfather—was a prosperous man. His inn was on one of the tributary roads that fed the main highway to Warsaw.

My father was the fourth of seven children, all boys. None of them received any formal education. Perhaps there were

5

no schools in the area. Perhaps my father's father did not believe in formal education. None of the scraps of talk that passed over my head when I was a child ever touched on this subject.

My father and his brothers worked in the fields that surrounded the inn, and while the passengers refreshed themselves, helped change the horses of the coaches that stopped on the way to and from Warsaw. I recall nothing about my father's feeling for farm labor, but I have a distinct impression that he liked working with the horses. This may be the reason why, when he was conscripted and went off at eighteen to serve for three years in the armies of Emperor Franz Josef, my father was assigned to the cavalry. I used to think this sounded romantic, but I doubt that it was. My father's services to the Austrian cavalry consisted of currying horses and cleaning stables. My feeling persists, however, that he enjoyed the work.

While he was away from home, going through his military service, my father's mother died. The only hard fact I can remember having heard about her deals with her death. One day, while carrying a tray of drinks out to the passengers in a coach that had stopped in the courtyard of the inn, she tripped and fell. Her head struck a stone. She was carried to her bed. Whether there were no doctors in the area, or whether my father's father felt about the medical profession the way he felt about formal schooling, I don't know. All I know is that my father's mother lay in a coma for four days. Then she died. When my father came home from the army at twenty-one, he discovered that his father had remarried. My father's stepmother was nineteen.

There is some confusion in my mind about the climate of this second marriage. In the scraps of talk that passed over

6

my head there were, I see now, many variations of the traditional jokes about the old husband and the young wife. Just how old my father's father was, I don't know. However, when my father came home from the army at the age of twenty-one, the oldest of his six brothers was twenty-nine. None was married. My father went back to work beside them in the stables and in the fields.

Why he did not remain with his family very long after his army service is not clear. My casual efforts to get information out of my relatives were not rewarding. Again, all I have is an impression. It tells me that none of these adults felt it was proper to satisfy a boy's idle curiosity with facts that, in their opinion, he was too young to hear. One of the facts I did hear was imbedded in somebody's indiscreet observation—hurriedly stifled by somebody else's sharply spoken *Shveig!*—that of my father's father's seven sons, the new young wife liked my father best.

Perhaps she liked him too much. In any case, a few months after he came home from the army, my father left the inn near Woloshonowa and set out for America. I suspect he did not leave with his father's blessing. He certainly left with none of his father's cash. The journey from Woloshonowa in Austria (or Poland) to Castle Garden in New York harbor took three years. My father worked his way.

At what, I do not know. He never spoke about these three years of his life. Neither did the relatives nor neighbors who sent out all those ultimately revealing scraps of sound over my youthful head.

It is difficult not to wonder about those three years. Why the silence? And it was, I see now, total silence. I never heard a word of complaint pass my father's lips. Of course, I never heard him utter a word of joy, either. I mean about himself.

7

He was always lavish with praise of his children, his wife, his neighbors, his bosses, his relatives, passers-by in the street. My father clearly held the firm belief that whatever evil existed in the world had not been created by the human beings who inhabited it. This was, of course, why there were those who called him stupid. As I consider the three years of his journey to America, common sense would seem to indicate that he must have been at least obtuse.

During the time he spent working his way across Europe and part of Asia, King Alexander I of Serbia, his queen, and many members of the court were destroyed in a bloody assassination; the repercussions of the Russo-Japanese War were shaking the complacent rulers of capitals from St. Petersburg to Vienna into a terrified hunt for scapegoats; Germany's Wilhelm II, on his way to Tangier to try to solve the Moroccan crisis, narrowly avoided three attempts on his life; Father Gapon's effort to lead a group of workers with a list of grievances to the Czar's palace gates ended in a savage massacre; street fighting broke out in Moscow; curfews for Jews were established in Warsaw and Berlin; the Young Turks, beginning to throw their weight around in their efforts to seize control of the Ottoman Empire, discovered the heady effects of anti-Semitism as an instrument of national policy.

It could not have been easy or even safe at this time for a penniless young Jew to keep himself alive—and accumulate the price of a steerage passage to America—during the course of a three-year trek across a couple of continents that were resorting desperately to repressive measures, many of them savage, designed to prevent themselves from coming apart at the seams. How my father managed it, I will never know. I am not altogether sure I want to know. I suspect it was the method of the management that sealed his lips. I believe it was his capacity to turn his back on evil, no matter how savage or degrading, that made it possible for him to survive the experience of those years and arrive in New York harbor with a smile.

The testimony to the smile was not, like most of my recollections, hearsay. There was an eyewitness. We, the members of my family, always called this eyewitness Uncle Yokkib. I didn't then know why, and I didn't care. I realize now that I hated Uncle Yokkib all the days of my life while he was alive. On learning a number of years ago that he had died, I remember being puzzled and distressed by the pleasure I got from the news. Two weeks ago, at my father's grave, I finally understood why.

It was Uncle Yokkib—so called, I am pleased to say, not because he was related to our family, but merely because he too came from Woloshonowa—who invented the oldest, if not the best, of the many jokes about my father that were told across my head when I was too young to understand them.

On the Castle Garden staff of the immigration authorities at that time there was a group of men known in Yiddish as "conductors." It was their job to conduct, to the homes of their nearest relatives or friends in the New York area, those immigrants who were not called for in person. The custom would seem to have been a sensible one.

Many, if not most, immigrants from Central Europe in those days were illiterate. Almost none spoke English. Very few had ever, save for the momentous journey that had just brought them to the New World, traveled very far from the small town, or *shtetl,* in which they had been born. Their innocence was, I recall quite clearly, often childlike. It is probably safe to say none arrived laden with the wealth of the Indies, but very few arrived totally penniless. Almost all had on their persons some pittance, the remainder of the tiny hoard that had paid their way to America. The pickings would seem to have been lean, but not so lean, apparently, that the underworld of the day was uninterested.

The continued robbery of the pitifully innocent in and near the dock areas might have continued indefinitely. The waterfront criminals brought the authorities down on their heads when they enlarged their activities to include white slavery: many of the female immigrants were, of course, pretty. The public protests began to make themselves audible. Into being came the system of sending out the unmet immigrant with a conductor.

Nobody was waiting for my father when he disembarked at Castle Garden. If anybody had been, it would have been a miracle; and perhaps he would not have been surprised, since my father knew, as most immigrants did, that he was journeying to a miraculous land. However, when my father set out from Woloshonowa, he told nobody he intended to go to America. It is possible that he did not know it himself. Pawing about among those scraps of sound that passed over my head as a boy, I get the feeling that when my father left home rather hurriedly, he had no destination in mind. He seems to have been sent on his way by one of man's oldest motivations: the desire to put space between himself and an unpleasant situation.

The desire to go to America—no immigrant, it seems, ever spoke of going to New York or Chicago or San Francisco, to anything less than the entire golden continent—must have taken shape in his mind sometime during his three years of wandering across Europe. I once heard him say that when he arrived in New York he believed he was the first citizen of

Woloshonowa who had ever set foot on American soil. He was wrong, of course, as the authorities at Castle Garden soon proved.

Out of an experience that was obviously strewn with repetitive patterns, they had worked out an effective cross-indexing system. Everybody had to come from somewhere. If you kept track of where everybody came from, you had the beginnings of a method for disposing of everybody who followed. It certainly did not take the authorities long to discover that over the years quite a few men and women had come to America from Woloshonowa. In even less time they established that one, a man named Yokkib Berlfein, had been conducted, when he arrived in New York several years earlier, to the home of another ex-citizen of Woloshonowa, also named Berlfein, on East Fourth Street, between Avenue D and Lewis Street. A Castle Garden conductor was assigned to take my father to the Berlfein home.

This proved to be a crowded cold-water flat on the sixth floor of what later came to be known as an "old law" tenement, and was always identified as a fire trap. The Berlfeins had never before seen my father, and he could not remember ever having seen any of them. But they all knew the Kramer inn outside Woloshonowa, and they made my father welcome. Years later, at a party in our own cold-water flat given by my mother—my father paid for it, but my mother "gave" it—to celebrate my bar mitzvah, I heard an account of this welcome.

I had carried into the safety of the bedroom the eight fountain pens, one pocket watch, and six five-dollar gold pieces that had been presented to me by various guests as mementos of the occasion. I concealed the gifts under the shirts in the one dresser drawer that was my private terrain, and turned to go back to the party. My way was blocked by Uncle Yokkib and a group of guests he was entertaining just outside the bedroom door.

Perhaps he saw me. Perhaps he didn't. In any case, he neither got out of my way nor did he stop talking. He did not send the words out over my head, either, as people did when they talked about my father in Deutsch's grocery or Lesser's drug store. If anything, it seemed to me Uncle Yokkib, noting that I was immediately behind him, raised his voice. I soon gathered that he was describing my father's first night on American soil. I don't know, of course, what he had said before I came up to the group. From what I did hear, however, it was not difficult to guess at the nature of what I had missed.

"There's schlemiels and schlemiels," Uncle Yokkib was saying in Yiddish to his chuckling audience. "And all right, naturally, a green one, he's just fresh from the ship, smart like you and me you don't expect him to be. But God in heaven, a dope like this, it's once in a lifetime you see a thing like this. Especially now, it's already after we showed him the toilet, and he asked for a piece of soap, so he could wash his hands in the pot, and then he put his finger in the gas to see what made it burn like that, so blue. So I said all right, now it's time to eat. But now you're in America, so now you'll eat only American food, so I gave him a banana. Everybody, we all watched, and this schlemiel, he never saw a banana before, so naturally, he turns it around in his hands like he's holding something, I don't know, a pistol maybe, he expects it should explode. Go ahead, I said, eat. It's good. It's American food. Eat. So this schlemiel, guess what he does? He puts the banana in his mouth, and he starts to eat it, with the skin on it and everything. He eats the whole thing, the skin and all!

12

And all the time, on his face, that stupid smile, like it's good! Like he's enjoying himself!"

It does not seem to have occurred to Uncle Yokkib that my father *was* enjoying himself. It did not occur to me until two weeks ago, standing beside his grave. Now, putting my mind on it, I see a young man who has just survived three years of a wandering struggle for survival across Europe and part of Asia. He finally achieves what must have long seemed impossible. He arrives on American soil. Why shouldn't he smile? A few hours later this same man, who has for so long been keeping himself alive on stolen scraps of garbage, is offered a piece of fresh fruit. Wolfing it down, skin and all, what could be a more natural reaction than a smile?

I suspect I might have done more than that. I can hear myself roaring with exultant laughter. But I have never attained what I see now was one of the central traits of my father's character: a becoming modesty. He was not an exultant laugher. He was a quiet accepter.

Having accepted America, and its fruit, with the smile that Uncle Yokkib thought foolish, my father turned to the next task: how to earn his keep in the Berlfein household, where everybody was welcome, even people who did not come from Woloshonowa, so long as they paid their share of the rent. My father earned his by finding a job the very next day, thus providing Uncle Yokkib with another funny story for his repertoire.

All the young immigrants who boarded with the Berlfeins on East Fourth Street worked in the men's clothing sweatshops on and near Allen Street in the shadow of the Brooklyn Bridge. A great proportion of New York's male immigrant population was, in those days, "in cloaks and suits." It was an industry that never seemed to have enough help. As a result, the owners of the factories were willing to take on un- trained men. The movements of most immigrants during their first few days in America rarely varied. First day, to the home of a friend or relative, for a reunion. Second day, to the shop in which the friend or relative worked, for a job. My father was either unaware of this pattern, or he did not find it attractive. At any rate, early on the morning after my father's arrival, when Uncle Yokkib awoke and looked for his new boarder with the intention of taking him to the shop where Uncle Yokkib worked, he discovered that my father was gone. If this fact caused any concern to Uncle Yokkib or the other members of the Berlfein family, it did not ap- pear in his version of what happened. I prefer my own.

My father was too excited to sleep. He lay awake for several hours after Uncle Yokkib and his audience had laughed themselves into insensibility. Shortly before dawn, unable to remain in the half bed that had been assigned to him, my father rose, dressed quietly, and tiptoed down into the street. He had no sense of fear. A man who had tramped from Warsaw to Moscow, from Istanbul to Marseilles was not likely to be intimidated by the streets of the Golden Land coming awake in the morning sun. My father started walk- ing. Everything he saw interested him, often because much of what he saw was not unlike what he had seen on the streets of Moscow and Warsaw and Marseilles.

A couple of hours after he left East Fourth Street, he stopped to watch a man unload baskets of oysters from a horse-drawn wagon. My father had earned many a meal in Marseilles by unloading oysters. The man asked my father to lend a hand. He did so, gladly. When the wagon was un- loaded, the man asked my father to join him at breakfast in

14

what proved to be the service kitchen of Fleischmann's Hotel on Lower Broadway.

Conversation did not languish. In those days everybody in New York talked Yiddish. Or so it seemed to my father. Indeed, so it seemed to me until I was almost five years old and my mother enrolled me in the kindergarten class of P.S. 188. Until then, Yiddish was the only language I knew. I still speak it in a manner that used to excite the ridicule of Uncle Yokkib: with the accents of my father's corner of Austria (or Poland). I have always liked the singing sounds made by that accent. So, apparently, did the people in that hotel kitchen. Before the luncheon crowd started coming in, my father was standing behind the oyster bar, wrapped in a white apron, his shucking knife at the ready.

Most of those who later said he was stupid had been led like captives by their cowed predecessors to the chains of their first jobs in the sweatshops of the Golden Land. My father had found his first job by himself. Not in a poorly lighted, badly ventilated, vermin-infested loft where the victims bent over their sewing machines like serfs cringing from the lash. My father had found his first job by himself, in a large room, gaily decorated with paintings and mirrors, full of the cheerful sounds of clinking glasses and laughing men, where he stood proudly upright, performing with dexterity and relish a difficult task that required great skill. He loved every minute of it, and his colleagues loved him. That, I see now, was one of the reasons, perhaps the only one, why Uncle Yokkib worked so hard to put an end to it.

Uncle Yokkib's arguments were persuasive. Jews were forbidden by Holy Writ to eat oysters. To handle them was, therefore, a sacrilege. Working for gentiles was not specifically enjoined. Neither was employment in an establishment that sold alcoholic beverages. The combination of the two, however, could not help but be frowned upon by God. It was true that my father had arranged to work on Sundays, so that he would be free to attend services in the synagogue on Saturday. But the fact remained that this arrangement was made possible only because the second oysterman, who happened to be a Jew without very strong religious convictions, preferred to take his day off on Sunday. My father was therefore, Uncle Yokkib pointed out, aiding in the destruction of the soul of a fellow Jew. And finally, of course, there was the economic argument. Shucking oysters in a saloon was not a skilled trade. It was true that my father was earning a bit more than an unskilled apprentice in cloaks and suits, but he would never become more skillful, and therefore he would never earn more than he was earning now. His job had no future. Until he acquired a skill, and was accepted in a trade where he could practice it, my father would never have a future. And without a future, what good was a man in America?

My father listened politely to Uncle Yokkib's arguments. None of the scraps of talk that passed over my head ever reflected on his manners. My father was always a good listener. Night after night he listened on East Fourth Street to Uncle Yokkib, and morning after morning he went off on foot to the oyster bar on Lower Broadway. Then, one night, perhaps a year after he arrived in America, my father came home from work and found in Uncle Yokkib's cold-water flat an argument he could not disregard.

Just as it was the common practice to lead most young men who arrived from Europe directly to the sewing machines "in cloaks and suits," girl immigrants were always

16

led to a "place." A "place" was the home of a family that wanted and could pay for domestic help. All "places" existed in that shapeless, uncharted land north of Fourteenth Street known as "uptown." Here people were rich. Here people were always looking for good servants. Not that the people who arranged for an immigrant girl to go into a "place" acknowledged even to themselves that they were getting her a job as a servant. What they were doing was handling a difficult problem in the best possible way for all concerned. Everybody had to work, even girls. But girls also had to be protected. They could not be turned loose in areas where they might be victimized by men. Most girl immigrants had no trades. In Europe, as a rule, they had done nothing more skilled than help their parents with the housework and, if they lived on farms, with the chores. What gainful work could such girls do in a crowded city where there were no cows to be milked or chickens to be fed? They could sweep. They could cook. They could wait on table. And they could take care of small children. To be able to do this in a respectable home, in return for bed and board, would have been considered a sensible arrangement. What made going into a "place" a desirable plum for an immigrant girl was that, in addition to her board and keep, she was paid a certain amount of money.

Therefore, the movements of most girl immigrants during their first days in America were as inflexible as those of the men. First day, to the home of a friend or relative, for a reunion. Second day, to the "place" that had been found for her long before she arrived. Anna Zwirn, like my father, was either unaware of this pattern, or she did not find it attractive. She had been born on a farm in Hungary near a town called Klein, or Small, Berezna. She had many brothers and

17

sisters. I have never been able to find out how many. There were certainly more than the farm could support, or needed, to get the work done. At the age of twelve, following a custom of the area, Anna Zwirn was placed in service with a family in the town or city of Gross, or Large, Berezna. She was given her board and keep, plus a small sum of money paid semi-annually. Every six months this money was divided into two parts: three quarters was sent to Anna's parents on the farm; one quarter was given to Anna for pocket money. She spent none of it.

After eleven years, at the age of twenty-three, Anna had saved enough to pay for a steerage passage to America. She left from Gross Berezna without informing her parents on the farm in Klein Berezna. She didn't inform anybody else, either. When she arrived at Castle Garden, there was nobody to meet her. The cross-indexing system set up by the immigration authorities turned up no recent arrivals named Zwirn, but during the past few years a number of Hungarian immigrants from the neighborhood of both Klein and Gross Berezna had arrived in America and had settled on East Fourth Street. A conductor was assigned to take Anna Zwirn to the home of one of her compatriots named Eckveldt. The Eckveldts lived in the cold-water flat on the floor below the Berlfeins in the "old law" tenement that almost a year before had become the home of Joseph Tadeus Isaac Kramer.

The Eckveldts welcomed Anna Zwirn as the Berlfeins had welcomed my father. With warmth: she came from their *shtetl*. With uneasiness: she was another mouth to feed. And with gaiety: a "green one" was always good for some fun. They got very little out of Anna Zwirn. When she was handed a banana, she peeled it.

During the course of that first evening, since no preparations had been made for the unexpected visitor, couriers roamed up and down East Fourth Street, hurriedly seeking information that should have been gathered leisurely during the preceding weeks. By bedtime the problem had been solved. A "place" had been found for Anna Zwirn.

In the morning the girl from Klein Berezna presented her hosts with their second surprise. Anna Zwirn refused to be conducted to the "place." She had not hoarded her pocket money for eleven years to earn her passage to the Golden Land in order to go back into the kind of degrading work to which she had already given half her young life in Gross Berezna. They could turn her out into the streets if they chose. She was not going to take a job as a servant.

Since she was not equipped to take any other kind of job —the immigrants of East Fourth Street didn't know of any other kind of job for a girl—the Eckveldts were faced with a terrible problem. They were, like almost everybody else on East Fourth Street, poor people. They could put up a stranger for the night. They could not support her indefinitely. On the other hand, they could not adopt the alternative Anna Zwirn had herself suggested. They could not turn her out into the streets. Mr. Eckveldt went upstairs to consult with his friend Yokkib Berlfein. By the time my father came home from work that night, the problem had been solved.

Uncle Yokkib led him into the front room of the Berlfein flat, which was used only on the Sabbath. Anna Zwirn was seated on a chair near the window. My father had never seen her before. Uncle Yokkib called Anna to the center of the room and lifted her up onto the round golden-oak table on which the Sabbath meals were served.

"This is the girl you are going to marry," Uncle Yokkib said. "It is your duty."

19

My father did his duty. To do it properly he had to change his way of life. As a bachelor, he had been able to withstand Uncle Yokkib's argument that there was no future in shucking oysters. As a married man, he could not.

A few days before the wedding my father said good-bye to his friends in the high, airy, gaily decorated, mirrored room full of the cheerful sounds of clinking glasses and laughing men, where for almost a year he had performed with dexterity and relish a difficult task that required great skill. The next morning he was led by Uncle Yokkib to a poorly lighted, badly ventilated, vermin-infested loft on Allen Street. Even those who said my father was stupid admitted that he learned soon enough how to bend over a sewing machine as though he were cringing from the lash. Perhaps there is not much to learn. For the rest of his life, almost until the day he died, my father was "in cloaks and suits."

I am only guessing, of course, but as guesses go it would seem to be a safe one: being "in cloaks and suits" could not have provided my father with very much in the way of a spiritual dimension for his life. Others seem to have found it in the fight against sweatshop conditions. My father joined this fight. In fact, he was a member of the small pioneer group that succeeded in wresting from "the bosses" the initial concessions that led to the establishment of the proud and wealthy labor union that now dominates one of the nation's major industries. But my father's participation, no matter what the physical risk, and all accounts of the period indicate that the physical risks were considerable, would not have been motivated by the revolutionary passion. It was simply, I am certain, a matter of shyness. My father was a retiring man. He shunned not only the spotlight. He cowered from the casual glance. To avoid it, to gain the protective coloration of the many, he would hurry to join the group, no matter what the group was doing. If the group happened to be going out on a picket line, my father's first thought would be, not that he might get his head broken, but that if he didn't go out, everybody would notice him hanging back. He never did.

"This is some dope," Uncle Yokkib once said to a few visitors in our house. They had dropped in to have a sympathetic glass of tea with my mother on an occasion when my father did get his head broken. "If somebody came running into the shop," Uncle Yokkib said, "and he screamed 'I'm the captain of a firing squad! I gotta have somebody to shoot! Hurry up, somebody! Let's have a volunteer to get himself killed!' What do you think would happen?" Uncle Yokkib had turned to the bedroom door, behind which my father lay under a turban of bandages. "Joe Kramer would be so ashamed for the captain because he had nobody to shoot, that he would jump up from his machine and say here, please stop looking so ashamed! Take me!"

It was, in my opinion, the lack of spiritual satisfaction he derived from the regularity with which he got his head broken, even though the cause was impeccably just, that led to the passion that ruled the remaining years of my father's life.

I know nothing of its origins that would pass the legal test of evidence. Without cooperation, the mind and the heart cannot be explored. The mind and the heart of another human being, that is. And while my father, if asked, would undoubtedly have been too shy or frightened to withhold the reasons for what he was doing, somebody would have had to ask him first. In his lifetime, nobody did. And now that he is gone, I can't.

Perhaps that is better. For my purpose, at any rate. Which is to explain for myself why my father did what he did, why he lived as he lived. For this, a man's own words do not always help. Indeed, they often confuse. What more eloquent explanation of his purpose could the inventor of the wheel achieve than to point mutely to his own invention? What could my father add in words to explain the reason for the invention of his one-man underground railway? All he had to do was point to the men and women whose lives he saved. He was never asked to do this. Hence these notes.

Almost every immigrant family, in those days on New York's Lower East Side, was engaged in a process known as "bringing somebody over." The somebody was almost always a close relative, a brother or sister, a son or daughter, a father or mother. And the place from which the somebody was being brought over was usually the town in Europe from which the immigrant already in America had himself or herself come.

The bringing-over process required a great deal of paper work, and what would today be considered a modest sum of money. It was far from modest by the standards of those days and the people who had to earn it in the sweatshops of Allen Street. Nevertheless, it was not the money that slowed down and often strangled the bringing-over process. It was the paper work. It was a rare immigrant who could understand or even read the documents that had to be filled in, sworn to before notaries, reproduced in varying quantities, mailed to consulates in Europe, supplemented by further documents demanded from abroad, and then, when files were lost, as they frequently were, start the tedious process over again. My father proved to be one of those rare immigrants. It was, in fact, because of the extent of his rarity that my father became an object of ridicule.

"You heard the newest?" I can still hear Uncle Yokkib telling a laughing group on the bench in front of Gordon's candy store. "This schlemiel, Joe Kramer, now guess who he's helping over?" The members of Uncle Yokkib's audience knew a rhetorical question when they heard one. Nobody guessed. "The brother from that Polack, he runs the stable on Fifth Street, Lesniak he's called!"

Even a boy could understand the exclamations and low whistles of disbelief. A boy who lived on East Fourth Street, anyway. It was a block inhabited exclusively by Jews. The notion that a Jew on Fourth Street would lend a hand with the bringing-over process of a Polish gentile on Fifth Street was unheard of. But most of the new aspects my father had brought to the bringing-over process had been unheard of until he began to devote himself to them.

He started, understandably enough, with the members of his immediate family. By the time my father began writing to them from East Fourth Street, his father had died in Woloshonowa, his oldest brother had married his young step-mother, and the happy couple was running the inn on the road to Warsaw. Perhaps that was why they refused my father's offer to help bring them over to America. Perhaps, remembering the reasons why he had left home, my father never made that particular offer. He did, however, make the offer to his other brothers. All five accepted. This annoyed my mother.

She said my father did not earn enough to support his own family. How could he afford to pay the passage money for five people? He couldn't. My father could not afford to pay the passage money for a single person. But he could afford to do the paper work. This did not involve money. The paper work of the immigrant bringing-over process required a certain amount of intelligence, and a great deal of patience. Nobody on Fourth Street was willing to grant my father the former. They could not, however, deny him the latter. So they made of it a weapon of derision.

"There he goes," they would say on Saturday mornings as my father set out on the long walk to Lafayette Street. "The neighborhood *Shabbes goy*."

A *Shabbes goy,* which translated literally means a "Saturday gentile," was a person who came into a Jewish home on Saturdays and, for a fee, performed those chores that were forbidden by Holy Writ to the orthodox on the Sabbath. On East Fourth Street this was, as a rule, limited to one: lighting the stove. In my experience this person was always, for obvious reasons, a gentile. The term was never applied to a Jew except as a joke. To hear it applied seriously to my father was something his family found unbearable. I was, of course, a member of that family.

My father was not called the neighborhood *Shabbes goy* for the obvious reason. He never in his life struck a match on a Saturday. But he did something that, on East Fourth Street, was considered worse. My father stopped attending Saturday services in the synagogue. He had to. It was the only time of the week when he could go to the Hebrew Immigrant Aid Society, known to generations of "bringers-over" as HIAS. Without regular visits to HIAS, the paper work involved in the bringing-over process always ground to a halt. In fact, without regular visits to HIAS, the paper work never got under way. It was here, in the long, low brown building in Lafayette Street, that the maddening complexities of the endless documents were reduced to sanity by patient clerks who understood the immigrant mind.

My father, like most men on East Fourth Street, could not go to HIAS on the days when he was earning his family's bread on Allen Street, and the helpful offices were closed on Sunday. Unlike most men on East Fourth Street, my father faced up to the issue: his God, or his passion. He knew it was sinful not to attend Sabbath services in the synagogue. He knew, also, that unless he stayed away from these services, he would be unable to get on with the paper work involved in the bringing-over process. There is no secret, as I have indicated, about how the decision went in my father's mind. What the decision cost him, I cannot say. I can, however, add two facts from my own observation. One, my father was a very devout man. And two, he never indicated, by word or sign, that he was aware of the derision and opprobrium heaped on him for his weekly act of sacrilege.

Both were intensified when it became known that my father, on his Saturday visits to HIAS, would work just as hard on the papers of a stranger as on those of one of his own brothers, that he would give as much attention to the documents of a gentile as to those of a Jew. He cared nothing about the origins, or character, or personality, or motives of the man or woman or child who was seeking to be brought over from Europe. All that was required to attract my father's services—which, with the practice of years, became extraordinarily skilled—was to ask for his help. He never denied it to anybody.

It was when my father's help moved into the second area of the bringing-over process that his family's embarrassment turned to shame.

Now that he is dead, and I am no longer ashamed, what

25

my father did seems eminently sensible. What good was all the paper work if after the months, sometimes years, of effort, it all came to nothing for lack of passage money? Since he could not himself supply the money, my father tried to get it from others. Very few people on East Fourth Street earned more than he did. Some not as much. Nobody could afford a contribution of fifty or seventy-five dollars to bring over an immigrant who was, in most cases, a total stranger and, in many, a gentile. But everybody could afford one dollar. Or less. They did not think they could afford it, and few of them wanted to contribute it. My father made it his business to persuade them. To this business he began to devote his Sundays.

He would set out early, when the Catholics of East Fifth Street were on their way to Mass, and then move on to other streets and other sects. Until late at night he roamed the streets of our neighborhood and others, buttonholing strangers as far west as Avenue A and as far south as Columbia Street, pleading the cause of a girl in Lemberg whose papers were all in order and who was only sixteen dollars short of escape from the next pogrom. Surely you could afford a dollar? A half dollar? A quarter? Even a dime will help. Where can you earn for such a low price a good mark in God's book? It's a bargain! It was also exactly what the people of the Lower East Side called it: begging.

Best of all, however, it was effective. My father kept no records, of course, and the members of his family were able to survive his passion only by pretending they were unaware of it. Two weeks ago, however, on the way home from the cemetery, my sister and I fell into a discussion of those early days. Out of our heads, decades after the events, we were able to put together a list of thirty-three men, women, and children, all now alive, who had reached America through my father's efforts before Hitler's holocaust swept across Europe. The list was far from complete. It included only those names that had lingered in our memories because my father's efforts in their behalf caused his family the most shame.

One thing we were spared: the unexpected arrival of a Castle Garden conductor with an unmet immigrant in tow. My father's interest in his charges did not stop with the completion of their papers and the collection of their fares. He kept track of the ships that carried them and the relatives who signed their documents. My father saw to it not only that one of these latter was waiting at Castle Garden when the stranger disembarked, but also that the relative had provided a job for the new arrival. Many of these arrived with a feeling of greater confidence in the man who had shepherded their papers for so long than in the relatives who came to pick them up at the ship. As a result, my father's relationship with many of the immigrants he helped to America continued long after they were here. Most of these relationships were economic.

My father had an almost mystical faith in compound interest. He had never heard of it until he came to America. He could not believe it existed anywhere else in the world. Only here, in this Golden Land, could a man take a dollar he had earned with his sweat, plant it in a marble building as he would plant a seed in the earth, and watch it grow. To each new arrival, just before he went off to his first job "in cloaks and suits" or she departed for her first "place," my father would deliver a lecture on the virtues of compound interest. I never heard it, but it must have been compelling. Almost every one of his listeners would bring him, on his or her first day off, some part of the first salary earned in America. Together, if it was a Saturday, they would set out on foot for the Bowery Savings Bank, which was not too far from the HIAS, and my father would help the immigrant start his first savings account. Many of them were so awed by the deposit book, they were afraid to keep it in their own possession. They asked my father to act as custodian. I can still remember the thick block of pale blue envelopes, held together with a piece of elastic discarded from one of my mother's old corsets, in the top drawer of the dresser I shared with my father. At one time or another he must have been the guardian of twenty or thirty deposit books. My mother, who disliked everything about my father's involvement in the bringing-over process, disliked most this end product.

The fiduciary relationship filled her with distrust. Taking care of other people's bankbooks could end in only one way: trouble. My mother, not for the first time or the last, was proved right.

Esta Mollka Unger was brought over from Poland by an uncle who lived on East Third Street and worked in my father's shop. My father aided with the paper work, helped collect the passage money, and saw to it—a process known as "*noodging*"—that Esta Mollka's uncle met her at the ship and had a "place" waiting for her. My father gave her his lecture on compound interest. She was impressed. She brought him her first salary, and he accompanied her to the Bowery Savings Bank. She asked my father to keep the book for her. He agreed. It was added to the block held together with the piece of elastic from my mother's corset. Once a month, when she received her salary, Esta Mollka would appear at our door, and my father would walk with her to the

Bowery Savings Bank, where she made her deposit. The relationship was no different from a dozen others that existed
between my father and the immigrants he had helped to
bring over.

Then, during Esta Mollka's third year in America, her
uncle died. He had been a childless widower. I do not know
how much affection there had been between him and Esta
Mollka, but it soon became apparent that she missed him.
During those three years she had come downtown from her
"place" to spend every Sunday with him. We had seen her
only once a month, and then very briefly, when she came to
our house for the walk with my father to the Bowery Savings
Bank to deposit her salary. Shortly after her uncle's death
Esta Mollka started showing up at our house every Sunday.
We soon learned why.

Her uncle had been her last surviving relative. Now she
was all alone in the world. She liked her "place." The people
for whom she worked were apparently kind to her and
pleasant to be with. Esta Mollka would happily have spent
her day off with them. However, they did not understand
this. They thought she, like any employee, looked forward
to her day off. Every Sunday, speeding Esta Mollka downtown with their good wishes for a pleasant time, they did not
realize they were speeding her into ten hours of loneliness
she did not know how to handle. It was inevitable that she
should turn to the only other family she knew in the new
land that had become her home.

At first, my mother was annoyed. Not because our social
life was complicated and Esta Mollka was disrupting it. We
had no social life. What we did have was what every family
on East Fourth Street had: a routine of existence that was as
invariable as the tides. Sunday was the day for catching up:

for me and my sister, with school homework; for my mother, with household chores such as mending and ironing; in the case of my father, when he was not out begging, with paper work involving the bringing-over process. Unexpected visitors upset the routine. They had to be entertained.

After her first few Sundays, it began to become apparent that Esta Mollka did not expect to be entertained. Making polite conversation, discussing the weather, commenting on the political situation, being offered glasses of tea, these things embarrassed her. One Sunday, when we were all feeling a bit desperate about how to entertain her, she showed us. She took off the jacket of her Sunday suit, rolled up the sleeves of her shirtwaist, and tackled my mother's ironing. Esta Mollka had it finished long before supper, so she went to work on the silver, which my mother had not planned to do until the middle of the week. From then on, Esta Mollka's Sunday visits were no problem. On the contrary. They were a convenience on which we all leaned. But none of us ever said so. On Sunday mornings, while my mother piled up the ironing, and my sister accumulated her stockings that needed darning, and I got out the sweater I wanted mended, there would be a great deal of weary sighing, long-suffering eye rolling, and hopeless shoulder shrugging. Esta Mollka, that boring dope, was coming.

One Sunday she didn't come. For an hour or so we were unaware of her defection. She always came in quietly. She always went to work without comment. By mid-afternoon, when it was clear that on this particular Sunday Esta Mollka was more than merely tardy, we all exploded with anger. All except my father. He was, as always, totally absorbed in a batch of documents he had brought from HIAS the day before. The rest of us, however, let the absent Esta Mollka have it. How dare she not show up? Who was going to iron the shirts? What about my sweater? And the stockings my sister had been counting on wearing that night? The least that stupid greenhorn could do, if she didn't intend to show up, was let us know. In our rage, we didn't suggest how she could have done this. Our tenement flat was not equipped with a telephone.

The following Sunday, when Esta Mollka showed up, looking pale and tired, and we learned that she had been in bed for almost a week with the grippe, we were properly sympathetic. But we also had the ironing piled up and waiting.

I cannot remember how long this relationship continued but I remember, as clearly and vividly as though it had happened this morning, the day Esta Mollka announced she was going to get married. She was standing at the ironing board in the kitchen, working on one of my shirts. My mother, my father, my sister, and I were seated around the kitchen table, finishing our breakfast. My mother, who was forcing more bread on my sister, looked up.

"What did you say?" she said.

"I'm going to get married," Esta Mollka said.

We all stared at her. I think that was the first time, after all those years, I really saw what she looked like. She was not a pretty girl. In fact, it occurred to me all at once that she was no longer a girl. She must have been in her late twenties when she arrived in America. At that time I had been in Miss Kitchell's 2A-1 class in P.S. 188. I was now in Miss Hallock's R.A.1 class in Junior High School 64. Six years had gone by. Almost seven. Esta Mollka was a woman in her thirties.

She was short, and stocky, and matronly. Her brown hair was done in a style that was popular at the time with young girls: two large puffs, one over each ear, called Castle Clips. They made Esta Mollka look ludicrous. Wondering why, and examining her more closely to see if I could discover the reason, it occurred to me that the attempt at a complicated, youthful hairdo merely underscored the round, innocent, simple face out of which Esta Mollka's guileless blue eyes stared with a look—

My mind seemed to jump, as though, rolling along smoothly in an attempt to put together a portrait, it had struck an unexpected bump in the pavement of my thinking. Innocent and guileless and simple were accurate enough, but not completely accurate. Simple-minded was more like it. It occurred to me, with a sudden small stab of terror, that there was something mentally wrong with this girl, this woman who had become almost a member of our family. All at once I could see the door in our schoolyard that was always kept locked on the inside, a door from behind which, as we filed up to class in long orderly rows after first bell, we could occasionally hear wild screams that clawed at the nerves like fingernails drawn down a blackboard. Nobody I knew could say what went on behind that door. The room the door shielded we all called "the crazy class."

"Who?" my mother said. "To get married, there must be a man. Who is he?"

"Monty," Esta Mollka said.

"Monty?" my mother said. "What kind of a name is that?"

"It's his name," Esta Mollka said, ironing away busily.

Suddenly suspicion clouded my mother's face. "He's a Jew?" she said.

Esta Mollka did not answer. She stared down sullenly at the ironing board.

"I asked a question," my mother said. "He's a Jew?"

32

"I don't know," Esta Mollka said, and even I knew she was lying.

"Jewish girls don't marry men called Monty," my mother said. "Watch what you're doing with the iron, there. You just broke a button on that cuff."

No more was said until Esta Mollka had finished the ironing, mended my sister's stockings, sewed my new merit badge on the sleeve of my boy scout uniform, polished the silver, laid out our Sunday supper, cleared the table, washed the dishes, and swept the kitchen. At ten o'clock, as she always did on her day off, Esta Mollka started putting on her hat and coat for the trip back to Amsterdam Avenue. There was one change in her routine on this Sunday night. After she had kissed each of us in turn, instead of going to the door, Esta Mollka turned to my father.

"Please, Uncle Joe," she said. "I want the bankbook."

"The bankbook?"

My father was obviously confused. Not my mother.

"Why?" she said sharply. "Late Sunday night, the bank is closed, what are you going to do with the bankbook on Sunday night?"

Esta Mollka had obviously expected resistance. Even more obviously, she had been briefed on how to meet it.

"It's my bankbook," she said in a voice that sounded strange in my ears. "It's my money. I want the book."

"To give to this goy," my mother said. "This Monty. You stupid fool. He's not going to marry you. All he wants is your money."

"That's a lie," Esta Mollka said, and now the voice once again sounded familiar, even though there were tears in it. "It's not the money."

"Then why do you need the bankbook?" my mother said.

"It's mine," Esta Mollka said stubbornly. "I want it."

"You listen to me, you stupid pudding head," my mother said. "If you take that bankbook and you give it to this Monty, don't you ever come into this house again. You hear?"

Evidently Esta Mollka did, because she hesitated. But not for long.

"It's my book," she said finally. "I want it."

"All right," my mother said. "But remember what I said. Never again in this house." She turned to my father. "Give her the book."

Now another strange thing happened. Strange to a boy who had never before seen his father contradict his mother.

"No," my father said.

"What?" my mother said in a startled voice.

"If it's a goy," my father said, "this Monty. If just for the money he's marrying you, then no. I won't give you the book."

Now clearly more surprised than angry, Esta Mollka said, "But it's mine. It's my money."

"It's your blood," my father said. "The years of work in your place, that's what's in that book. The years. Not money. Your blood. Your blood you're not giving away to somebody I never saw. For this I didn't help your uncle, he should rest in peace, he should bring you over from Poland. This Monty, he wants to marry you, he wants your bankbook, let him come here like a man, on his own feet, and ask for it."

When he did, the following night, the surprise was so great on so many levels that for a while I was more concerned with sorting them out than with understanding what was happening.

34

The Head of the Family

For one thing, Esta Mollka came with the man called Monty, and I found this difficult to grasp. I had never seen her "place" or any other immigrant girl's "place." But for years there had been in my mind a picture—I didn't really know where it had come from—of Esta Mollka and all those other girls being kept under lock and key for six days, as though they were in a prison; then, on Sundays, the gates unlocked and the girls allowed out for a few hours. How had Esta Mollka managed to get out on a Monday?

Another thing that confused me about Monty was his appearance. I knew absolutely nothing about marriage except what my mind, unaware that it was doing so, had recorded from my observation of the married people by whom I was surrounded. These observations indicated, among other things, that husbands were usually older than wives, and wives were usually more attractive than husbands. Neither was true in the case of Esta Mollka and this man called Monty.

He was tall and slender and handsome, with broad shoulders and powerful hands. I don't know, of course, how old he was, but he looked much younger than Esta Mollka.

The most startling thing about this strange couple now standing in our kitchen, however, was the fact that I could not see them as a couple. Esta Mollka looked like a terrified, feeble-minded peasant in one of those Russian newsreels I saw occasionally in the American Theatre on Third Street, Monty looked like the young bodyguard—his knowing eyes glinting steel, flashing to right and left—who walked a couple of steps behind the leader of the mob in the gangster movies. Even before Monty opened his mouth, I knew my mother had been right. It was impossible for a man who looked like Monty to marry a woman like Esta Mollka.

"I hear you said if she wants her bankbook," he said to my father, "I should come with her to get it."

At least his voice was no surprise. He sounded exactly like those tough-talking gunmen who shielded the leader from the hoods of the rival mob.

"That's right," my father said.

"Okay," Monty said. "I'm here. Get me the bankbook."

"Show me first the marriage certificate," my father said.

"How's that?" Monty said.

"Esta Mollka says you and she, it's going to be a wedding," my father said. "To her husband I'll give the bankbook. Not to anybody else. Come back with a marriage certificate, your name on it and hers, and I'll give you the book."

Monty lifted his huge right hand, closed it into a fist, and smashed the fist into my father's face. He fell back against the icebox. My mother screamed. My sister yelled something and started toward my father. I followed her. With one hand Monty grabbed me by the seat of my pants, and with his other hand he caught my sister's elbow. He shoved us back, toward my mother, and the three of us tumbled to the kitchen floor. As I went down, I caught a glimpse of Esta Mollka's face. Tears were rolling down her cheeks, but she had not moved.

"Get the bankbook," Monty said.

"When you come back with the marriage certificate," my father said through his bloody lips.

Monty reached out, pulled my father away from the icebox, and again smashed his fist into my father's face.

"Get the book."

"No," my father said.

The Head of the Family

After the fourth blow, my mother screamed, "I'll get it! I'll get it!"

She ran out into the bedroom and came back with the small pale blue envelope. Monty took it, slid out the bankbook, examined it for a moment, then put the book into his pocket.

"Come on," he said to Esta Mollka.

She followed him without a word.

About a year later an employee of the city's Welfare Department came to see my father. An unidentified woman had been found wandering in the rain on Third Avenue near Forty-second Street. She did not know who she was. She could scarcely speak. The words she uttered were unintelligible. In her sodden purse they found a ten-year-old receipt for a steerage passage from Antwerp to New York. It had been made out to Esta Mollka Unger in care of Joseph Tadeus Isaac Kramer at our address on East Fourth Street. My father accompanied the social worker to Bellevue. The woman was Esta Mollka, all right.

She did not recognize my father. She did not recognize him for thirty years. During all that time he never failed to visit her twice a year in the upstate asylum to which she was committed: once in February, on the anniversary of her arrival at Castle Garden; and again in late August or early September, just before the High Holidays.

My father always brought with him a homemade sponge cake. My mother always grumbled, but she always baked it. For the last ten years of Esta Mollka's life, during which my mother's accelerating arthritis began to make it difficult for her to do any baking, my father would always go down to Delancey Street, on the day before his semi-annual trip to the asylum, and buy a sponge cake. It had to be golden yellow, not dark brown, and it had to come with the crinkled paper in which it had been baked still stuck to it. These details were important, and Delancey Street was just about the only place left where you could get a cake like that.

On the day Esta Mollka had been brought to her uncle's home on East Third Street from Castle Garden, the people who had gathered to celebrate her arrival from Poland had eaten slices of golden yellow sponge cake cut from a loaf still sitting in the nest of crinkled paper in which it had been baked. It was the only detail Esta Mollka remembered of her six lucid years in the Golden Land.

When she died, a year ago, my father was the only person who went up from New York to attend the funeral. Out of his Social Security check, he set aside a five-dollar deduction every month to pay for the stone that will ultimately mark Esta Mollka's grave. He arranged, through the rabbi of his synagogue, to take on the burden of saying *Kaddish,* the prayer for the dead that must be said daily, morning and night, for a full year to insure the safe passage of the soul of the departed into heaven.

About a month ago, when I saw him alive for the last time, my father told me he still had six weeks of *Kaddish* ahead of him before Esta Mollka's soul would be safe.

As I figured it, when my father dropped dead sixteen days ago he had worked off a little over two weeks of this period, thus leaving the soul of Esta Mollka one month short of the sanctuary my father wanted her to achieve.

That night at sundown, and every night after that, I knew where I was going. For about four weeks, anyway. With a little effort I was able to make it sometimes in the mornings, too.

2

Draft Status

Whenever I hear or read a reference to the First World War, my mind leaps to the subject of sugar cookies. I haven't eaten or even seen one since I was a boy on East Fourth Street. It seems odd to recall that once they were as regular a part of my life as the chore of going down with my father to the Fifth Street dock every summer Thursday, buying a ten-cent lump of ice, trundling it home in the wagon my father and I had constructed from an old egg crate and four discarded skate wheels, and then, when the ice was in the icebox, wrapping it carefully with old copies of the *Jewish Daily Forward*. This, it was believed on our block, made the ice last longer.

Every mother on East Fourth Street did the week's baking for her family on Friday, and my mother was no exception. What she baked was almost exactly what every other mother on the block baked: two loaves of ceremonial white bread for the Sabbath (store-bought rye was eaten only on week-days); a honey cake, or *lekach,* to last through the week for male guests who dropped in for a talk with my father and for a glass of his homemade Passover wine; a sponge cake for women guests; and sugar cookies to go with the glass of milk my sister and I were forced to drink every afternoon when we came home from school.

My mother felt about milk the way I imagine the Rockefellers feel about oil. She believed in it. The sugar cookies were a bribe to get us to share her belief. The bribe must have worked. I still drink milk with pleasure, and somehow drinking milk always reminds me of the day when I was struck by the sudden realization that the world as I had known it all my life had taken a sudden and unexpected turn into the terrifying unknown.

On that day I had come home from P.S. 188, where I was one of the three best raffia-basket weavers in Miss Kahn's kindergarten class. On the kitchen table was set out my mother's usual afternoon treat: two old jelly jars full of cold milk and, between them, a plate of sugar cookies. My sister had not yet come home, but this was not unusual. Her class was 1A on the "girls' side" of P.S. 188, and while I did not really know what went on there, I knew it was different from the activities on my, or the boys', side of the school.

On the girls' side, for example, they had a club called "The Blue Birds for Happiness." I learned years later that it had been inspired by Maeterlinck's famous play, but I never did learn just what the members of the club did, or why it kept my sister in school after classes were dismissed. I was not interested, either, because it did not affect the sugar cookies.

My mother always placed six on the plate. Three for me, three for my sister. It did not matter how late she came home.

The rules had been laid down, and we both observed them. After I finished my third cookie, if I wanted more, I asked my mother. My sister's three were never touched. What shocked me that day into an awareness that the world I had known all my life had suddenly changed was the fact that unlike every other afternoon I could remember, I had no desire to touch my sister's three cookies, or even finish my own.

Sugar cookies, as I had known them until that day, were pale lemon-yellow discs about four inches in diameter, with a deliciously soft, chewy center, topped by lumped little mounds of snow-white sugar. Nothing Brillat-Savarin ever put together can possibly come near what happened when a great big bite of one of these cookies from my mother's stove met a great big mouthful of cold milk from Mr. Deutsch's grocery store. It did not happen on that fateful day.

"What's the matter?" my mother said.

She always said this when the normal routine of her rather primitive existence was in any way, however slightly, jogged off course.

"Nothing," I said.

This was what I always said when questions from the adult, or enemy, world started coming through my carefully constructed barricades.

"You're not eating the cookies," my mother said.

"I'm not hungry," I said.

"You're sick," my mother said. "I'll get the Bolls Rolls."

Bolls Rolls were a laxative sold by Mr. Lesser, the corner druggist, that looked like dirty golf balls, tasted like sour figs, and were used by the mothers of East Fourth Street on their children the way a salesman uses the word miscellaneous on his expense account.

41

"No, don't," I said. "I feel fine."

"Then why aren't you eating the cookies?" my mother said.

"It's the sugar," I said. "It's not white."

For the first time in my experience with sugar cookies, the lumped little mounds on the delicious yellow discs were not white but brown.

"Mr. Deutsch doesn't have any more white sugar to sell," my mother said. "It's the war. Don't you know there's a war?"

Of course I knew there was a war. On Friday nights, when my mother always served stewed prunes for dessert, didn't I carefully collect all the pits, wash them at the kitchen sink, dry them all weekend in the sun on the window sill, and then take them to school on Monday so that when during recess Miss Kahn marched her class out to the corner of Lewis and Houston Streets, I would have something to toss proudly into the U.S. Army collection box that Miss Kahn said was helping to supply our brave boys with gas masks? And every Wednesday, didn't I bring a dime to assembly so that a War Savings Stamp could be pasted into my Liberty Bond Book? What I did not understand was why the war should suddenly make it impossible for Mr. Deutsch to supply my mother with the white sugar she had always bought from him for making her sugar cookies.

"I could go for you to Leopolstadt on Avenue C," I said. "He sells everything."

I had heard Henny Leopolstadt, who was two classes ahead of me in P.S. 188, say this many times about his father's grocery store, and of course I believed it.

"I went already to Mr. Leopolstadt," my mother said. "And to Sheffler's on Lewis Street. I went every place. Nobody has white sugar."

42

The statement shocked me. I did not at the time understand why. I am fairly certain that my mother's cookies, made with brown sugar, were just as delicious as the cookies she had always made with white sugar. The answer, I think, is in the word "always." I was only five years old, but those five years added up to a lifetime, the only lifetime with which I was intimately acquainted, and it was my first encounter during that lifetime with the sudden and inexplicable cessation of the familiar.

Years later the father of a boy who sat next to me in Intermediate Algebra at Thomas Jefferson High School jumped out of his office window the day after the stock market crashed in 1929. I happened to mention this to Mr. Fisher, my homeroom teacher, saying I didn't understand why a man would do a thing like that.

"People get used to things," Mr. Fisher said. "Like a nice steady flow of money. Then the things they've gotten used to, one day they stop flowing in, and it scares the hell out of them."

Suddenly I understood what had happened to me at the age of five on East Fourth Street. There had always been a nice steady flow of white sugar. Then one day there was no more white sugar, and it scared the hell out of me.

Fortunately, thanks to my mother's Uncle Berel, my terror did not last long.

Uncle Berel was our rich relative. He had come to America from Hungary during McKinley's first administration and somehow found his way to Waterbury, Connecticut, where he got a job delivering cases of bottled soda for a manufacturer of carbonated beverages. By the time McKinley was assassinated, Uncle Berel owned the bottling plant. At the age of five I had never yet met him, but I knew he was fond

43

of my mother. He was always sending her presents. These rarely pleased my mother. I could not understand why. What was wrong with receiving, as we once did just before Passover, a crate containing one hundred pounds of matzohs? It's true, they did fill the kitchen and half the front room of our three-room tenement flat, and we had to eat matzohs until long after Yom Kipper, but for a few days I was a person of some importance on East Fourth Street. Nobody else on the block had an uncle with such spectacular ideas about presents.

"It's because when he sends a present he doesn't think of the person he's sending it to," my mother said irritably. "He thinks of himself, so everybody, when they see the present, they'll know how rich he is."

This may very well have been the reason why, a few days after the change in my mother's sugar cookies struck unexpected terror to my heart, an American Express Company truck arrived on East Fourth Street with a two-hundred-pound sack of white sugar addressed to my mother. It caused a sensation.

At a time when nobody else could purchase so much as "half a quarter"—on East Fourth Street nobody ever heard of an eighth of a pound as a unit of measurement—my mother had two hundred pounds of the food product nobody on the block had ever before done without. Even though my mother implied there was something mysterious about this, it was actually quite simple. As a manufacturer of perhaps twenty different flavors of charged soda water, Uncle Berel manufactured huge quantities of syrup, and to make syrup you must have sugar. When the Archduke Ferdinand was assassinated at Sarajevo, my mother's Uncle Berel had a great deal of white sugar stockpiled in his warehouse in

Waterbury. When it became obvious at the Marne that the war was going to be a long one, and the civilian shortages that are always a result of long wars started to creep across the Atlantic, my mother's Uncle Berel saw, and seized, the opportunity to make a characteristic gesture. My mother's response was equally characteristic.

"Two hundred pounds of sugar," she said irritably, staring at the big fat sack standing in the middle of our small kitchen. "What am I going to do with it?"

The question was, of course, rhetorical. My mother never asked anybody for advice. She didn't seem to need it. I cannot remember a single instance when she even appeared to be in doubt about a course of action. She was not, as I recall, a generous woman. This statement is not intended as a reflection on her character. Generosity, at least in matters involving physical objects such as food, is almost totally dependent on wherewithal. You can't give away what you haven't got, and food was the item that received the most constant and troubled attention of every housewife on the block. It was not a street of rich people. I can remember only one family, a childless young couple named Mr. and Mrs. Mishig, who seemed to be free from the constant preoccupation of most women on East Fourth Street with the problem of getting three meals a day onto the family table. That is why I was so astonished by the way my mother handled her Uncle Berel's unexpected gift.

"Get the *shep leffel*," she said to me.

The *shep leffel* was a blue and white porcelain ladle with which on Friday nights—when we had our evening meal, not as on weekday nights at the kitchen table, but at the big round oak table in the front room—my mother served the noodle soup from the pewter tureen she had brought with her from Hungary. When I brought the ladle from the side-board in the front room into the kitchen, I found that my mother had opened the sack of sugar with her noodle knife, and she was setting the pewter tureen on the kitchen floor.

"Get the ice pail," she said.

The ice pail was a flat, badly chipped, once-white enamel basin that sat under the icebox. In warm weather it caught the water as the ice wrapped in the *Jewish Daily Forward* melted slowly up above. Uncle Berel's gift had arrived in March, however. Between late October and early May, foods that needed refrigeration on East Fourth Street were kept out on the fire escape. The ice pail was empty and dry. I dragged it from under the icebox and watched while my mother filled it with huge scoops of sugar from Uncle Berel's sack. She then turned to the pewter soup tureen. When it was full, my mother rose from her knees and wiped her hands on her apron, one of several she had made by tearing apart and re-sewing old Hecker's flour sacks.

"All right," she said. "You take the ice pail, and we'll start from the ground floor."

I picked up the ice pail, my mother lifted the tureen, and we started downstairs from our rooms on the fourth floor. The tenement in which we lived, at the corner of Lewis and Fourth Streets, was known as a double house: two six-story structures separated by a narrow court, one building facing the street, the other facing the court. On every floor of each house there were six sets of "rooms." (The words "apart-ment" and "flat" did not cross my path until I received my first borrower's card at the Hamilton Fish Park Branch of the New York Public Library and I started to read novels.) The sets of rooms in both houses were all exactly alike: a bedroom and a front room separated by a kitchen, all three strung out in a straight line. There were no bathrooms, but ours was considered a very desirable building because it was "with toilets in the hall," meaning one on each floor, serving only six families. Almost every other tenement on East Fourth Street was "with toilets in the yard," meaning in the court that separated the front building from the rear building. How many families used each one I cannot remember, but I do remember that in our building there were thirty-six families in the "front house" and thirty-six in the "back house." Until the day my mother received Uncle Berel's present, I believe the only person who ever visited all seventy-two sets of rooms in our tenement on one day was Mr. Koptzin, the landlord. On the first of every month he showed up early in the morning, while my sister and I were still getting dressed for school, and went from door to door, collecting his rent and scribbling receipts that were then laid away in the bottoms of bureau drawers with as much care and reverence as citizenship papers and prayer clothes.

It never occurred to me that knocking on seventy-two doors could be exhausting, probably because the notion of knocking on seventy-two doors had always been associated in my mind with the way Mr. Koptzin's pockets grew fatter and fatter as he moved up the stairs and his collections increased. Checking accounts were unheard of on East Fourth Street. All transactions, from the purchase of a penny-pack of Three-X chewing gum to the payment of the month's rent, were on a cash basis, and every family kept its cash where my mother kept hers: in a small, tightly rolled tube tucked into the top of one of her stockings. One of the stockings she was wearing, that is. Money was never left in a place that was not within immediate reach of the family member who was in charge of its finances. The rolled top of my mother's

47

stocking was known in our family as Mama's Avenue B Branch of The Standard Bank. When Mr. Koptzin showed up on the first of the month, she stepped modestly behind the half-opened door and unpeeled the month's rent. Mr. Koptzin never seemed tired when he accepted it. Probably he did not, while making his rounds, carry an ice pail full of white sugar. Nor did Mr. Koptzin say what my mother said when the woman on whose door she knocked opened it.

"My crazy uncle from Connecticut," my mother said, "he sent me a great big sack of white sugar. Even for a factory it's too much. Who can use it all? Would you like some?"

Every woman did the same thing. She looked suspicious. Every woman then said the same thing: "How much a pound?"

"In the grocery business I'm not," my mother said. "I got it for nothing, so I'm giving it away for nothing. Go bring something to put it in."

By the time my ice pail and my mother's tureen were empty, we had worked our way up to the third floor of the front house of our seventy-two-family tenement. We went back to our rooms, refilled the ice pail and the tureen, and returned to our tour. I didn't realize it was hard work, even though I was aware that I was getting tired, until I happened to notice my mother's face. We were about halfway through the back house, after five refill trips to our own rooms, when she staggered slightly. This was most unusual. My mother was not a large woman, but she was strong. I had never seen her stagger. I looked at her in surprise and saw that she looked exhausted. This reminded me of the way I felt, so I said, "Ma, I'm tired."

"We have only two floors more," she said. "I want everybody in the building should have some."

She may have been exhausted, but she sounded cheerful. It was obvious that she was having a good time. I suddenly realized that so was I. Thinking back on it, the reason seems obvious. Neither of us had ever been in a position to give away anything of value. The opportunity to do so, watching the faces in the open doors change from suspicion to incredulity to gratitude, was heady stuff. I think when we reached the top floor of the back house, and my mother knocked on the last door, she and I were both slightly drunk. The door opened and Mrs. Mishig looked out at us.

"What do you want?" she said.

"Who wants?" my mother said cheerily. "I'm giving!" She made her jubilant little speech about her crazy uncle in Connecticut, then said, "Go get a pot or a bag and you'll have enough white sugar till General Pershing he makes the Kaiser drop dead."

"Get out of here," Mrs. Mishig said in a cold, hard voice. "We don't want nothing from people they're draft dodgers running away from Furtz Luchel."

She slammed the door in our faces. I was, of course, stunned. For more than two hours, carrying our ice pail and pewter tureen through the front and back houses of our tenement, my mother and I had been received at door after door the way—I later gathered from reading the books to which my Hamilton Fish Park Branch borrower's card gave me access—General Baden-Powell had been greeted when his relieving column entered Mafeking. I do not actually know how my mother felt about the response of Mrs. Mishig to our generous—I don't think the word is inappropriate—offer because I was not really thinking about my mother. I was thinking about myself. I was not only shocked. I was confused. Not by the refusal of Mrs. Mishig to take some of the white sugar every other tenant we had visited had so eagerly accepted. I was confused by what she had said.

Furtz Luchel was the way people on East Fourth Street pronounced Fort Slocum, a U.S. Army installation not far from Manhattan to which the men were sent when they were drafted. I knew as little about Fort Slocum as I knew about the war that had brought it into existence, but I knew the name meant something unpleasant, something people on our block tried to avoid, like visits to Dr. Jacobowitz, the dentist on Avenue C. I could not understand why the words had been hurled so angrily at me and my mother, and why Mrs. Mishig had slammed the door in our faces. Above all, I could not understand why anybody would refuse a gift of several pounds of white sugar. I asked my mother.

"She's crazy," my mother said, but there was no conviction in her voice. My mother sounded the way she had for the last hour or so looked: exhausted. The fun of giving had vanished. "Let's go back," my mother said. "Forget that crazy woman with her crazy words."

I tried, but it was impossible. The savage contempt in the voice of Mrs. Mishig seemed to linger in my head, like an unpleasant echo, all day. I thought my mother would tell my father about it when he came home from work that night. The conversation in our house in the evening consisted of my father telling my mother what had happened during the day in the shop on Allen Street, and my mother telling him what had happened on East Fourth Street while he had been gone. Sometimes I was asked what had happened in Miss Kahn's class, and my sister was asked what the members of The Blue Birds for Happiness had been up to, but this was rare. Most of the talk across the kitchen table was between my father and mother, and by listening to it, I had learned most of what I knew, it seemed to me then, about everything. Their conversation was always more interesting, to me, at any rate, than mine or my sister's. It always contained something surprising.

Nothing, however, was more surprising than what my mother's conversation that night did not contain. She explained the presence in our kitchen of the now three-quarters-empty sack of white sugar, and she described the tour through the tenement she and I had made with the ice pail and the pewter tureen. She did not mention Mrs. Mishig or what had happened when we knocked on that strange young woman's door.

Actually, there was nothing strange about Mrs. Mishig. She was a small woman with a disapproving look who clearly thought herself much too good for her neighbors, and apparently to prove it, rarely came out of the set of rooms, top floor back, in which she lived with her husband. He was the strange one.

He was a very tall, broad-shouldered, powerful young man with a look of sinister elegance. This was probably due to his custom-made clothes and the fierce look with which he stared out at the world through hard, bright black eyes that seemed to have no pupils. Nobody else on East Fourth Street had a mustache like Mr. Mishig, either. It stood out from his upper lip in two distinctly separated sections, like a set of miniature bull's horns painted black to match his eyes. But it was not the custom-made suits and the striking mustache that made the people of our block feel there was something strange about Mr. Mishig. What puzzled us was that nobody could figure out what he and his wife were doing on East Fourth Street.

First of all, he was a Turk, and East Fourth Street was

51

a colony of Hungarians sprinkled with a few Austrians. Secondly, they were obviously rich. Mrs. Mishig owned a Hudson seal coat. The only other woman who had ever owned a fur coat on East Fourth Street, in my time, anyway, was Mrs. Shumansky, whose husband owned the chicken store on the Avenue C corner, and as soon as she got the coat, the Shumanskys moved uptown to the Bronx. Nobody on the block thought this was an act of snobbery. It was the natural thing to do. East Fourth Street was no place in which to spend your life. It was a way station. People lived there because living there cost less than living in other places. As soon as you could afford one of those other places, you left East Fourth Street. To my knowledge, nobody ever did it with regret. That's why everybody on the block wondered why Mr. and Mrs. Mishig lived among us. They obviously could afford to live elsewhere.

Even more obviously, they did not enjoy living on East Fourth Street. They never mixed with their neighbors, and their neighbors never stopped wondering what Mr. Mishig did to earn the money with which he bought his custom-made suits and paid for his wife's fur coat. When my father left our tenement at six-thirty in the morning, everybody knew he was going to the shop on Allen Street where he made pockets. When Henny Leopolstadt's mother came out of the tenement across the street a few minutes later and started up the block to Avenue C, everybody knew she was going to open the family grocery store. This sort of information was common knowledge about every family on the block. When Mr. Mishig came out in the street every morning, however, and with his proud, arrogant stride started stalking west toward Avenue C in his expensive suit, nobody on East Fourth Street knew where he was going.

Another thing nobody knew about him was why Mr. Mishig seemed impervious to the threat that hung over every childless man on the block: Furtz Luchel.

As I recall the attitude of East Fourth Street toward the first war through which I lived, it had very little in common with the spirit that animated Ethan Allen and his Green Mountain Boys. To the immigrant population of East Fourth Street, wars and conscription were unpleasant but commonplace facts of life. Many of our neighbors had escaped from their native lands to avoid military service. Like most of his neighbors on East Fourth Street, my father saw very little difference between Franz Josef and Woodrow Wilson. Both, in their desire to put people into uniform, were threats to his existence. This attitude was so general that the busiest man on the block seemed to be Mr. Tannenbaum, the marriage broker. There were several weddings every week, in those days. Nevertheless, as the army's need for men increased, marriage was not enough to keep a man safe at home. New young husbands were constantly being snatched away for the trip to Fort Slocum. Only the childless young Mr. Mishig seemed to be safe from the draft.

Naturally, there was a great deal of talk about it. From this talk, I knew that my father was not involved in the general threat because, like the fathers of my classmates, he had become a father long before Miss Kahn had started urging us to save prune pits and buy War Savings Stamps. It was this knowledge that troubled me about the furious words Mrs. Mishig had hurled at my mother when she spurned our offering of white sugar. How could she call my father a draft dodger? He was the father of two children.

The next day, on my way to school, I ran into Henny Leopolstadt. Or rather, he ran into me. We were not close friends. This was due partly to age and partly to geography. Henny, who was my senior by two years, had left raffia baskets behind, and was struggling with arithmetic in Miss Kitchell's class. Also, he spent most of his spare time in his father's store on Avenue C. This was only a block further west than the piece of East Fourth Street on which I lived, but Henny's attitude implied clearly that the gap was not unlike what one would find between the average desert oasis and Mecca. He was certainly more sophisticated than any of my real friends, and he had a tendency to be contemptuous of boys whose parents bought their groceries from his father's rival, Mr. Deutsch. Henny had never, however, been openly hostile to me, and on this morning, to my pleased surprise, he was openly friendly. In fact, he had obviously been waiting for me. I soon learned why. Henny had heard about Uncle Berel's present, and what my mother had done with it.

"I hear every tenant in the building, they got a couple pounds pure white sugar free," he said.

"Everybody except Mrs. Mishig," I said.

"How come?" Henny asked.

I told him.

"What the hella you care what names she calls you," Henny said contemptuously. "As long as your old man don't get one of them brown suits. How's about your mother giving me a few pounds of that white sugar?"

"Sure," I said. "Come up the house after school with a pot or something." We turned the corner into Lewis Street, while I worked my way back through Henny's comment on Mrs. Mishig. There was something wrong with it. "Listen," I said. "What did she mean she don't want nothing from draft dodgers? My father ain't in the draft."

54

"No, but if the war goes on long enough, he could be," Henny said. "They're running out of guys, see? So they're starting to take married men with only one kid. Next they'll start on married men with two kids. That's why your old lady is having a baby. With three kids your old man's got a better chance to stay out of Furtz Luchel than with only two."

At this point we reached the school entrance, and I was pleased by the opportunity to end the conversation. I did not want Henny to know that this was the first I had heard about my mother having a baby. It was a process about which I knew no more, probably, than most five-year-olds, although on East Fourth Street this could have been a good deal more than in some other places. What I knew most clearly was that while the process was going on, you were supposed to feel thoroughly ashamed of your mother for having become involved in it. I had seen more than one fight start in the P.S. 188 schoolyard, or on the Forest Box & Lumber Company dock, when one boy accused another of having a mother in the condition Henny Leopolstadt had just advised me my mother was in. I thought it very decent of Henny to have slipped me the information as delicately as he had, burying it in an explanation about my father's draft status rather than taunting me with it. That afternoon, when Henny came into our kitchen with an empty butter tub from his father's grocery store, I filled it to the brim from Uncle Berel's sack of sugar.

"Are you crazy?" my mother said when she came home later with the paper sack of vegetables from her daily shopping visit to the Avenue C pushcarts. "You gave him enough for a dozen families. Now his father he'll sell it in his grocery store for God alone knows how much a pound!"

This had not occurred to me, but now that I saw this was probably why Henny had waited for me on the way to school that morning, I didn't care. Henny had warned me about something that might have been sprung on me unexpectedly from a hostile source. My only problem now was to wait out the shameful period of gestation.

I had no idea how long it took to have a baby, but I knew it did not happen overnight. For all I knew, it could take years. Although I didn't really know how long a year was, I knew several of them would have to be lived through before the shame was lifted from my family.

I lay awake for hours that night, plotting ways and means of survival, but worked out only one practical device. Instead of going to school as I had always gone, around the corner from our tenement into Lewis Street and up to the Third Street entrance to the boys' side of P.S. 188, I would go west up Fourth Street to Avenue C, south on Avenue C to Third Street, and then work my way cautiously down Third to the school entrance. In this way I would meet fewer, perhaps none, of the boys who knew me and my family well enough to be aware of the shameful secret I had just learned from Henny Leopolstadt.

The device worked. The next morning I managed to get to the school entrance without meeting anybody I knew, and in the afternoon, following in reverse the same new route on the way home, I was just as lucky. This lifted my spirits a little, and as I opened the door of our rooms, I was thinking hopefully that perhaps I might survive the appalling period of trial that stretched ahead. The thought did not last long.

Our kitchen was crowded with people who did not belong

56

in it. Not at that hour, anyway. My father should not have been there until four hours later. He always came home from work at seven-thirty. Dr. Gropple, who charged fifty cents for an office visit to his brownstone on Fifth Street and a dollar for a house call, should not have been washing his hands at the tap in our kitchen sink. Above all, at three-thirty in the afternoon, my sister should have been doing something on the girls' side of P.S. 188 with The Blue Birds for Happiness, not pouring glasses of my father's Passover wine for a dozen neighbors who, when you thought about it for a moment, should have been in their own kitchens, preparing the evening meal for their families.

"Take him into the bedroom," Dr. Gropple said cheerfully. It occurred to me from the sound of his voice that perhaps my sister had served him first. "Show him his brand-new brother."

They did that, and even though he wasn't much to see, the sight was a great relief to me. There was nothing wrong on East Fourth Street about new babies. It was waiting for them that was shameful. My relief was so great that it confused my sense of gratitude. I didn't know whether I should be grateful to my mother or to my new brother or to Dr. Gropple, but I did know that I was grateful for being spared the long shameful period of waiting. I entered cheerfully into the share of the celebration that was assigned to me, and it seemed highly appropriate that the person chosen to assist me should be Henny Leopolstadt.

"Henny is here he should take you to his father's store," my father said, handing me a list he had scribbled on the blank space above the masthead of a copy of the *Jewish Daily Forward*. "Come back quick because the guests are already coming, and we have only in the house wine and leftover sugar cookies from Friday." My father then gave Henny five two-dollar bills. "If it costs more," my father said to Henny, "I'll come in tomorrow and pay, tell your father."

Henny did not get a chance to convey this message, because when we came into his father's store Mrs. Mishig was standing at the slicing counter, holding her Hudson seal coat tightly wrapped around her with both hands and arguing with Mr. Leopolstadt about the way he was carving her order of belly lox.

The reason my mother did not patronize Mr. Leopolstadt's store regularly was that, unlike Mr. Deutsch, Henny's father was not really a grocer. He owned what was known on East Fourth Street as an appetizing store. Mr. Leopolstadt sold smoked fish, fresh olives, and other spiced delicacies, items that the people of East Fourth Street could afford only on special occasions, such as the one on which my own family was at the moment embarked: celebrating the birth of a new baby. Mr. and Mrs. Mishig, to my knowledge, were the only people on our block who were rich enough to shop regularly at Mr. Leopolstadt's, and in spite of my excitement about the party that was about to take place in our house, there was room in my head to note how appropriate it was for me and Henny to find the small, arrogant young woman not only buying belly lox, the most expensive kind of smoked salmon Mr. Leopolstadt sold, but also to be arguing about the way it was being sliced. She stopped when Henny and I came into the store, because his father, a large, cheerful man, released a roar of laughter and waved the large knife over his head as though it were a baton.

"To the new brother, a big hello!" Mr. Leopolstadt

58

shouted. "And to the new mother, go give my congratulations!"

"Some citizen you are," Mrs. Mishig said coldly. "To go around congratulating people they're having children so they can stay out of the draft!"

"Why people have children, it's not my business to ask," Mr. Leopolstadt said. "All I know, when they have them, I give them the congratulations, and I sell them the sturgeon and the *muslinniss* for the party. That's why you came," he said to me. "No?"

I nodded and handed over the list my father had given me. Henny handed over the five two-dollar bills. I didn't speak, because the look on Mrs. Mishig's face made me uncomfortable. Also, I could not forget the savagery in her voice when she had slammed the door in my mother's face two days before.

"Your father, the whole block he must have invited," Mr. Leopolstadt said, looking up from the list. "Ten pounds knubble carp, I never yet had in the store so much at one time. Henny, you go with him to Shmeelick's, and tell them it's for me for the store. By the time you come back with the knubble carp, the other things on the list, I'll have them ready."

"Okay," Henny said to his father, and to me, "Come on."

"They should be ashamed of themselves," Mrs. Mishig said in a loud, clear voice as Henny and I turned to go. "Giving parties with knubble carp because they got a new baby to keep the father a draft dodger out of Furtz Luchel."

"Mrs. Mishig," Mr. Leopolstadt said, "I don't with my belly lox for the same price give my customers advice, but you and Mr. Mishig, a big healthy young man like your husband, nobody knows how long this war it'll last, a baby or two if you had, it wouldn't hurt, you know. A married man, with no children, I'm surprised they didn't grab him up to Furtz Luchel long ago already."

As Henny and I went through the door of his father's store into Avenue C, I saw Mrs. Mishig do something I never heard about until years later when I began to read novels: she tossed her head.

"Mr. Mishig is not afraid of Furtz Luchel," she said. "When his country wants him, Mr. Mishig will go. Mr. Mishig and I have decided not to have children until the war is over, so nobody can say he's a draft dodger!"

The door of Mr. Leopolstadt's appetizing store slammed shut behind me and Henny. I did not, of course, understand why it was such a terrible thing to be called a draft dodger, but I did know that for the second time in two days the wife of the only man on East Fourth Street who was not open to the accusation had insulted my father, and I had done nothing about it. I felt awful. Henny must have understood this, because as we walked up the street he made a short remark about Mrs. Mishig that though it was not new on East Fourth Street, I did not then know was universal. It seemed wise to change the subject.

"What's Shmeelick's?" I said.

"He's the wholesaler they give my father his stuff for the store," Henny said. "It's on Houston Street."

I was familiar with Houston Street. The part that came down to the East River formed the southern boundary of P.S. 188. Shmeelick's, however, was near First Avenue, a part of Houston Street I had never before visited. Henny Leopolstadt said he had been there many times, on errands for his father. For this reason he did not seem to be as interested as I was in the neighborhood. It was not, like the part of Houston Street I knew, a residential area. The further west we moved, the more warehouses and trucks we were surrounded by. Shmeelick's looked like most of its neighbors: a gray, evil-smelling building with a loading ramp and an office tucked away at one side of the arched entrance. A woman with several pencils stuck into her mound of white hair listened to Henny for a couple of moments, then pulled one of the pencils from her hair and scribbled something on a pad.

"We're all out of knubble carp," she said. "Go over to Friedlander's on Fourteenth Street and give them this order." She tore the top sheet from the pad and handed it to Henny. "You won't have no trouble finding the place. It's between Sixth and Seventh Avenue."

We didn't have any trouble, but I was afraid we might, and I think Henny shared my fear. Neither of us had ever before been in this part of town. We walked slowly, and examined everything we passed with care. There was a great deal to see. The Sixth Avenue El, for example. This was my first glimpse of it. The piece of it that loomed up ahead of us as we walked west on Fourteenth Street did not look different from the First Avenue El or the Third Avenue El, both of which I had seen many times. But because it was new to me, there were things about the Sixth Avenue El that looked different. At the bottom of the long flight of steps that led up to the green station house, for example, I saw something I had never seen at the bottom of the steps that led up to any of the stations on the First and Third Avenue Els with which I was familiar.

A man was sitting on the sidewalk, his back against the railing, one elbow resting on the lowest step. His clothes were ragged, his face dirty, and his hair matted. In his lap he held a filthy old brown felt hat. As people passed him on their way up the steps to the El station, some would pause, dip their hands into their pockets, pull out a coin or two, and drop them into the man's hat. As Henny and I came closer, I saw that the man had a sign hung around his neck. In crude letters, it read, "Please Help I Am A Cripple." A moment after that, I recognized the man's mustache. It had been rumpled, like his hair, but there was no mistaking those two distinctly separated sections that stood out from his upper lip like a set of miniature bull's horns. Then I saw the trouser leg pinned up over the stump that helped keep the felt hat full of coins steady against the young man's good leg.

I did not realize Henny had seen what I was seeing until I heard him say, "Jesus Christ, no wonder he's not afraid of Furtz Luchel!"

My own reaction was entirely different. I don't know why. I remember thinking, "So this is how he pays for those expensive suits and his wife's Hudson seal coat!" Then the fierce look that came out of those bright black eyes that seemed to have no pupils swung toward me and caught my glance. It must have caught Henny's, too, because we both turned and started to run at the same time.

I don't know when Henny told his father about what we had seen on Fourteenth Street, but I waited until Dr. Gropple said it was all right for my mother to get out of bed. Since this happened on a Friday, the first thing she did, after she gave my new brother his bottle, was start the week's baking. When I came home from school in the afternoon, the two jelly jars of cold milk and the plate with six sugar cookies were set out on the table.

"The week while I was in bed," my mother said as I bit

into the first cookie, "guess who moved away from Fourth Street?"

I did not have to guess. The day after we brought the ten pounds of knubble carp from Friedlander's, Henny Leopolstadt and I had watched the Mishig furniture being loaded into the wagon from Weltner's stable. But I remembered the hurt look on my mother's face the day Mrs. Mishig refused to accept some of Uncle Berel's white sugar from the wife of a draft dodger. I remembered the savage contempt in the voice of the only woman on East Fourth Street who owned a Hudson seal coat. It seemed to me my mother was entitled to the satisfaction of breaking the news.

"Who?" I said.

3

A Kid
or a Coffin

When I was a boy on East Fourth Street, Monroe Klein was known, in Yiddish of course, as "The Knife with Hair on It." The last four words were intended to distinguish Monroe from his father. Mr. Klein was totally bald. Mr. Klein was also the first professional politician I ever met, but at the time I didn't think of him that way.

At the time, which was shortly after the First World War, I didn't think very much about anything that was happening around me. I just accepted it. I was approximately eight years old, and what was happening around me seemed perfectly reasonable. After all, it was also happening to everybody else.

I say I was approximately eight years old, because at that time on East Fourth Street, birth certificates were a hit-or-miss proposition. Women in labor did not go to hospitals. They screamed for a neighbor. As I put together the verifiable facts about my entrance into the twentieth century, when my mother screamed, Mrs. Lichtblau responded.

It was around noon. Even though I have no way of nailing down the exact moment with the sort of historical fidelity practiced by the biographers of our martyred Presidents, there are reliable compass points. The city's garbage collection trucks, for example. In those days they managed to make it to East Fourth Street only once a week, on Tuesdays, and, for no reason I can sensibly explain, around noon.

Two weeks ago, when Mrs. Lichtblau came to my father's funeral, we discussed the day of my birth. Mrs. Lichtblau was ninety-three last year, and she was having trouble with her upper plate, but she remembered the event clearly.

"It was a Tuesday," Mrs. Lichtblau said. "I know it was a Tuesday because the day before I put the saltpeter in my corned beef pot, and I always put in the saltpeter on a Monday because to make corned beef right, it has to be with the saltpeter five days. No more, no less, just five, and I always put in the saltpeter on a Monday so I could remember always to take off the stone from the meat and spill away the saltpeter on Friday just before I used to light the candles. Lighting the candles on Friday night, that you never forget. So anything you have to do just before you light the candles, that you'll never forget either. So if you put in the saltpeter on a Monday, and it has to stay in five days, you couldn't make a mistake. That's how I know you were born on a Tuesday. The day after I put in the saltpeter and the stone on my corned beef, I heard your mother scream. The same time I heard the scream, I was sending *my* Benny downstairs with garbage, because I just heard the garbage truck in the street. So like that, from the saltpeter I know it was a Tuesday, and from the garbage truck I know it was twelve o'clock, because that's when they always came. Twelve o'clock. I ran across the hall to your rooms," Mrs. Lichtblau said. "I took one look at your mother, and I ran back, and I screamed down in the street from my window to *my* Benny, forget the garbage, run quick, go get Dr. Gropple."

Dr. Gropple lived and practiced in a brownstone on East Fourth Street just in from the Avenue C corner, going toward Avenue B. He did not have office hours. Nobody ever made an appointment to see him. For one thing, nobody on East Fourth Street had a telephone. Not even Dr. Gropple. For another, he did not own an engagement book. When you were sick, you walked over and sat in the front room of his parlor floor until he was ready to see you. You carried your fifty cents with you. If you were too sick to be trusted with holding the money, your mother wrapped the coin in a piece of paper and pinned the paper to your coat. Dr. Gropple never sent out bills. He had no time to write bills. He worked around the clock. He had no nurse. He did everything himself. He never refused to make a house call. He never delayed a house call, either. The moment he was summoned, day or night, he went. No, he ran.

Years later, when I was the senior patrol leader of Troop 224, Dr. Gropple's son Morris explained why. Morris was the leader of the Beaver Patrol, and he had asked me over to his house one night for a meeting at which we were to lay out the program for an elimination knot-tying contest that Mr. Osterweil, our scoutmaster, felt was the only fair way to select the team that would represent our troop in the annual all-Manhattan rally. Morris and I were working with a pad and a pencil at the Gropple kitchen table in the basement of the brownstone. Suddenly the iron areaway gate clanged noisily. Morris ran out to see what was happening. A couple of moments later I heard him running upstairs to the waiting room on the parlor floor. I went to the window and looked out into the night. On the sidewalk, under the lamppost in front of the Gropple stoop, a man was standing and staring up the brownstone steps to the Gropple front door. He was shivering, which was not surprising, since it was January and he had obviously come running from his home without pausing to dress. He was wearing pants and a sleeveless undershirt. But he was shivering with more than the cold. The man looked terrified.

A couple of moments after I got to the window, Dr. Gropple came running down the brownstone steps, carrying his little black bag and adjusting his pearl-gray fedora. On East Fourth Street the effectiveness of a doctor depended to a large extent on the clothes he wore. Dr. Gropple dressed like Woodrow Wilson. When a man who dressed like Woodrow Wilson told an immigrant woman to take two of these every hour, and never mind how bitter they tasted or if they were kosher, she took them. Dr. Gropple's pearl-gray fedoras, which I learned years later he bought uptown at Dobbs, were just as important on an East Fourth Street house call as his stethoscope.

He seized the arm of the frightened, shivering man and they hurried off toward Avenue C. A few moments later, when Morris came back to the kitchen, I asked him what had happened. Morris shrugged as he picked up the pencil. "Who knows?" he said. "But you can be sure it's either a kid or a coffin. The people around here, before they'll

68

spend a dollar on a house call, it's either somebody is getting born, or somebody is getting ready to croak."

I had no idea that I was about to croak on that day, so few years after I was born, when Dr. Gropple made his second house call to our tenement flat.

Ten days before his appearance in the bedroom I shared with my father and younger brother, Miss Kitchell had taken her P.S. 188 class for a walk during recess to what was known in our neighborhood as the "Roof Garden." This was a dark green structure, the color of a dirty park bench, with many uselessly decorative spires and turrets. This structure partially enclosed the dock that jutted out into the East River at the end of Third Street. It was actually no more than a foolishly fancy shed that the city, for perhaps perfectly sound reasons, had built soon after the Civil War. By the time Dr. Gropple brought me into the world, those reasons had long been forgotten. By the time Miss Kitchell took her class out for a walk in the bright June sunlight, I had seen the Roof Garden used for only two purposes.

During the war soldiers had on several occasions been disembarked on the Third Street dock, then put through some sort of drill or inspection under the dark green shed before they were marched up Third Street to that mysterious and to me as yet unexplored region called "uptown." Also, two or three times every summer, on Sunday afternoons, a group of men in gold-braided uniforms appeared on the Third Street dock, carrying musical instruments and metal folding chairs. They would arrange these in a square at the far or river end of the Roof Garden, tune up their instruments, and start to play.

Nobody seemed to know where these men came from, or why they were playing. They did not live in our neighborhood, and they did not play any of the songs my mother had learned as a girl in Hungary, and had later taught me and my brother and sister on East Fourth Street. These songs were different. Some were strange. The older people, however, especially boys and girls who had graduated from P.S. 188 and were now earning money uptown, seemed to like these songs. After a while, I found I did, too. I didn't dance to them, of course, the way the older boys and girls did. By the time I learned to dance, I no longer lived on East Fourth Street. It was from these Sunday afternoon band concerts, however, listening to the young—but to me at the time very old—couples singing as they danced under the Roof Garden, that I learned all the words to "K-K-K-Katy," "Over There," "Apple Blossom Time," and "The Star-Spangled Banner."

On the day Miss Kitchell took her class for a constitutional, I learned something else: why rules and regulations, the raw material that fed the minds of men like Hammurabi and Clarence Darrow, come into existence. It was quite a lesson to learn from a tiny, humpbacked lady with white hair and dark brown eyes as bright as shoe buttons. Miss Kitchell couldn't possibly have weighed more than eighty pounds and she never raised her voice. Except in the morning when, after sounding the correct note on her pitch pipe, Miss Kitchell led the class in singing "Dear Lord, Who Sought at Dawn of Day" or "By Roads That Wound Uphill and Down," her two favorite hymns.

My own favorite was "Fling Out the Banner! Let It Float" because Monroe Klein, who was twelve years old, almost ready for his bar mitzvah, and went to Junior High

School 64 on Ninth Street, had invented a set of obscene
lyrics to the melody. When adults were not within earshot,
he would sing his version to us. I did not then understand
all of the words, and it is possible that Monroe didn't understand all of them, either, but I wouldn't bet on it. I think
I grasp now what I merely responded to then, namely, the
ambiance of leadership. Monroe had it. As I look back on
other people I've known who had it, it seems to me much
of it consists of precocity. If at five you can play the violin
well enough to make Mischa Elman sweat, other musicians
are bound to look up to you as a leader. If at twelve you
can rewrite a deeply religious and very moving hymn with
words out of the gutter, your associates are almost certainly
going to think of you with a certain amount of awe. I know
that's how I felt about Monroe Klein on the day Miss
Kitchell led us out of P.S. 188 for a walk at recess, and we
reached the Roof Garden on the Third Street dock. Monroe
was coming toward us, trundling a wheelbarrow full of
coal for his father's hardware store on Avenue C. Monroe
played hookey regularly to go down to the docks and pick
up from the moored barges items his father wanted for the
store.

"Hey, kids," Monroe said. "Look! It's the Floating
Coney!"

This was East Fourth Street's name for the only mobile
link in the city's chain of structures designed to keep the
immigrant population of the Lower East Side in a reasonably sanitary condition. This was no small task.

I, for example, never saw a bathtub until I was eleven.
Neither did my mother. As a girl on the farm in Hungary,
however, she had grown accustomed to a weekly scrub-
down in a tin washtub set near the kitchen stove. The

kitchens of the East Fourth Street tenement flats were less spacious. In my years on East Fourth Street, I saw a great many of these kitchens.

They were all exactly like ours: a twelve-foot square, with a black dado running around the four walls, about four feet from the floor. Below the dado the walls were painted dark green; above, somewhat lighter green. The ceilings were always pale brown or dark yellow. It was difficult to tell which, because they were painted so infrequently that what my mother felt was yellow darkened by years of accumulated dirt, my father believed was once white paint turning brown with age. The color of the floor depended on the tenant's taste in linoleum. My mother in those days favored the sort of unadorned dark brown used in the corridors of public buildings because "it didn't show the dirt." The tenant could, of course, add to the room any furnishings he chose, but the landlord provided only three: a large coal stove against one wall, a metal sink in the corner nearest the single window, and a gray cement rectangular washtub, four feet by two. This was divided in the middle by a cement wall to form two square tubs, two feet by two. One tub was for soaping the family laundry, the other for rinsing, and this was how most housewives on East Fourth Street used this piece of standard equipment. Not my mother.

Soon after we moved into our rooms at 390 East Fourth Street, she borrowed a small sledge hammer from the janitor and smashed to bits the cement wall that separated the two sections of the washtub. After my father carried the pulverized cement down to the garbage cans on the sidewalk in front of the tenement, my mother used an old bread knife to smooth down the places where the demolished cement wall had once divided the washtubs. On our first Saturday night in 390, I was the first member of the family to take a bath in the improvised bathtub. My father, who followed, said he felt a bit cramped in the four-by-two space, but it was the depth that counted, and from then on, my mother saw to it that none of us missed a turn at least once a week. Many of our neighbors expressed their admiration for my mother's ingenuity, but none so far as I can recall followed her example. The general feeling seemed to be that it was the government's problem. If the city administration did not want the entire Lower East Side to smell like a locker room, it was up to the city to do something about it, and of course the city had done something about it.

The city had built a series of public bathhouses. The one I knew was on Rivington Street. You had to bring your own towel, but for a penny a civil service employee in dirty white pants and an even dirtier sleeveless undershirt gave you a sliver of soap and access to a room lined with open stall showers. Each was equipped with hot and cold running water and, on the gray marble walls, graffiti of astonishing ingenuity. I was describing them to my friend Henny Leopolstadt one day soon after my first visit, and my mother heard me. It proved to be my last visit. The same was true of my first visit to the Floating Coney, but for a different reason.

The Floating Coney was named, of course, after the only seaside resort most people on East Fourth Street had ever visited or even heard about: Coney Island. It was a barge, in outer appearance not unlike the barges that were brought by tugs up and down the East River every day to be eased into their moorings at the Fourth Street dock so that their loads of lumber and coal could be transferred to the storage

73

yards of the Forest Box & Lumber Company and the Burns Coal Company, which I could see from the bedroom window. Outward appearance, however, was the only resemblance between these barges and the Floating Coney.

I have never been able to find out whether the city intended it to serve as a sanitary facility or a recreation center. In any case, when the Floating Coney came to our neighborhood, it served as both. It was a large floating swimming pool. The central body of the barge was a huge rectangle with wooden sides and a sort of latticework bottom. Through this bottom the waters of the East River ebbed and flowed. Around the four sides of this open pool stretched a series of lockers, painted the inevitable dirty park-bench green.

Long before I saw the Floating Coney for the first time, I had heard from Monroe Klein and others that, beginning with the first day of June, the city sent the barge on a slow tour of the docks that surrounded Manhattan. The Floating Coney would be towed to a mooring by one or more of the city's tugs. The barge would be made fast. And for a week or so, before it moved on to another part of the city, the people who lived near the particular dock would be free to board the barge between the hours of nine in the morning and sundown for a swim in the wooden pool.

No charge. No keys to the open lockers, either. Fortunately, these all faced the pool, and none had doors. It was possible, therefore, while swimming in the river water that flowed through the center of the barge, to keep an eye on your clothes. This was important. If they were stolen you were in trouble. Visitors to the Floating Coney swam naked. There were, naturally, Men's Days and Women's Days. The day I first saw the Floating Coney was neither. When Miss

74

Kitchell's class reached the Roof Garden on the Third Street dock, the barge was being eased into the slip between Third and Fourth Streets by a city tug.

"Notice the skill with which the captain of the tugboat uses the power at his command," Miss Kitchell said as we stood in two neat rows and watched. "He does not turn loose the full force of his engines. He thrusts and stops. He thrusts and reverses. He thrusts and stops. Then he thrusts and reverses again. In this way he keeps the movement of the enormously heavy barge at a slow and steady pace, easing it gently to its mooring. If he did not do this, if the captain of the tugboat used all his power and used it thoughtlessly, he might damage both the barge and the dock, perhaps even destroy them. There is a lesson in this for all of us."

I waited eagerly to hear what it was. I was impressed by Miss Kitchell's lessons. They were totally different from the ones I was taught at home. Or rather, the method was different. My mother, for instance, did not say, "Never come into the house wearing your muddy rubbers. Take them off and leave them out in the hall before you come into the house." What happened was that one day you came into the house wearing your muddy rubbers. Before you got very far into the house, wham, you caught one across your rear end. As you started to cry or protest or merely pull yourself together, there was your mother, laying down the brand-new law: "Never come into the house wearing your muddy rubbers. Take them off and leave them out in the hall before you come into the house." It was a good method. Anyway, it worked. You never came into the house wearing muddy rubbers.

Miss Kitchell's method was refreshingly different. One

day you came clumping into her classroom wearing your muddy rubbers. Miss Kitchell would descend on you and begin chirping and buzzing like a house fly trying to get through a window screen.

"Oh, my, what a mess we've made! Here, let me help you take off those muddy rubbers. There, that's better. Now, we'll just put them outside the door, so they can dry in the hall. There we are. And now we'll take this rag and clean up this mess we've made, won't we? There we are. And now, children, let's all remember what just happened, because there's a lesson in this for all of us. Never come into the classroom wearing your muddy rubbers. Always take off your muddy rubbers outside, and leave them in the hall before you come into the classroom. We'll try to remember this lesson, won't we, children?"

I don't recall that it was necessary to try very hard. As soon as Miss Kitchell started chirping about a lesson, I found myself beginning to listen eagerly. On that June day, however, before she could tell us what lesson was concealed in the way the tugboat captain was maneuvering the Floating Coney to its berth, Monroe Klein spoke up.

"When they got it docked, Miss Kitchell," he said, "how's about you let your class go on for a swim? Recess is a whole hour."

I remember my first reaction. Admiration. I wasn't surprised. Monroe Klein's suggestions were all brilliant. I was puzzled by how few of them Miss Kitchell adopted. Especially since she obviously shared my feeling that they were brilliant. Monroe was too old, of course, to be in Miss Kitchell's class, but he always seemed to be around. Perhaps because he was a born politician. Anyway, even though Miss Kitchell never actually said Monroe's suggestions were brilliant, I could tell she admired them because she always found a lesson in them.

"I'm glad you made that suggestion, Monroe," Miss Kitchell said. "Because there is a lesson in it for all of us. Very few people realize how dangerous it is to swim in the East River. Even the city authorities do not realize it. Or perhaps they do not care. If they did, they would not invite the citizens of the city to come on board a boat like this and bathe in the polluted waters of the river. We have it on good medical authority that bathing in the East River is an open invitation to mastoids, scrofula, diphtheria, tuberculosis, meningitis, typhoid fever, German measles, typhus, and many other diseases. I am glad you made your suggestion, Monroe, because it has given me this opportunity to warn you all about the danger of bathing in polluted river water. We'll try to remember this lesson, won't we?"

I tried, but it was not easy. The weather, which had been very warm, turned hot that week. On Men's Days, as soon as school was over, all the older boys on the block headed for the East River dock. Even some of the fathers, when they came home from work, went over for a dip on the Floating Coney. Not my father. And, on Women's Days, not my mother. As for my sister and me, we were forbidden to go anywhere near the swimming barge.

"You and your big mouth," my sister said bitterly on the first Saturday afternoon after the Floating Coney docked at Third Street. She was watching her friends disappear around the Lewis Street corner on their way to a swim. "It's all your fault."

She was right. It was all my fault. My admiration for Miss Kitchell was such that every night as we ate our dinner around the kitchen table, I would tell my family

in detail what new lesson she had taught her class that day.
The day the Floating Coney docked at Third Street, I gave
an account of Monroe Klein's suggestion, and the lesson
Miss Kitchell had drawn from it for the class.

"She's right," my father said. "I remember once it happened in *da heim*."

The literal translation of these two Yiddish words is "the
home." To my father, as well as to my mother, the words
meant something larger: *their* home. And to each of them
their home was more than a house, and not the house in
which they were then living. When my mother or father
uttered the words *da heim,* there was in the two small
sounds the clear implication that, for both of them, all other
homes were temporary resting places on the long journey
back to the only home that mattered.

"With my brothers and other boys," my father said, "I
remember we went swimming in a place behind the forest.
The water had a bad smell, and my mother used to say
don't go, you'll get sick, but you know how it is with boys.
They don't listen. So we went, and we swam, and three
days later my older brother and one of the other boys, they
got sick, and then a few days later they were gone."

"You heard what Papa said," my mother said. "Nobody
from this house is going in that dirty water. You hear?"

My sister and I nodded, and that would have been the
end of it, if Monroe Klein had not been a dutiful son,
proud of his father's role in the life of East Fourth Street,
and eager to help him. Mr. Klein earned his living in the
hardware store on Avenue C, but what he lived for was the
Democratic Party. He was the local captain of the Sixth
Assembly District.

Every year, as the summer started to edge up on Labor

Day, Mr. Klein and the Republican captain, a man named
Diener, would begin to lay their snares for the votes that
the citizens of East Fourth Street would cast on the first
Tuesday after the first Monday in November. Mr. Klein
had one advantage over his Republican rival: he lived on
East Fourth Street. Mr. Diener, who lived on East Seventh
Street, had one advantage over Mr. Klein: the Republicans
had more money. Anyway, Mr. Diener seemed to have more
to spend. He was certainly more generous during the initial
phases of the bargaining.

Years later, when I had reached voting age and started
to cast my ballot for Franklin Delano Roosevelt and believed like so many others of my generation that there never
would be anybody else to vote for, I began to realize that
it was wrong to describe the polling process as bargaining.
When I was growing up, however, that's how the machinery
of democracy functioned on East Fourth Street, and nobody
thought it was wrong. Certainly not Mr. Klein.

He would drop in some evening late in August, tweak
my sister's cheek, run his hardware-store-toughened hand
through my hair and my brother's hair, and ask my mother
what she would like to have "for the cold weather." The
approach was, of course, correct. Winter was the difficult
time on East Fourth Street.

The tenement flats were not equipped with central heat-
ing. The coal stove in the kitchen, which the year round
was used for cooking, in the winter provided the only heat.
This meant that the further you moved from the kitchen,
the colder you were. After November, for example, only
about one third of our front room was habitable. It was
the third near the door, which opened directly into the
kitchen. Similarly, one third of the bedroom was reasonably

comfortable. Again, it was the third near the door, which also opened directly into the kitchen, at the other side of the stove. I have been inside butchers' iceboxes that were more comfortable than this bedroom. It was at the end of our railroad flat. By the time you got to the middle of this room, all exposed parts of your body began to tingle. By the time you got to the end, your eyes teared, your cheekbones stung, and your nose ran.

What Mr. Klein and Mr. Diener had to offer in exchange for the votes they coveted was protection against what winter could do to you on the banks of the East River. The form of protection was, of course, a matter of choice. Some voters asked for heavy underwear for their families. Others preferred rubber boots. Mrs. Lichtblau, I remember, always held out for a winter coat for *her* Benny, enough wool with which to knit thick sweaters for herself and her husband, and four bottles of Stoke's Expectorant.

"The only thing you can be sure on East Fourth Street it'll happen in the winter," I remember her once saying to my mother when they were comparing notes on their negotiations with Mr. Klein and Mr. Diener, "you can be sure the whole family they'll start coughing. You got enough Stoke's in the house, you'll live through to Passover."

My mother's price for the two votes she was able to deliver was always the same: two tons of anthracite. She did not call it anthracite. She called it what everybody on East Fourth Street called it and very few could afford: hard coal. It was more expensive than soft coal. It did not throw off as much soot. And it burned longer. Two tons, my mother had learned, would get us comfortably through the winter, and for two tons she was willing to learn how to recognize the names of either Mr. Klein's or Mr. Diener's candidates when she entered the polling booth so she could place her "X" in the proper place. She could not read.

There was nothing very delicate about these negotiations, and yet they were carried on, with all the formality of a minuet, in a series of moves that never varied. Mr. Diener, for example, never came calling before Mr. Klein. Perhaps because Mr. Klein lived right there, in our building, whereas Mr. Diener had to come all the way from East Seventh Street. Perhaps because the two men had an understanding. Mr. Klein, even though he always ended by giving my mother the two tons she demanded, always began by saying two tons were more than he could afford, and he would have to think it over. While he was thinking it over, Mr. Diener showed up. He always seemed more hurried than Mr. Klein, so my sister was spared the cheek tweak, and my brother and I didn't have to go through the hair rub. Mr. Diener, perhaps because he was rushed for time, never wasted any of it.

"Whatever Klein said he'd give you," he always said, "I'll give you more."

My mother's reply was also always the same. "I'll think it over," she said.

I don't think she ever did. Because she always, in the end, did the same thing. As a result, I never found out what the "more" was—three tons? four?—that Mr. Diener offered. Before he could get around to naming the size of his larger offer, my mother always accepted Mr. Klein's two tons. One of the reasons for this was clear. For the rent he paid on his rooms, every tenant in the building was entitled to the use of a *kemmerel* in the cellar. A *kemmerel* was a crudely constructed wooden bin designed for storage. I

81

suppose they would have been adequate for storing Chippendale furniture and Bristol glass, but I don't recall ever seeing a *kemmerel* put to this test. Almost every tenant in our building used his *kemmerel* for the same purpose: storing coal. Our *kemmerel* could take two tons comfortably, and two was all we needed to get through the winter. Why take more and create a storage problem for yourself? So, I think, my mother's reasoning went on practical grounds.

About how her reasoning went on political grounds, I am not certain, and I was never able to get her to tell me. Her reticence is my only clue. My mother was not a very complex person. That is, once you grasped how her mind worked in pursuit of the things she wanted. The things she wanted were always things she needed. For herself and for her family. And the things she needed, she had learned during her hard youth in Europe, were the things that kept you alive.

I never, for example, heard her mention, much less discuss or covet, finery for herself. But I have watched her scheme to get soup bones free out of Mr. Kanervogel, the butcher on the Avenue D corner, by promising to urge the women in our building to patronize him rather than Mr. Gottlieb on Lewis Street. My mother never kept the promise, and even at my then tender age I knew she wouldn't when I heard her make it. She had got what she wanted. No, what she needed. That ended her interest in the matter. A discussion of ethics, the pros and cons of keeping a pledged word, was to my mother a waste of time. Time that could better be devoted to the acquisition of something else she needed to keep herself and her family alive.

I don't think it bothered her that she never kept her promise to Mr. Klein. I think what troubled her was the fact that my father knew she made the promise every year. My father was a socialist. He detested the candidates for whom Mr. Klein and Mr. Diener solicited votes. My father worked and voted for people like Jacob Panken, August Claessens, Meyer London, Victor Berger, and Eugene Debs. He did it out of conviction. My mother voted for them, too. Out of loyalty to my father. What upset her may very well have been the knowledge that he was aware of her annual lie.

I am certain, however, that she refused to discuss it, even with me when I was older and seeking information, because she understood the danger of gossip. Talking about it might have spread the news of her duplicity to the ears of Mr. Klein and Mr. Diener. In their justifiable anger, they might have ceased buying her two votes every year. She would then have had to use money desperately needed for food to pay for equally desperately needed coal. One of the unfailing constants, therefore, in the minuet of negotiations for our winter fuel was the role played in them by my father. As soon as Mr. Klein or Mr. Diener entered our kitchen, my father left. He did not leave in that equipage of the Victorian novelist known as a huff. My father was a quiet man. He left quietly.

I can still see him on that hot summer Saturday looking up from his copy of the *Jewish Daily Forward* as the kitchen door opened. Mr. Klein came in, followed by his son Monroe. Monroe always accompanied his father on visits to families that had children. Both parties to the bargaining process must have felt they were indulging in an activity that it was better for the young not to witness. It was Monroe's job to remove the young witnesses from the scene of the negotiations.

"Hello, hello, hello," Mr. Klein said. He always spoke as though he were making carbon copies for his files and the files of the home office. "Could a person come in for a little quiet talk?"

"You'll excuse me," my father said to my mother. "I forgot something to do."

He folded his newspaper, tucked it under his arm, and left the house. Mr. Klein looked into the front room, and then into the bedroom off the kitchen.

"Where's the other children?" he said.

My mother explained that my sister had taken her baby brother with her to a Blue Birds for Happiness Club meeting at P.S. 188.

"So what's left then," he said, taking another stab at my hair, "why shouldn't my Monroe take him to the bios?"

The "bios," I figured out years later, must have been an abbreviation for the word "biographs." On Fourth Street it means the American Movie Theatre on Third Street, between Avenue C and Avenue D. I had been inside only twice in my life, both times as the guest of Mr. Klein and in the company of his son Monroe, on days when the Democratic captain of the Sixth Assembly District had begun his negotiations for my mother's votes.

"If he wants to go, why not?" my mother said.

Mr. Klein handed Monroe two dimes. Monroe took my hand and we left. We walked in silence. Monroe, in the service he rendered his father, was always conscientious, but he did not enter into many conversations with his young charges. Perhaps he had no small talk. Perhaps he preferred his own thoughts. I wouldn't have blamed him. Although my wife says I have made up for it since, in those days I had very little to say. I wouldn't have known how to express it at the time, but I see now that I, too, preferred my own thoughts. Some of them still make me wince.

"Hey, look at that," Monroe said suddenly.

He was pointing to the Third Street pickle stand. It was one of my favorite sights. I never tired of looking at it. It consisted of a broad plank, perhaps twelve feet long, set on three wooden horses. On the plank were ranged thirty or forty small wooden buckets full of pickles, spiced tomatoes, fresh black olives, and red and green peppers in various sizes. Some of the buckets were covered with smaller planks on which were arranged pyramids of sliced pickles and tomatoes. From each pyramid, and out of each bucket, a small spatula-shaped piece of wood stuck up into the air with a price lettered on it. For one cent you could buy a slice of pickle, a quarter of a large green tomato, half a red pepper, or a small tomato. Entire pickles started at two cents and, depending on size, went up to a nickel.

Mr. Meyerson, who owned the pickle stand, kept his planks, horses, and buckets in the cellar under the tenement at the corner of Third Street and Avenue C. Every morning, when the pushcart peddlers started to arrive and set up the vegetable and fruit market that lined both sides of Avenue C, Mr. Meyerson brought out his planks and buckets and set up his pickle stand. To the housewives who came out every weekday morning with their shopping bags, Mr. Meyerson's pickle stand was more than a place where they chose a few items to add spice to the evening meal they would prepare later in the day for their families. It was also a gathering place for the exchange of gossip and a pause for refreshment. They would stop, buy a slice of pickle for a penny, and spend a few minutes discussing the weather, impending marriages, recent deaths, and the cost of living. On the Sabbath, of course, the pushcart market was not set up along the curbs of Avenue C. Mr. Meyerson, however, always set up his stand after he came home from synagogue, because on Saturday afternoons a great many young people went to the bios and, on the way, paused to buy a delicacy from Mr. Meyerson's buckets. My own favorite was the small green tomato, about the size of a golf ball, into which you had to bite with care because it squirted. I did not know which of the delicacies on display was Monroe Klein's favorite, but I could see that he thought the sight was as beautiful as I did.

I could see something else, but I did not then know what it was. Monroe was only twelve years old at the time. To me, however, that put him in the same class with grown-ups, especially since he was tall. I had not yet learned the importance of making a conscious effort to separate one grownup from another. I had learned, however, that all people who were older and taller than myself shared a few basic characteristics. One of these was certainty. They always seemed to know what they wanted or were going to do. I was surprised, therefore, to see the expression on Monroe's face as he stared at the pickle stand. He seemed to be going through some sort of inner struggle. I did not know then that I was watching something from which I, too, would one day suffer: the crisis of temptation.

"You want one?" Monroe said finally. I nodded quickly. The marvelous vinegary odor from the buckets was intoxicating. I could hardly speak. "What would you like?" Monroe said. "A penny slice?"

"No," I said. "That."

I pointed to the mound of small green tomatoes. Monroe took one down, handed it to me, and chose a fat three-cent

86

pickle for himself. He handed Mr. Meyerson one of the two dimes Mr. Klein had given him. Mr. Meyerson counted out the change from the pocket in his burlap apron. I waited until Monroe bit into his pickle before I attacked my tomato. I did it carefully, and managed to catch the delicious squirting juice in my mouth. Monroe then led me up the block to the American Theatre. By the time we reached it, my tomato was gone and Monroe had finished his pickle. He seemed troubled as he stared at the gaudy poster. He pulled a handful of coins from his pocket and stared at them.

"Listen," he said. "How about another tomato?"

I could scarcely believe my luck. I had never in my life had more than one at a time.

"Sure," I said.

We went back to the Avenue C corner. Holding my hand, Monroe bought another tomato for me, and another pickle for himself. Then he took me around the corner, into Avenue C, and he said, "You know something about that picture, kid. It's got no fighting."

Fighting meant fist fighting. On East Fourth Street it was the sole yardstick of cinema excellence. When a new bio arrived at the American, the first boy or girl who saw it was eagerly asked, "Zit gotnee fighting?" If the answer was yes, everybody schemed to go. If the answer was no, everybody lost interest.

"No fighting?" I said.

I had not meant to sound dubious. It was simply that I had heard a couple of my classmates say the new movie at the American had a lot of fighting. I was disappointed to learn I had been misinformed. Monroe apparently interpreted the disappointment in my voice as criticism.

"You calling me a liar?"

Years later I could still hear the cold, metallic, menacing sound in his voice, and I understood more clearly why Monroe Klein had been known on East Fourth Street as The Knife with Hair on It. I was suddenly frightened.

"No, no," I said. "It's just I heard—"

"Never mind what you heard," Monroe said. "The picture stinks." Then his face changed. "Anyway, it's too hot for the movies. Y'ever been on the Floating Coney?"

My heart leaped. I forgot all about the movies. Unfortunately, I also forgot my mother's stern injunction.

"No," I said.

"Come on," Monroe said.

He led me down Third Street to the Roof Garden on the dock. The Floating Coney rose and fell gently at its mooring. We went up the gangplank to the deck, where an attendant stood guard over a turnstile.

"Lockers on the left," he said.

Monroe pushed me through, and came through behind me. We emerged on a wet boardwalk that ran around the four sides of the wooden pool. It was full of boys and men, splashing, yelling, and laughing. I followed Monroe along the boardwalk until he found an empty locker. We took off our clothes and hung them on pegs.

"You know how to swim?" Monroe said.

"No," I said.

"Then let's go down the low end."

Here, in the shallow water, I had my first swimming lesson. Monroe must have been a good teacher, because by the time he said we'd better get dressed, I was able to stay afloat for a few moments, and I could even take several strokes before I went under. I had been having such a good

88

time that I did not notice, until we started to get dressed, that both of us were streaked with oil slick.

"Don't tell your mother where we were," Monroe said when we were out on the dock, heading for home.

"She'll smell me," I said.

Monroe walked in silence for a while, then said, "Tell her there was a leak from the ceiling in the movies. Tell her a lot of people got it. Me, too."

My mother had a suspicious nature, but when I made this explanation, she accepted it without question. From this I guessed that in my absence her negotiations with Mr. Klein for our winter coal supply had gone well. It was the last rational deduction I was to make for some time.

The process of learning to swim has undoubtedly always involved swallowing a certain amount of the water in which the lessons are given. I had been aware, as I thrashed around on the Floating Coney, that what I was swallowing tasted unpleasant, but I was too excited to make any effort to swallow less. During our evening meal, I began to taste the oil slick through my mother's noodle soup. It was not a good combination. I was sick all night.

By morning my mother decided I had a fever. We did not, of course, own a thermometer. Even if we had, nobody in the family would have known how to read it. By poking at my forehead, however, my mother knew that the time had come to spend a half dollar. She wrapped the coin in a piece of paper, pinned it to my shirt, and sent me off to sit in Dr. Gropple's waiting room. I remember getting as far as the sidewalk in front of our tenement, and that's all I do remember. I apparently collapsed.

My next recollections are confused. I recall that my joints ached. My eyes could not seem to focus properly.

My bed was suffocatingly hot, then freezing cold. I could not keep down the food my mother brought in from the kitchen. And then suddenly Dr. Gropple was bending over the bed.

At once I knew I was dangerously ill. My mother would not have spent a dollar on a house call unless my life was in danger. With this realization, which terrified me, the clarity of the outside world vanished. Again everything became confused. I don't know how long I remained in this state, but I see now that it couldn't have been very long, because when I next became aware of what was going on around me, Mr. Diener, the Republican captain, was standing with my mother at my bedside.

"You know who did this?" he said.

"Who?" my mother said.

"The Knife with Hair on It," Mr. Diener said in Yiddish. "Mr. Klein was here by you on Saturday, no?"

"So suppose he was?" my mother said.

"And he sent Monroe to take him to the movies, no?" Mr. Diener said, nodding toward me.

"So suppose he did?" my mother said.

"So they didn't go to the movies," Mr. Diener said. "Monroe spent the money for pickles by Mr. Meyerson's pickle stand on Avenue C, and then when there was no more money to go in the movies, he took your son swimming on the Floating Coney. That's why he's sick. That dirty water, it could kill a horse."

"How do you know this?" my mother said.

"A dozen people saw them first eating the pickles on Avenue C, and then swimming in that dirty water, that's how I know it," Mr. Diener said. "A man like that, his son makes your son so sick he could maybe die, for such a man you'll give your two votes in November?"

"I didn't say I'm giving Mr. Klein my votes," my mother said. "He only came to talk. Like you just came."

"So I'll talk, too," Mr. Diener said. "I'll do like this. Whatever Mr. Klein promised you for your two votes, I'll give you the same, but also I'll pay for a specialist from uptown."

"Who needs a specialist?" my mother said.

"Your son," Mr. Diener said. "With your own eyes you can see how sick he is. For a sickness like this, Gropple is not good enough. He doesn't know. He was here already two days, no? And the boy is better? Better, I'm saying? I must be crazy. He's sicker, that's what he is. He could maybe die. What he needs, he needs a specialist from uptown. You say you'll give me the two votes in November, and I'll give you also the coal, but first I'll go fast bring the specialist. So say yes or no."

"All right," my mother said.

Later that day, or perhaps it was the next day, a strange man appeared at my bedside. He wore what was known on East Fourth Street as an uptown suit. It was double-breasted. In his tie there was a small golden horseshoe set with tiny diamonds. I trusted him at once. He made soothing noises, some of which may actually have been words, but they made no sense to me. I don't remember how long he remained or when he left. I remember clearly, however, that when I next became aware of my surroundings, my mother and Mr. Diener were staring anxiously down at me.

"He'll get better," Mr. Diener said. "He's got to. From a specialist, people always get better."

He did not sound very convincing. I think it was at this moment that the concept of death invaded my mind. Most people, I have noticed, believe until well into their forties that they are going to live forever. Illness, death of contemporaries, the appearance of more and more familiar names on the obituary page, these all contribute to the slow realization that the phrase "nobody lives forever" also includes you. I am the only person I have ever known to whom this realization came at such a tender age. I recall my reactions: terror and resignation. I didn't want to die, but I knew I was going to. If that man in the uptown suit with the diamond horseshoe could not save me, nobody could. I clearly remember doing something I have since read about many times but have never actually seen: I literally turned my face to the wall.

What caused me to turn back were the sounds of an argument out in the kitchen. I listened in astonishment. Never before had Mr. Diener and Mr. Klein appeared in our house at the same time.

"You with your specialists!" Mr. Klein shouted. "What good did he do?"

"You with your son!" Mr. Diener shouted back. "If it wasn't for your Monroe, the boy wouldn't now be dying!"

"Who says he's dying?" Mr. Klein said. "I'll save him! The Republicans, what good are they? To send specialists that can't help, that's what good they are! But you wait and see! By the Democrats he'll be saved!"

The snarling voices became confused as my mother's voice rose in an effort to quiet them down. She may have succeeded, or perhaps she merely led the combatants out of the kitchen into the front room to keep the noise from disturbing me. In any case, the sounds had sunk to a distant murmur when Monroe Klein came into the room. He paused to look back toward the kitchen, clearly making sure he was not being observed, then he tiptoed to the bed.

"Don't worry, kid," he said to me in a low voice. "My father is getting the Democratic Club to put up the dough for a *Siem ha Seifer*."

At that time I had never heard the phrase. I had no idea what it meant. I learned later that it was the name for a ceremony in which a new Torah is presented to the synagogue. The presentation is either an expression of gratitude to God for something good that has happened to the donor of the Torah, or an appeal to God to prevent something bad from happening. The *Siem ha Seifer* arranged by Mr. Klein and paid for by the Democratic Club of the Sixth Assembly District fell, naturally, into the second category.

I don't know how long it takes, or used to take, to prepare a *Siem ha Seifer*. Ordinarily, I have been told, it is a lengthy process, since the rolled parchment of the Torah must be hand-lettered. My mother's own recollections are not totally reliable since she was in a state of terror about my imminent death. She told me later, however, that she believes Mr. Klein arranged to have the Democratic Club acquire, for a bonus payment, of course, a Torah that was almost completed for somebody else's *Siem ha Seifer*. It was a celebration of gratitude that could, without injury to the grateful donor, be postponed. I was very sick. My *Siem ha Seifer* could not be postponed. It wasn't.

On Saturday night, soon after sundown, Mr. Klein and his son Monroe appeared in my bedroom with my mother and father. I was too sick to realize that the mere fact that my father had remained at home after one of the district's political leaders had come in was in itself an indication that something unusual was afoot. My mother wrapped me in a blanket.

"All right," Mr. Klein said to his son. "Pick him up."

Monroe took me in his arms and carried me through the apartment to the front room. My parents and Mr. Klein followed. My mother pulled a chair to the window that looked out on Fourth Street. Monroe sat down, still holding me in his arms, and arranged me in his lap so I could look out the window.

"Okay, everybody," Monroe said. "You all go ahead."

My mother and father seemed uneasy and hesitant.

"It's all right," Mr. Klein said. "My two votes in November they should be in such good hands like your son is."

After a few more awkward moments, the Democratic captain led my parents out of the room.

"They're going to get the Torah," Monroe said. "You and I, we're gonna watch from here."

I did not know what to watch. The synagogue was across the street and to my left. Pollack's livery stable faced our tenement slightly to the right. The street in between was empty. Suddenly a group of men, I think there were ten, came racing up the block on horseback. Several were carrying lighted kerosene-soaked torches that shed sprays of fiery sparks behind them. All were dressed in the uniforms Teddy Roosevelt and his Rough Riders had worn on San Juan Hill. The clatter of the horses' hooves brought people to the windows of the tenements facing us. When the riders reached the synagogue, they reined in their horses, shouted a few unintelligible words from a *brucha,* or prayer, and then kicked their horses into a fresh gallop.

By the time the horsemen turned the corner into Avenue D and disappeared, an ice wagon loaded with Indians in full headdress had come into Fourth Street around the Lewis Street corner. As the wagon plodded up the street toward the synagogue, the Indians released wild war whoops and shot arrows tipped with flaming cotton up into the air. Boys and girls from the crowded sidewalks screamed and laughed as they chased the falling arrows. The wagon did not stop at the synagogue, although the Indians stopped the war whoops long enough to shout a *brucha,* because they were being hard-pressed by a group of mounted hussars, with shakos topped by ostrich plumes, who had come prancing into Fourth Street behind the Indians. They were singing "The Star-Spangled Banner" and waving sabers over their heads.

By the time they reached the synagogue my eyes had been drawn to the brass band in circus uniforms that had entered Fourth Street and kept swaying left and right to make room for a couple of clowns who tumbled over each other and juggled great red and green balls as they danced up the block to the band's ear-splitting rendition of "Tipperary."

I had never before seen a parade, and I was too young and too sick to do much thinking about it, but I knew at once as I squirmed with delight on Monroe Klein's lap that I was having an experience to which I would always look forward with eagerness. I still do. Of all the parades I have seen since then, however, none contained the moment when, behind a group of Bedouin chieftains and in front of a somewhat erratic enactment of Custer's Last Stand, a blue velvet canopy with golden tassels was carried into Fourth Street. The poles were held up by four *yeshiva buchers,* seminary students from uptown with long side-curls and broad-brimmed *shtrahmels.* Under the canopy, moving with slow, measured, pious grace, marched Mr. Klein. Tenderly, as though it were a delicate child, he carried in his arms the Torah the Democratic Party of the Sixth Assembly District was donating to the Fourth Street synagogue as an appeal to God for my recovery. Mr. Klein was flanked by my mother and father. Both looked grave. Both kept their eyes on the ground. Both were praying. I could see their lips move.

"You're gonna be all right, kid," Monroe Klein said to me. "God's gonna put that cross in the right box on your ballot."

That night my fever broke. Four days later I went back to school. For almost half a century I wanted to ask my mother how she cast her vote that November. I never had the courage to phrase the question.

4

A Correction

One of the difficulties about growing older is the acquisition of self-knowledge. The slow but relentless realization that certain inadequacies of character and intellect will never be corrected. They can't be. Time has run out. You'll never live long enough.

I, for example, have never been able to conquer a life-long tendency to believe everything I read in print. Especially if it is printed in my morning newspaper. Until, of course, I read the next morning's newspaper and come across those discreet little boxes, tucked away among the American cross-stretch brassiere ads and the Danish blue cheese recipes, captioned "A Correction."

I enjoy reading these corrections, indeed I seek them out, because for years I have kept alive a hope that some day I will read one about Srul Honig.

Now that I have entered my fifties, however, it seems reasonable to assume that this hope is vain. For one thing, I don't think that any New York newspaper is likely to provide itself with an opportunity to get any facts wrong about Srul Honig. He is no longer news. In fact, Srul has not been news for almost forty years. Secondly, even if a New York newspaper should print something about Srul Honig, and get any of it wrong, I think I am probably the only person still around who would recognize the errors. I would not like to see anybody be unfair to Srul. On the other hand, I don't think even he would want me to spend the rest of my life poised at the starting line, so to speak, waiting to break out in "A Correction" about the things that happened in the days when we were both much younger. The time has come to hang up my gloves in that particular fight.

What I liked about Mr. Honig, and what still makes him so pleasant a memory of my youth, was that he brought a breath of fresh air into my life. This figure of speech may seem odd to anybody who has ever spent time in a blacksmith shop. It occupied the street level of a squat red brick building facing our tenement on the corner of East Fourth Street and Lewis Street.

East Fourth Street in those days was, among many other things, a commercial route between the traffic of the East River, on the banks of which my life was centered, and the business world of uptown, which at that time I did not even know existed. The East Fourth Street dock was occupied by two commercial enterprises. Every square foot of the northern, or uptown, side was almost totally covered by the enormous drying stacks of the Forest Box & Lumber Company. The southern, or downtown, side of the dock was jam-packed with the derricks and mountainous black piles of the Burns Coal Company.

The lumber and coal were shoved by tugs down-river to

the docks in barges and were then fed out to different parts of the city in horse-drawn wagons. I don't know how many wagons these two companies owned or how many horses drew them, but there must have been a great many. It seems to me, or to my usually not totally unreliable memory, that the wagons never stopped moving up and down our block, piled high with lumber and coal on the way west, empty on the way east back to the river barges. Every one of these horses was shod by Srul Honig.

He was a great big pork of a man. The word came to me years later when I was visiting my married sister in Portland, Oregon, and we happened to walk down a street of butcher shops. In every window, spiked at the throat on large steel hooks, hung a string of wax-colored gutted pigs. My sister who, like her brother, had been raised "kosher" on East Fourth Street, said it was enough to turn your stomach. Hers, perhaps. Not mine. What the sight did for me was bring back a picture of Srul Honig as I had known him when I was eleven.

His great height and girth were underscored by a number of things by which a boy of eleven could not help being impressed: a skullcap of closely cropped hair the color of a fresh pomegranate; a scarred black leather apron; biceps as thick around as a lamppost; a mat of red hair on his chest, so thick that it seemed a substitute for the shirt Mr. Honig never wore. Winter and summer he worked naked to the waist, and he worked in full view not only of passers-by but of anybody on the block who happened to look out the window. Blacksmith shop patrons need plenty of room on their way in and out, and the forge in front of which Mr. Honig worked would have been a hot background even for the asbestos cat who, in the nursery jokes I learned in kindergarten class in P.S. 188, was always stalking the tallow rat in Hades.

Mr. Honig at work was an arresting sight. He worked with his back to the horse. He maneuvered his humped back between the horse's buttocks, lifted the horse's leg between his own legs, and pulled from a slot on his leather apron the pair of pliers with which he tore away first the old nails and then the old shoe they had held to the horse's hoof. With the last nail the old shoe went flying out in a wide arc to the far corner of the smithy. From another slot in the black leather apron came a short, wide-bladed, murderous-looking sharp knife.

With short, hard, perfectly directed strokes, Mr. Honig cut away from the horse's hoof the horn that had accumulated since the last horseshoe had been nailed on. The pieces flew out in a spray of ivory-colored slivers. Having cleared the area of operations, Mr. Honig put the knife back into his apron, and from the white-hot fire in the forge, pulled the long iron rod to the end of which was attached the glowing red horseshoe. With delicate precision Mr. Honig now set the red-hot horseshoe on the horse's hoof. A whitish sizzling smoke rose up to the red hair on Mr. Honig's chest. It reminded me, again years later, of the smoke that floats up in a London pub when the waiter plunges his hot poker into a mug of ale. The smell in Mr. Honig's smithy, however, was different. It was probably enough, as my sister said of the gutted pigs in Portland, to turn your stomach. Again, however, not mine. I was accustomed to the smells of East Fourth Street.

By the time Mr. Honig had the shoe set, and with another pair of pliers plucked from another slot in his black leather apron had snapped the iron rod from the still red-hot horseshoe, this particular smell had faded into the overall smell that was composed of many ingredients. The two strongest were Mr. Honig's sweat and the manure of his charges. I don't know why, but getting a new set of shoes relaxes a horse's sphincter muscles. Now came the exciting part.

From a pocket in his apron Mr. Honig brought out a handful of horseshoe nails and thrust them into his mouth, blunt ends protruding. The first three, two at the tail ends of the horseshoe and one at the top of the arc, went in with a dexterity and speed that still makes me marvel. Mr. Honig had to pluck those nails from his mouth, set them in place one at a time, pull his short but heavy-headed hammer from still another slot in the leather apron, and drive the three nails home through the red-hot horseshoe with single, powerful blows. This done, he began to shape the shoe to the horse's hoof. It was like watching a fireworks display. Each blow of the hammer sent up a shower of sparks. They spattered against Mr. Honig's face and naked chest, but he paid no attention. The shoe had to be in place, and all the rest of the nails sunk flat with the metal, before the cooling shoe turned gray. It always was.

For me, today, the most fascinating aspect of this performance was that I did not then consider it a performance. I do not think I ever stopped to watch Mr. Honig shoe a horse. I accepted what he was doing as part of the landscape. The way I accepted the wagons loaded with coal and lumber moving slowly up from the dock under the bedroom window toward a world that had for me at the time as little shape or meaning as China must have had for little Marco Polo when, with his first paddle, he was learning to maneuver a gondola along the canals of Venice. It was this total acceptance—it may even have been indifference—to my surroundings that made my friendship with Mr. Honig, when it happened, so startling. One day he stepped out of the landscape and became a human being. Literally.

I was coming down Fourth Street from Avenue D on my way home from school on what had until then been a perfectly normal, uneventful day. I was, as I recall, worrying about my work with integers and multiplicands in Miss Moerdler's arithmetic class—my work in this area at the time was not distinguished; I was doing better with fractions—when I heard a voice shout.

"Hey, kid, c'mere!"

I stopped and turned toward the voice. It had come out of Mr. Honig's blacksmith shop. Indeed, as I learned a moment later, out of Mr. Honig's throat. He called again.

"Hey, kid, c'mere!"

It seems sensible to add that he said it in Yiddish. And he was holding the bridle of a rearing horse just inside the double-door, wide-open entrance to his blacksmith shop.

"Huh?" I said.

"Grab this," said Mr. Honig.

In Yiddish.

"What?" I said.

In English.

"Grab this, you stupid little bastard," said Mr. Honig.

In Yiddish.

"What?" I said.

In I forget what.

But I had grabbed the bridle, which I think was actually a lead strap attached to the bridle, and was hanging on. In subsequent years I have had a certain amount of traffic with people who bet on horses. From them I have picked up a certain amount of information about how to handle horses. They do, it is true, panic easily. But it is equally true that they calm down easily. Like human beings, apparently, all they want is to be assured they are loved. I had never noticed that they calm down when you grab their bridles and utter, in English or Yiddish, phrases like, "Okay, boy. Steady, now. Take it easy, kid. That's the boy." And so on. On that day in 1924, when I grasped the bridle Mr. Honig shoved into my hands, it worked.

Probably, I think, because the horse was scared by something I had not at the moment noticed. Another horse plunging around insanely near the forge. As soon as I took the bridle Mr. Honig shoved at me, he leaped for the head of this other horse, and in a matter of moments had him, or her, under control. With the same Yiddish phrases. "Okay, boy. Steady, now. Take it easy, kid. That's the boy." And so on. In a few moments, therefore, there we were, man and boy, facing each other from under the heads of two calm Percherons.

"Thanks," Mr. Honig said.

"You're welcome," I said.

"They're okay," Mr. Honig said. He stroked the neck of his huge horse. It was like patting the cables of the Brooklyn Bridge. "It's just they get excited," Mr. Honig said.

Today, I think, my reply would have been: "Who doesn't?" But then, remember, I was only eleven. It is wrong to say I did not know what I was doing. It is, however, completely accurate to say I did not know what was going on. I stroked the neck of my horse as steadily and easily as I stroked my hair when I ran my comb through it.

"You know horses," Mr. Honig said.

I didn't. This was the first time in my life I had ever been

103

this close to a horse. I plowed through my mind for some observation that would deflect Mr. Honig from further praise of a talent I did not possess.

"My father was in the Austrian cavalry," I said.

"That's where you learn," Mr. Honig said.

I sensed at once that he had confused my father's service in the Austrian cavalry with my instinctive knowledge of horses. I sensed something else. Life offers you very few dividends of this kind. My reaction came from the age beyond innocence: I took advantage of Mr. Honig's obviously innocent remark.

"There's nothing like a horse," I said.

In Yiddish.

"Yeah," said Mr. Honig. He stroked the neck of the horse he was holding. "You wanna make a nickel?" he said.

"Sure," I said.

"Take this horse down the dock and deliver to Walter," Mr. Honig said.

He handed me the bridle.

"What about the nickel?" I said.

"When you come back," Mr. Honig said.

"Okay if I leave this?" I said.

I lifted my batch of schoolbooks and my pencil box. They were lashed together by the yellow leather strap every parent on East Fourth Street provided for his or her school-age son or daughter.

"Sure," Mr. Honig said. Gravely, as though he were laying down the terms of an important business deal, he added, "You come back in one piece, you can take this horse, too, and you got yourself another nickel."

It was the expression on his face that made me laugh. Which meant I liked him.

104

"Okay," I said.

Not in Yiddish, of course. The two syllables do not really translate at all.

"I'll have this second one ready when you come back," Mr. Honig said.

I took the bridle of the first horse. Mr. Honig crouched down and hunkered himself in under the buttocks of the second horse. He was lifting the horse's left hind leg up between his knees as I led the first horse out into Fourth Street and down toward the dock.

"These four things and nothing more," Kipling wrote. "Women and horses and power and war."

He was, of course, stating the code of the natural man. Perhaps he did not intend to state the code of the natural boy. But he touched something to which I know I responded as a boy.

Power had never crossed my path. War was still two decades ahead of me. Women were already on the horizon, but only in a vague, undefined, troubling way. Horses, however. Horses. There they were. Or rather, there was this one. In my hand, so to speak. The bridle, anyway. And the huge, beautiful locomotive that was made of flesh and blood and rippling muscle came right along. Under my command. Giving me a sense of exhilaration I had never experienced before and I have never encountered since. When the days go brown, I force my mind back through the years to that incandescent moment. The sky lights up at once.

It did just the opposite when I reached the Fourth Street dock. The sky seemed to come down on me and the horse I was leading like a collapsed circus tent. I had not been paying any attention to the weather. As I recall, on East Fourth Street almost nobody did. It was never pleasant.

Always hot or cold, meaning too hot or too cold. Something you had to live through, not with. I suppose I should have noticed that a storm was coming up, but I had been too absorbed in my meeting with Mr. Honig and the discovery of horses, not to mention the two nickels I was in the process of earning, to pay any attention to the weather. When the sky opened up, I found it was too late. The horse started to buck.

"Okay, boy. Steady, now. Take it easy, kid. That's the boy."

The soothing words astonished me. They had not emerged from my throat. And they were not spoken in Yiddish. I swung around, into the suddenly belting rain, trying to get a better grip on the bridle, and saw that it was not necessary. Walter had come out of his cottage and had taken charge.

I suppose he had a second name, but I had never heard it spoken aloud. Perhaps because the words that were always spoken after his first name were assumed by the people of East Fourth Street to be his last name. He was known as "Walter from the Docks."

I had never met him until that day when Srul Honig asked me to deliver my first Percheron to the Fourth Street dock, but I knew a great deal about Walter. On second thought, no, not a great deal. What I mean is that I probably knew as much as most people on East Fourth Street knew about Walter, which was not much. I knew he was the custodian of the stable on the dock that was apparently jointly owned by the Forest Box & Lumber Company and the Burns Coal Company. I knew he lived in a small white cottage with green shutters that sat at the top of the dock area, separated by a narrow patch of vegetable garden from

106

the dark brown, almost shapeless mass of sprawling old beams in which were housed the horses that hauled the coal and lumber wagons west from the river barges to the customers uptown.

It seems strange to me now that the few things I did know about the man we called Walter from the Docks should not have seemed strange. The house he lived in, for example. I never saw anything like it until, years later, I paid my first visit to Cape Cod. How did that sunny, bright little New England fisherman's cottage land on a dirty dock jutting out into the East River in the shadow of the most unsunny, unbright, dirty gray stone tenements ever built by Western man?

As for vegetable gardens, what in God's name were they? Vegetables came out of the pushcarts on Avenue C. But not, apparently, for Walter from the Docks. For him, tomatoes, potatoes, scallions, carrots, and plumed ears of corn came out of the sliver of fenced earth that kept the ugly dock stable from toppling onto and obliterating the shining little white cottage in which Walter lived.

With whom? I don't believe anybody really knew. As I recall the scraps of talk that passed over my eleven-year-old head, it was generally believed that Walter from the Docks was married. I think, although I am not sure, I heard occasional references to a female figure in a blue and white checked housedress who was seen at regular intervals crawling about on her knees in the narrow strip of garden. Now, of course, I know that she was not crawling about. She was weeding. Or gathering some of the ingredients for the evening meal. I don't know.

I have, since my early days on East Fourth Street, spent some time as a householder in the country. Like most middle-aged men who have endured the suburban experience, I have learned how to cut a lawn, trim a hedge, and pay a bill for sheep manure. But I have never learned to like any of it. My wife says I have four thumbs. Not one of them, however, is green. So I did not really have much interest in Walter from the Docks and his way of life until that day when I met Walter for the first time in the rainstorm that had suddenly exploded around me.

"You go on in the house," he said to me. "I'll take care of the horse."

He did it with a skill that aroused so much of my admiration, I forgot all about the rain. I stood there, sopping up water, and watched him soothe the plunging horse and lead him into the stable. When they disappeared, the door of the white cottage opened and a woman's voice shouted at me.

"Do come in out of that rain! You'll catch your death!"

A hand came clawing out of the partially opened white cottage door, grabbed my ear, and dragged me into the house. At that time I did not weigh much. I think probably somewhere between sixty and seventy pounds. But that is an awful lot of weight to come in behind a skinny, almost transparent kid's ear. I screamed. The unmanly noise had the most satisfying manly result.

A pair of deliciously soft arms reached out and drew me toward a bosom that I must confess set a mark toward which I have without total success been shooting for most of my life.

After all these years, and I have had almost half a century to think about it, I believe some experiences can come too early. All things considered, I think it would have been better if I had met the wife of Walter from the Docks when

I had reached, if not the age of discretion, at least my teens.
Eleven was too young.

"You poor, poor lad! You are soaked to the skin. Sit
here, love."

For several moments I did not know what was happening. I do not want to give the impression that I was stupid.
I may not have been as bright as I would like to think I
was, and indeed am. But physical circumstances do affect
intellectual capacities. I was eleven, remember. And soaking wet. Flushed with the discovery of horses and cleavage.
Even today, with a lifetime of experience behind me, I feel
I could be excused for not being completely with it.

For example, the instructions to "Sit here, love" were
not exactly that. I felt myself flung into something that
could have been a chair. It proved to be a small couch with
a high back. I sensed a glow of warmth on my face. It
proved to come from an open fire. And then I felt the
hands of somebody who smelled as delicious as my mother's
lekach, or honey cake, tearing the clothes from my body.

As clothes go, these were not much. A cheesy sweater
knitted by my mother? A pair of what we then called
knickerbockers sewed by my father? A pair of long black
ribbed stockings that dug deep streaks into my flesh all the
way up from ankle to thigh? A set of Dr. Posner's Hygienic
Health shoes that had been resoled so often it was hard to
tell where the original last began? A sudden blast of icy
air hit me in a sensitive place. I screamed again.

"What are you doing to him?"

I turned toward the voice. It had come from the throat
of Walter from the Docks. He had come through the front
door of the cottage. The blast of icy air had come from the
open front door.

109

"I must get him dry. The lad will catch his death."

Walter from the Docks shut the door. My sensitive places calmed down. The woman with the cleavage and the wonderful smell threw a blanket around me. She tucked the edges in under my sensitive places, and stood back to admire either me or her handiwork. I did not worry too much about which it was. I was taking my first look at her.

She was plump and round and tiny. A combination that may sound physically impossible. It is not. The wife of Walter from the Docks was plump, and round, and tiny. A combination that made her look delicious. Not only to me. After all, at that particular moment I did not count. As I have been careful to point out at several crucial moments in this history, I was only eleven. Walter from the Docks must have been about the same age as Srul Honig. Mid-thirties? Pushing forty? Certainly no more than that. And all you had to do was catch a glimpse of Walter's face to know he, too, thought his wife looked delicious. If you looked in the opposite direction, which I did, you realized at once that she thought pretty highly of him, too. How could she not?

In retrospect I know now, of course, that he was one of the handsomest men I had ever seen. At the time, however, Walter merely looked odd. He did not belong to the world of Jewish immigrants who made up the population of East Fourth Street any more than his shining white and green cottage belonged in the shadow of the ugly gray stone tenements in which everybody else on East Fourth Street lived. He was tall and dark, with jutting, overhanging heavy black eyebrows, and one of those thin, deeply lined, strong faces that seem to have been hacked out of a log somewhere west of the Alleghenys with a few clean strokes of an axe by some primitive artist making up souvenirs of Abraham Lincoln. Even his clothes were an anachronism on East Fourth Street. Walter wore olive-green corduroy pants tucked into high black rubber boots and a khaki brass-buttoned doughboy's tunic from which the insignia had been carefully cut away.

His plump little wife wore the checked blue and white gingham dress in which she had been reported to have been seen crawling about on her hands and knees in the tiny garden. I don't know how she looked on her hands and knees among the carrots, but standing up in front of an open fire, with a bright pink and white smile, and a compact little head that seemed to be held together neatly by coils of tightly laced braided yellow hair, Walter's wife looked as though that blue and white gingham dress was a part of her. I never saw her wear anything else. Forty years later I still find it impossible to think of her in any other color.

"What the lad needs, Walter, is a nice hot cup of tea," she said. "I'll get it while you hang up his clothes to dry."

I wonder if these two commonplace remarks by Walter's wife convey the totally uncommonplace, indeed the almost explosively extraordinary, world they opened up for me. It was not unlike Alice being plunged down the rabbit hole. Nothing around me seemed in any way connected with the way things had been before Srul Honig offered me a nickel if I would lead the big Percheron down to the dock and deliver the horse to Walter.

Consider.

Homes on East Fourth Street were heated by whatever warmth managed to travel on its own, without direction, from the coal stove in the kitchen that was lighted only for cooking. I had never seen an open fire before. I was confused by the roaring flames, and not a little frightened by them, but I had no trouble enjoying the warmth. As for tea, this was a beverage served on East Fourth Street in a glass to adult visitors, who sipped the hot brew through small nibbles of lump sugar. It was never served to children, except as a laxative, but that was another kind of tea, and it was never served to anybody in the sort of delicate white china cup decorated with tiny red roses that Walter's wife now set before me on a folding table. She pulled up a chair, and when Walter finished draping my wet knickerbockers and sweater and stockings over the brass fender in front of the fire, he pulled up another chair.

His wife brought over a silver tray on which, in plates that matched the teacups, were set out a number of things I had never seen before: sliced hard-boiled eggs, each oval of yellow yolk crossed with what looked like tiny dark brown stunted herrings and proved to be anchovies; slivers of buttered bread as thin as one of my mother's freshly laundered handkerchiefs; diced bits of vinegary red vegetable that Walter's wife later identified as beet-root salad; a mound of horrid brown paste that proved to be delicious goose liver; slabs of brown cake that looked like my mother's homemade honey cake, but were jammed with bits and pieces of fruit, including bright red glazed cherries; tiny white triangles Walter's wife called cucumber sandwiches; and at least seven or eight other items—Walter's wife called them comestibles—I had never seen before but had no trouble getting down in rather large quantities. It was, of course, my first encounter with an English tea.

112

Walter was a Yorkshire stable hand who had been gassed at Passchendale and emigrated to America after the war. His wife was a Cockney barmaid he had met while on leave in London at something I think she once called the Lord Palmerston Arms in Brondesbury.

By the time I got to the end of the platter of cucumber sandwiches—Walter's wife insisted I have the last one—I had, without knowing it, reached a turning point in my life. Deep down in the place where people learn things, I had learned without phrasing the lesson for myself that the world was larger than East Fourth Street. And the astonishing thing about the lesson was that I had learned it on the East Fourth Street dock. By the time my clothes were dry, and Walter and his wife had helped me get back into them, and I set out to bring in the second horse Srul Honig was shoeing, I knew in my heart that East Fourth Street would never be enough for me.

When I came out of the white and green cottage the rain had stopped. When I came into Srul Honig's blacksmith shop he had finished with the second horse. He handed me a nickel.

"For the first delivery," he said in Yiddish. "Here's for the second one." He dropped a second nickel into my hand. "Just to show I trust you, this one I pay in advance."

When I brought the second horse out onto the dock, both Walter and his wife were waiting in the scrap of garden between the cottage and the stable. She looked like a mirror. Her face, I mean. As though the rain had polished her.

"Good boy," Walter said, taking the lead rein from my hand. "I'll just get this one into the stable." As he led the horse away he said to his wife, "Maybe he'd like another cup of tea."

113

"Would you?" she said to me.

I thought about the cucumber sandwiches. The tea had been just tea. But the cucumber sandwiches had been an experience. Walter's wife seemed to understand that.

"I could make some more cucumber sandwiches," she said.

I understood something else. This was a welcome I did not want to wear out.

"Thanks," I said. "But I better get home."

"Will you come tomorrow?" she said.

"Well," I said.

She smiled. "Mr. Honig is having trouble shoeing the horses and also delivering them," she said. "And Walter has too much to do here to go up the street for the horses. I'm sure Mr. Honig will be pleased to have your help. Aside from the nickel, whenever you come, there will always be a cup of tea waiting." She smiled again and touched my forehead. "And cucumber sandwiches, of course."

Every day, after school, I stopped in at Srul Honig's blacksmith shop. He always had at least one horse ready for delivery to the stable on the dock. Sometimes two. After he taught me how to handle two, there was more time for cucumber sandwiches and tea with Walter and his wife. Sometimes, between cups and sandwiches, I went back for another horse. Often for two more. At that age I did not spend much time sorting out my emotions. I just sort of rolled along with them, enjoying the pleasures of nickels earned, delicious foods consumed, and the delight of being liked by a couple of delightful people.

Then—well, what happened was this. When I came into the blacksmith shop one day after school Srul Honig had a big black horse tethered near the door, and he was ham-

114

mering a shoe on the back right leg of a smaller brown and white horse.

"Take the black one," Srul said.

"How near finished are you with the brown?" I said.

"No, take the black and come back for the brown," Srul said.

I didn't like the delay. I wanted to get to Walter's cottage and that tray of cucumber sandwiches.

"I'll wait," I said.

"No," Srul said. "The black one is a *mishimid*."

There is no precise translation. The word means a bad person. It does not quite fit a horse, but then neither does it fit a cobra or a bean-ball pitcher. If you understand Yiddish, however, you understand the word *mishimid*.

"Okay," I said. "I'll be right back."

I untied the rope, took a firm grip on the bridle, and led the black horse down Fourth Street to the dock. Maybe I did it a bit too gingerly. If you're scared of a horse, stay away from him. He'll know you're scared before you do. And what's terrible about it is that knowing you're scared, the horse gets scared. And scared horses are the only horses that ever cause trouble. It doesn't seem the sort of thing a boy of eleven would learn on East Fourth Street, but that's where I learned it, and I wish I hadn't. Because when I handed the lead rope to Walter in front of the stable on the dock, I did it with a feeling of relief. I remember that clearly. I remember everything else, too.

"Where's the brown and white?" Walter said.

"Mr. Honig is finishing him up," I said. "He told me to deliver the black first, and come back for the brown."

"Tea's ready," Walter said. "Why don't you go in and have a cup before you go back for the brown?"

I hesitated. This was a mistake. I don't think Walter knew it was a mistake. I believe now that he thought I was being shy. But the horse knew. The horse had known I was scared from the moment I led him out of Mr. Honig's blacksmith shop. As Walter turned toward the door of the white cottage with green shutters, the black horse blew a blast of terror through its steaming nostrils and turned its back on Walter. I screamed, but it was too late. The enormous hooves kicked out backwards. The metal shoes, brand-new, hammered into place by Srul Honig only minutes ago, sharp as paring knives, caught Walter in the back of the neck, and tore his head from his body. I saw it happen.

I saw everything else, too. But I'm not going to set it down. After you've seen a human head roll across a dock and drop into a river with a splash, as though you have been watching a dribbling basketball, you have gone as far as you want your powers of description to take you.

The next hour or so may be buried mercifully under the word hysteria. Mine. The wife of Walter from the Docks'. Strange men's. I did not know then that these men were officials of the Forest Box & Lumber Company and the Burns Coal Company. A couple of white-coated strangers', who were obviously connected with the Bellevue ambulance. It was because of this general hysteria that Srul Honig stands out most clearly in my recollection of the horror. He was not hysterical.

This astonished me, and my astonishment saved me. I had never seen Srul Honig outside his blacksmith shop. Standing in front of the blazing forge, naked to the waist, his huge biceps streaming with sweat as he banged the blunt-headed hammer up and down on the white-hot horseshoes and the sparks showered all over him, he had always been a

116

figure of violence. When he arrived on the dock, still wearing his black leather apron and still wet with sweat, Srul Honig was suddenly a figure of serenity. He moved around quietly. He helped the doctors carry the corpse to the ambulance. And it was only when Srul Honig was free to go into the green-shuttered cottage to soothe the widow that her violent sobbing finally stopped.

I stood around on the dock for a while, not quite sure of what I was supposed to do, or even wanted to do. I did not realize at the time that for the past few months my life had fallen into a rhythm, and now the rhythm had been broken. The ambulance, the doctors, the lumber and coal company executives, the few curious people who had been drawn to the dock by the sound of the ambulance bell, all were gone. I was alone in front of the small white cottage with the green shutters. I thought I would wait until Mr. Honig came out and ask him what to do. But he didn't come out. So, after a while, I went home.

The next day, when I came down East Fourth Street from school, I stopped in at the blacksmith shop. Srul Honig, spraying sweat in all directions, was banging a shoe into shape on a horse's hoof. He looked up.

"What do you want?" he said.

And so I knew an interlude in my life had ended.

"The horse," I said. "You want me to take him to the dock?"

"Where's there to take?" Mr. Honig said. "Walter is dead."

At eleven my grasp of economics was still primitive. Mr. Honig's reply seemed logical to me. Walter from the Docks had been the person to whom for months I had been delivering the horses Srul Honig shod. Now that Walter was gone, there was nobody to receive the horses. It had not occurred to me that the delivery of those horses was part of a commercial enterprise. I had not connected the work Srul Honig did at his forge and the work Walter had done in the stable on the dock as part of the coal and lumber yards on the dock. I had assumed the whole process had been set in motion so I could earn a few nickels and eat a lot of cucumber sandwiches. How dumb can you be at eleven?

Well, this small chronicle may provide at least one answer.

I don't know what I missed most. The cucumber sandwiches or the plump girl with the delicious smile who served them. Considering the appetites of most eleven-year-olds, it is probably accurate to say I missed them both in equal proportions. That is why, when I got home that day and spread my schoolbooks on the table in our front room, where my mother occasionally allowed me to do my homework, I spent more time looking out the window than looking into my arithmetic text.

Thus, perhaps ten or fifteen minutes after I left him, I saw Mr. Honig lead out of the smithy the horse he had been shoeing. I saw him walk down East Fourth Street to the Lewis Street corner, cross to the top of the dock area, and lead the horse into the stable next to the green-shuttered white cottage. I can describe my state of mind most accurately, I believe, by saying that questions not only came to but actually assaulted it.

To whom was Mr. Honig delivering that horse? Now that Walter was dead? Somebody must have been in that stable, because a few moments later Mr. Honig came out of the stable minus the horse. He stepped across to the white cottage and knocked on the door. It opened. Mr. Honig entered the

118

cottage. The door was pushed shut from the inside. I did no arithmetic homework that day. I sat at the table and stared down at the cottage on the dock until Srul Honig came out. This was before the days when I owned a watch, so I can only guess how long he had been in there. It was not a short time.

I was jealous, of course. But not in the way that a grown man would be jealous. I think what I was jealous of, at that moment in my eleventh year, was the throat down which those cucumber sandwiches were going. They were really good.

They must have continued to meet the high standard Watler's wife had set when she served my first one. Because, during the next few weeks, from the windows of our front room, when I should have been doing my arithmetic homework, I noticed that Walter's widow was attracting a great many customers. What else would they be coming for, if not her cucumber sandwiches?

I hoped she was getting a good price for them. From the words I heard crossing over my head, uttered in Yiddish by my parents and their neighbors, the death of Walter from the Docks had left his wife penniless. These men who started dropping in on her to buy her cucumber sandwiches were her only source of income. Nobody was very happy about Srul Honig's role in the new business venture. None of the older people, anyway. They were all, like Srul, immigrants from Austria and Hungary. There was nothing wrong with selling his skills as a Jewish immigrant to the gentile "men of the docks." It was a new world. A man had to eat. Especially a great big barrel of a man like Srul Honig. But to become friendly with the men of the docks?

Shaking of heads. Clucking of tongues. Sidelong glances at me. Had the boy understood what was being said over his head?

The answer of course was no. A small indication of how dumb you can be at eleven. Although I wasn't all that dumb. I knew what, in the eyes of my parents and their neighbors, was wrong with the men of the docks. They were a rough crew. They came from nobody quite knew where, out of the river, riding the coal and lumber barges to the East Fourth Street dock. They worked the cranes in the dock yards. They drove the wagons that carried the coal and lumber west into the city. They played cards. They shot craps. They drank. And they were gentiles.

They lived together, on the barges, and they played together, in the dock saloons. They came and went with the movement of the river traffic. They never touched the lives of the Jewish immigrants on East Fourth Street. The Jewish immigrants of East Fourth Street were careful not to touch the lives of these men of the docks.

I had not violated this unspoken arrangement when I started delivering horses to Walter from the Docks, because my boss was Srul Honig. It was a Jewish immigrant who had paid me my nickels. Just what I had violated when I started entering the white and green cottage and eating cucumber sandwiches made by Walter's wife, I don't know. Neither did my parents. I had never said a word about the things I had enjoyed most during my trips to the dock with Srul Honig's freshly shod horses. I had an uncomfortable feeling that some of the delicacies Walter's wife set out along with the cucumber sandwiches were not kosher. Neither was Srul Honig's conduct.

About a month after the death of Walter from the Docks,

A Correction

I was coming down Fourth Street on my way home from school. I walked, as I had every day since Walter's death, on the south side of the street. I did not want to pass the open door of the blacksmith shop. I didn't have to. Srul Honig had apparently been waiting for me.

"Come on over," he yelled from the other side of the street. I hesitated, but crossed over. "I got a horse for you," Srul said.

I followed him into the smithy. A big gray horse was tethered near the door. Mr. Honig pulled a nickel from his pocket under the black apron.

"Payment in advance," he said through the troubled frown that was his customary expression. From another pocket under the leather apron he pulled a small folded piece of paper. "Here," he said. "Give this to her."

"I'll have to leave my schoolbooks," I said.

"I'll hold them," Mr. Honig said.

He took my strapped bundle of books. I took the nickel and the piece of paper. He untethered the horse and I took the bridle. It was all simple, direct, matter-of-fact, the way it had always been, and yet, of course, it was not. I have often wondered what I could have been thinking as I led the big gray horse down Fourth Street and out onto the dock. Nothing that comes back to me is very satisfactory or even trustworthy. I think I remember a sense of anticipation. I was going back, under the auspices that had directed me there originally, to a place where I had once been happy. I think I thought it might happen again.

I came out at the top of the dock area and led the horse toward the stable. At once I saw that something was different. Walter had always kept the stable doors open. The stable was always empty when I arrived with the horse or horses

121

Srul Honig had just shod. At that time of day the other horses owned by the Forest Box & Lumber Company and the Burns Coal Company were harnessed into the shafts of the big wagons, dragging lumber and coal across the city. Now the stable doors were closed.

I stood in front of them, holding the horse's bridle, and trying to decide what to do. If you give it a moment's thought, as I did, you don't knock politely on a closed stable door the way you knock on the door of a friend's apartment where you have been invited to dinner. On the other hand, what was I going to do with the horse? I could lead it back up the street to Srul Honig, but then I would probably have to return the nickel. What broke the impasse was an odor. The smell of thin slices of cucumber bedded down on richly buttered slices of thin white bread.

I turned toward the white cottage with green shutters. Four or five steps, and the horse and I had circled the tiny garden. I knocked on the door. No answer. The smell of cucumber sandwiches, however, was now irresistible. I knocked again. Curious, unidentifiable sounds started to work their way through the smell. One sound was readily identifiable. Bare feet slap-slapping hurriedly across a linoleum-covered floor. The door opened.

"Oh," Walter's widow said, "it's you."

I stared at her in some confusion. I had never, as I already stated, seen her in anything except the checked blue and white gingham housedress. She was in it now, but she wasn't very far in it. She kept tugging at buttons, trying to bring them across to buttonholes, as she smiled down at me.

"He sent me with a horse," I said. "Mr. Honig the blacksmith."

Across the room, through the door that led to the bedroom, came a man in a gray turtleneck sweater. He, too, was barefoot, and he, too, was not very far into his demin pants.

"What the hell is going on?" he said as he struggled with the buttons.

Walter's wife turned and said, "It's the boy from the blacksmith."

Then the man, who could have used a shave as well as some help with his buttons, saw me in the open doorway and the big gray horse behind.

"Son of a bitch," the man said. "I told that red-headed Jew bastard not to deliver the horse till after five o'clock."

He strode across the room, pushed Walter's widow aside, seized the lead strap from me, and pulled the horse away to the stable.

"I haven't seen you for a long time," Walter's widow said.

"Mr. Honig doesn't send me with any more horses," I said. "He brings them himself."

"He was supposed to bring this one himself," Walter's widow said. "Why did he send you?"

"He said I should give you this note."

I handed it over. She unfolded the paper, studied it for a moment, then looked up with a frown.

"It's not in English," she said.

I took back the paper. It sure wasn't in English, and I understood why Srul Honig had wanted me to carry it for him.

"It's in Yiddish," I said.

"Can you read it?" she said.

Srul Honig knew damn well I could read it. That's why he had asked me to carry it for him.

"Sure," I said, and I did read it. Out loud. "*I can't stand how you are living. I'm a blacksmith, yes, and I smell from horses, but no worse than the men on the dock. I'll buy more soap. I'll do anything you want. Just so long as you stop the way you are living and marry me. Please.*"

I read it out loud. Just like that. There are a lot of things you can do at eleven that you can never do again.

"Would you like a cup of tea?"

"Thank you, yes," I said to Walter's widow.

She nodded toward the tray in front of the fire. "Have a cucumber sandwich while I put the kettle on."

Before she went out through the other door, the door that led to the kitchen, she crumpled Mr. Honig's note and threw it into the fire. I picked up a cucumber sandwich and took a bite. I was disappointed. It didn't seem to taste as good as I remembered. The front door opened. The man who needed a shave came in.

"What the hell you doing?"

"Walter's wife asked me to have a cup of tea," I said.

"She ain't Walter's wife any more," the man said. He grabbed me by the collar, dragged me across the room, and shoved me out onto the dock. "Beat it," he said. "And don't ever show up around here."

I remember thinking, as I walked back up the dock, that Srul Honig had been right. He smelled no worse than this son of a bitch who had thrown me out of the cottage. I lifted the cucumber sandwich for a bite, but the man had stained this odor, too. I had just reached the top of the dock. Before I stepped out into Fourth Street I did two things: I threw the sandwich into the river, and I waited until Mr. Honig turned away from the open doors of his blacksmith shop to pluck a red-hot horseshoe from the forge before I slipped quickly across the street into our tenement. I did not want to take a chance on being asked to return that nickel. The only thing I understood about what had happened on the dock was that I had earned my money.

The next day I learned the rest. During the night somebody had entered the white cottage with green shutters on the dock and killed Walter's widow, the unshaven man who had thrown me out of the house before I could get my cup of tea, and two men—at that time still unidentified—who had late in the day helped bring in a coal barge that had been logged steadily at every check point on the Erie Canal the week before.

Walter's widow had apparently been entertaining all three men when the murderer came in and killed them. Anyway, that's what it said in the *Jewish Daily Forward.*

In the *Daily News,* which Chink Alberg showed me during school recess, it said a blacksmith was being sought. The blood-covered murder weapon, found on the bedroom floor of the cottage, was a short-handled, heavy-headed hammer. The sort of thing used by blacksmiths all over the world.

They caught him, of course. When the cops arrived Srul Honig was asleep in the small room behind the forge that I had never known existed. I remember my surprise on learning he had a life outside the blacksmith shop. I had never thought of Mr. Honig as a man who had a home.

The trial was widely reported in the press. Naturally it had a special interest for me. Every night, after my father came home from work, and while my mother was washing the evening-meal dishes, he would read aloud to us large slabs of testimony from the *Jewish Daily Forward.*

I think I understood most of it, but one thing was puzzling. The charge on which Srul Honig was tried, it said in all the papers, was man's laughter. Very odd, I thought. Mr. Honig was a man who had never smiled, much less laughed.

125

5

Mafia Mia

If I understand what I read in the newspapers, the country in which I was born and have lived for more than half a century is now run by a network of Sicilians who wear Savile Row suits, get the time of day by consulting the world's thinnest wrist watches, and operate under the sort of names ordinarily associated with the labels on the sides of cardboard boxes containing uncooked spaghetti.

I am not surprised. Any more than I think Henry Ford was surprised whenever he walked into his plant and saw the assembly lines cranking out all those tin lizzies. After all, Henry had been in at the beginning. So was I, although I didn't know it at the time.

Today even kids of eleven are not ignorant. They know that schoolteachers are cynical civil servants relentlessly bucking for security, their cold calculating eyes so firmly fixed on the pension up ahead that they have no interest in seeing to it that the kids milling about down around their knees learn how to read. Anyway, that's what I read in the papers.

In those days, when I was eleven, I did not read the papers. I never saw them. My father could afford to buy only one: the *Jewish Daily Forward*. I knew how to read the *Forward* —you did it by going backward—but I spent very little time with it. I had reached the age where I was more interested in reading English, a language I had learned only a few years earlier. As a result, all I knew about teachers was what I saw with my own eyes and experienced with my own senses. It still is, as it was then, the best way to fall in love.

It is also the least expensive. No bills for sending flowers. No dinner checks in expensive restaurants. No scalped theater tickets. Not even a taxi fare. All you had to do was walk from your tenement at the corner of East Fourth and Lewis Streets to your school on Ninth Street between Avenue C and Avenue B, walk into Rapid Advance Class 7-1, and there she was: Miss Anna Bongiorno.

Today, of course, I don't think she would attract the eye of even a desperate casting director. Unless, perhaps, he was looking for someone to play the part of Miss Havisham in *Great Expectations*. Miss Bongiorno was not a young woman. I might as well be frank. She was an old lady. In her mid-sixties, I would guess. With strong, not particularly feminine features and the sort of dark complexion that I am trying to avoid calling swarthy. I can't. Miss Bongiorno was a dead ringer for a movie actor whose memory still makes me glow: Eduardo Cianelli. But, and it is a but I want to emphasize, she had snow-white hair. It was my first experience with what snow-white hair does to an Italian face. It made Miss Bongiorno beautiful.

I did not know this when we first met. How could I? I was scared stiff. After six years in P.S. 188 on Houston Street I was suddenly, without warning, transferred to J.H.S. 64 on

Ninth Street. I still don't know why. I suspect the city's public school system was beginning to suffer the early twinges of congestion, and one of the first efforts to ease the crowding was to move some of the brighter students—I may have been ignorant but my mother assures me I was not stupid—out of the regular, evenly spaced routine into schools that were experimenting with rapid advance classes. Two terms for the price of one, so to speak. I didn't want to advance rapidly. I wanted to remain in the comfortable nest I had made for myself in P.S. 188. My wants, however, were not taken into consideration.

Not even by Miss Bongiorno. She was clearly annoyed by the arrival of a new boy in the middle of the term, and she did not conceal her annoyance. She was not exactly mean to me, but Beth out of *Little Women* she wasn't, either. Until the day we did a scene from *Henry V*.

Even today, when the things that go on in our elementary schools would no longer surprise either Dr. Kinsey or Thomas De Quincey, I think a seventh-grade class, rapid-advance or slowpoke, doing *Henry V* would probably raise an eyebrow. Not, however, if Miss Bongiorno were still around. She flourished at a time when "departmental" was just beginning to appear in the school system.

Up to then teachers who received their pupils at nine in the morning and dismissed them at three in the afternoon broke up the six hours of their stewardship to suit their own convenience, predilections, or prejudices.

So much time for arithmetic. So much for spelling. History? Well, if the teacher was fond of dates and battles, her pupils might spend more time on history than on long division. If she—I never had a male teacher until ninth grade—did not like dates and battles, her pupils had to wait until they were older to learn about Magellan and Bunker Hill. "Departmental" changed all that.

Under this new system the school day was divided into six equal sections of fifty minutes each. The ten minutes that completed each hour were allotted to the flow of traffic in the school building as in a psychoanalyst's office they are allotted to the change of bodies on the old leather. The pupils moved from room to room, where different teachers waited for them with reservoirs of knowledge about multiplication, diagramed sentences, the proper treatment of the alimentary canal, the short- and long-range causes of the Revolutionary War, the boundaries of Manhattan Island, and a thing called "elocution."

This thing called "elocution" is defined in the *Shorter Oxford English Dictionary* as "The art of public speaking as regards delivery, pronunciation, tones, and gestures; manner or style of oral delivery." Not bad. If the compilers of the *Shorter Oxford* had consulted me, however, I could have cut the definition down to seven words. "Elocution: the passion of Miss Bongiorno's life."

God knows how many of the six hours every day during which the education of her pupils was in Miss Bongiorno's hands before "departmental" came in were devoted to flogging them into declamations of *The Vision of Sir Launfal,* and acting out *The Idylls of the King.* When I came to J.H.S. 64 "departmental" had just been set in motion, and so I came under Miss Bongiorno's spell for only one hour, or fifty minutes, every day. But what an hour, or fifty minutes, it was, or they were!

I used to sit there during these first weeks, listening to the majestic thunder of English literature break all around me, and I do mean English. Miss Bongiorno did not exactly sneer at Longfellow and Washington Irving, but it was to Shake-speare and the *Oxford Book of English Verse* that as a girl she had given her heart. She remained faithful. She belonged to a school of elocution that has gone out of fashion. Miss Bongiorno taught her students to declaim.

"These words are among the greatest ever written," she used to say to a boy who was not reciting loudly enough to suit her taste. "Let's hear them."

There were times during those first weeks when it seemed to me everybody in the school building could hear them. It never occurred to me that anybody might object or even mind. I did not, of course, understand all the words, but the noises they made in my head were thrilling. I became im-patient with my role as spectator. I was dying to get up there and yell my head off along with the others. Miss Bongiorno, however, continued to disregard me. Until the day Abraham Pincus had his appendicitis attack.

Abraham Pincus was Miss Bongiorno's favorite. He was a small boy but he had a large voice. So large that Miss Bongiorno always assigned to him the major roles in per-formances involving two or more actors. As for solo recita-tions, it was Abraham Pincus all the way. When the class did "The Ancient Mariner" it was not the role of the Wedding Guest that Abraham played, and Miss Bongiorno was never overcome by the desire to hear Kipling's "If" on days when Abraham was home sick. This happened quite often, much to Miss Bongiorno's distress. We never really knew what was wrong with Abraham, except that he seemed to be plagued by a series of bellyaches, until the day Miss Bongiorno called on him to recite the "a mighty charge" speech from *Henry V*, Act III, Scene i.

Abraham went to the front of the room, faced the class,

131

raised his right hand in the commanding gesture I had seen him make at least a dozen times: "*Once more unto the breach, dear friends, once more,*" Abraham bellowed, "*Or close the wall up with our English dead.*"

Abraham opened his mouth wide for the next line, but it did not come. Instead of Shakespeare, what emerged was a terrible scream. What made it so terrible was not the obvious pain that had triggered the sound but the fact that Abraham's voice, overwhelming in normal declamation, was terrifying in agony. It seemed to terrify him, too.

After the first blast he could not seem to listen to any more. He clutched at his belly with both hands, doubled up, fell to the floor, and began to thrash about. Miss Bongiorno jumped from her seat at the back of the room.

"Frank!" she said sharply. "Ira! Take Abraham to the nurse!"

Frank and Ira ran to the front of the room, grabbed Abraham, hoisted him to his feet, and hustled him out the door. What happened next has always been for me one of the most astonishing and puzzling recollections of my youth. Without plan, indeed without thought, I slipped from my seat, ran to the front of the room, raised my hand the way Abraham had raised his, and I started to recite, taking up where Abraham had stopped: "*In peace there's nothing so becomes a man,*" I bellowed, "*As modest stillness and humility.*" I kept right on going, without hesitation, all the way to: "*Follow your spirit; and upon this charge/Cry 'God for Harry, England and St. George!'*"

At this point I stopped. Not because I had come to the end of the speech. More accurately, not because I knew that was all Shakespeare had written for Henry. I stopped because those were all the words I knew. I wondered, for a few

132

moments, how I knew them. Miss Bongiorno was apparently similarly puzzled.

"Ralph," she said in a tone of wonder. "I didn't know you had memorized all that."

It did not seem the right moment to tell her my name was Benjamin.

"Well," I said. "I've, uh, I've been sitting here for a few weeks sort of, you know, sort of listening."

I was not quite sure what I was saying, but I sensed I was on the right track. I did not then know how to say what I was just dimly beginning to grasp. At eleven I was already what people in the theater call a quick study. I still am. For things I like, anyway. After almost thirty years I cannot remember the address of my dentist, who happens to be a close personal friend. But all I have to hear are the words "Up from the meadows rich with corn, Clear in the cool September morn," and I need very little urging to embark on all the twenty-nine couplets of "Barbara Frietchie" that follow, right down to "And ever the stars above look down, On the stars below in Frederick Town." Or if someone merely murmurs within my hearing "The curfew tolls the knell of parting day," the murmurer is in for all thirty-two stanzas of Gray's "Elegy," including the epitaph.

I learned them—and I don't know how many more—in Miss Bongiorno's elocution class, and I learned them not by a conscious effort at imbedding the words in my memory, but by listening to the words spoken aloud by my classmates and our teacher. Listening, I must add, with delight. It is the only way to learn.

That was how I learned the "a mighty charge" speech at a time when I did not know who Shakespeare was. There had been music in Abraham Pincus' bellowing, even though he

133

may not have known who had put it there. Another thing he did not know was that when he collapsed after the first four lines of that speech, he was changing two lives: his and mine.

"Ralph," Miss Bongiorno said to me. "Would you mind doing it for us again?"

"No, ma'am," I said.

She went to a seat at the back of the room, sat down, and folded her hands on the desk in front of her. She smiled at me across the heads of my classmates, and my heart turned over. I could not understand why I had never seen it before. She was beautiful.

"Could you perhaps do it a little louder this time?" the white-haired old lady said. "These words are among the greatest ever written. Let's hear them."

She heard them, and Miss Bongiorno must have liked what she heard, because the next day, when my class marched into her room for our fifty minutes of elocution, and she said she thought today, boys, it would be nice if we did "The Ancient Mariner," guess who was called upon to do the central role? Correct. And I knew all the words, too.

Three weeks later, when Abraham Pincus, fully recovered from his appendicitis attack, returned to class, I did not return to my seat at the back of the room.

I have never been quite sure why Miss Bongiorno shifted her affection from Abraham Pincus to me. The fact that I could recite louder than Abraham undoubtedly had something to do with it. Two other facts probably helped. I was a little taller than Abraham, and much thinner. Miss Bongiorno may very well have felt this made me look more like King Henry and The Ancient Mariner than Abraham did. Whatever the reason or combination of reasons, by the time *The New York Times* announced the sponsorship of a city-wide oratorical contest about the Constitution of the United States, and Mr. McLaughlin, our principal, appointed Miss Bongiorno to supervise the selection of the boy who would represent J.H.S. 64, Abraham Pincus was not even in the running.

I do not wish to imply that Miss Bongiorno was unfair. Not so anybody could notice it, anyway. She was meticulous in maintaining the appearance of impartiality. She announced in morning assembly, to the entire student body, that any boy who wanted to enter the contest was urged to submit to her within two weeks a written speech of no less than one thousand words and no more than two thousand on any aspect of the United States Constitution. I chose the Constitutional Convention in Philadelphia. I made the choice after a private meeting with Miss Bongiorno at which she pointed out that this was an aspect of the Constitution that none of the other boys would think of. She was right. I still remember the opening line of my speech: "In the drama of history there has never been, and there probably never again will be, so crucial a year as 1787." If Miss Bongiorno were alive today, I'm sure she would remember it, too. She wrote it.

The rest of the speech was pretty much my own. If the words ended up in more graceful arrangements than I had given them, or was capable of making, it was due to the time and trouble Miss Bongiorno took to correct and polish my crude first draft. I felt it was a measure of her generosity that she did all this correcting and polishing after class, when we were alone together. I don't think Miss Bongiorno ever told me not to say anything to the other contestants about the help she was giving me with my speech, and I don't believe I felt there was anything wrong with her giving me this help, but even at the age of eleven I already had a well-developed instinct for knowing when to keep my trap shut.

On the day the school contest closed, when Miss Bongiorno announced in morning assembly that my speech was the best submitted to her, and thus gave me the right to represent the school in the city-wide contest, I was not surprised, therefore, that nobody complained. If any of my classmates knew or suspected that I was not exactly the sole author of the fifteen hundred words with which I was going to enter the lists, it seems likely that they, too, had already learned when it was sensible to shut up.

My energies during the next three weeks were directed by Miss Bongiorno in the opposite direction: to speaking up. What had drawn us together originally, as I have indicated, was the volume of sound I was able to send forth with my vocal cords. Even without trying I could fill every corner of the classroom. Now Miss Bongiorno started to teach me the difference between a classroom and an auditorium.

Every afternoon, when classes were over, I would meet her in the downstairs hall where morning assembly was held every day, and she would drill me for an hour or more. Miss Bongiorno taught me how to control my voice, how to keep the volume up without loss of breath, and, most important of all, how to gather and hoard energy for my best shots. These were chosen by her.

She marked every line of the speech for the words on which to pause, the areas where my voice was to sink, which were not many, and the places Miss Bongiorno called "the real sockdologers." For these she would step out of the assembly hall into the corridor and pull the heavy doors shut. If she was smiling when she came back in, I knew my voice had

136

reached her. If she was frowning when she came back in, I had to try again.

After ten days I could go through the entire rehearsal session without seeing a single frown on her face. Miss Bongiorno felt I was ready for gestures. She inserted these with the precision of a watchmaker and sank them into my consciousness with the efficiency of a Marine Corps drill sergeant.

To this day, almost half a century later, when I hear the word "history" spoken aloud I must restrain myself from raising my right hand, palm upward, to the height of my ear. And nobody had better be carrying a bowl of hot soup within my reach when the words "founding fathers" are uttered in my presence. On hearing the first "eff" my arms sweep out automatically and my eyes turn toward the sky in a gesture I have learned, since Miss Bongiorno taught it to me, is more appropriate to a rainmaker testing for the results of his most recent effort.

The effort Miss Bongiorno poured into me seemed to please her. The day before the southern Manhattan eliminations, which was to be my first public appearance, she told me we would skip our regular rehearsal.

"You're perfect right now," she said. "I don't think we should do any more practicing. Overtraining can be just as harmful as undertraining. Between now and tomorrow night I want you to relax. Don't even think about the contest."

This was not easy. I had been thinking about nothing else for weeks. What astonished me when I came home from school that day was to learn that my mother had been thinking about it at all.

My life at school, on the street, anywhere outside our tenement flat, was something to which she paid no attention.

137

So long as I brought home satisfactory school report cards my mother did not seem to care what I did while I was not in her presence. Subsequent years of troubled thinking have led me to conclude that she did care, probably desperately, but her desperation I now believe was motivated by the fear that she might, if she probed even casually, uncover things about this New World to which she had fled from the Old that might be worse than the horrors she had left behind in Europe. At the time I did not understand this, mainly because I was not interested in exploring it, but I accepted it. Perhaps out of fear for parental authority. Probably out of laziness. Undoubtedly selfishness had a lot to do with it. I was living my own life. I was having fun. The desire to share it with my immigrant, illiterate, and (I can't avoid confessing, I must at the time have felt) my stupid parents never crossed my mind. I was astonished, therefore, when I came home from school the day before my first public appearance in *The New York Times* oratorical contest to find my mother waiting for me in the kitchen with a flat rectangular parcel wrapped in tan-colored glazed paper.

I was not astonished by her physical presence. She was always waiting for me in the kitchen when I came home from school. My mother left our flat only once a day—while my father was working in the pants shop on Allen Street and I was in class at J.H.S. 64—to shop for the ingredients of our evening meal at Deutsch's grocery and the Avenue C push-carts. She was, therefore, never out of the house when I came home. What I was always met with when I came home from school was the usual glass of milk and plate of sugar cookies. The flat rectangular parcel wrapped in tan-colored glazed paper was, therefore, a surprise.

"What time tomorrow night it takes place this contest?" my mother said.

In Yiddish, of course. I do not know to this day if, at the time, she understood English, or if she was capable of speaking some fragments of the language. All I know is that she never did.

"What contest?" I said.

I didn't really say it. I merely uttered the syllables in a sort of rumbling mutter of astonishment. How did she know I was involved in a contest? I had never mentioned it at home. She had never asked about the after-school hours of practice I had been spending with Miss Bongiorno. The word contest itself was so alien to my life in the tenement flat, as opposed to my life on the streets and in school, that in Yiddish translation it did not sound like an exploration of American history sponsored by a distinguished New York newspaper. My mother made it sound like a pogrom.

"The speech," my mother said. "What time tomorrow night?"

"Eight o'clock," I said.

"Here," she said. "I want you to wear this."

She gave me the flat rectangular parcel wrapped in tan-colored glazed paper. It came, of course, from what was known on East Fourth Street as "the Chinks." The Chinks was a Chinese laundryman named, somewhat improbably but on the whole not inappropriately, James Jew. He functioned in a store on Avenue C, between Fifth and Sixth Streets, and his function was a puzzle to me.

On East Fourth Street soap was looked upon as an item that had to fight for its life on the family budget along with bread, butter, milk, and rent. For laundry purposes, therefore, my mother, like most housewives on the block, bought the cheapest kind. It may have been the best kind because, as I remember it, the shirts I wore to school were always clean. So were the shirts of my classmates and the shirts of our fathers. All, of course, were washed at home. Professional laundries were a luxury that had just begun to appear in the neighborhood. They were all what was then known as wet-wash laundries. You could always tell when a family on the block was doing well. Two or three times a month the horse-drawn wagon of the Demand Wet Wash Laundry, Inc., would arrive from Lewis Street. The driver would collect the family laundry in a dry white canvas sack. A few days later he would deliver it in the same sack, which now seemed to contain bricks, because he carried it bent over. The laundry inside was soaking wet. The prosperous housewife, spared the work of scrubbing and rinsing, still had to hang out her laundry to dry on a clothesline, and then iron it. Nobody, not even prosperous housewives, ever sent out what was known as flat, meaning laundry that was returned dry and ironed. This was a luxury that on East Fourth Street was considered a criminal waste of money, and conceivably a sign of certifiable insanity. Who, then, were the customers of James Jew? How did the proprietor of the shop known as "the Chinks" pay his rent?

The hint of an answer suggested itself on that afternoon when I came home from school the day before my first public appearance in *The New York Times* oratorical contest. The flat rectangular parcel wrapped in tan-colored glazed paper contained one of my white shirts. Or rather, what looked like one of my white shirts. My mother never used starch. Perhaps because it represented an additional cost in the laundering process. In any case, my shirts, like my father's, were always ironed soft. My mother had obviously felt that this, while adequate for normal shirt-wearing occasions, was inadequate for the occasion toward which Miss Bongiorno's preparations had been pointing me. My mother had turned over the preparation for my public appearance to James Jew.

I was deeply impressed. Not only by the way the shirt was folded around a piece of cardboard, and sealed with a pink paper band on which was printed "James Jew Hand Laundry," but also by what James Jew had done to the collar and cuffs. He had converted them to the appearance, consistency, and flexibility of ceramic tile. I could not believe James Jew's income was derived from boys in the neighborhood who participated in public contests and, therefore, needed a shirt for the occasion prepared in similar fashion. It occurred to me with a sense of astonishment that there must have been people in the area who had their shirts similarly treated for lesser occasions.

"What's the matter?" my mother said. "You don't like it?"

"No, it's fine," I said. "I was just wondering how much it cost."

"Fifteen cents," my mother said. "So you better win."

All of that evening, and all of the next day, I wondered uneasily if she intended to come along and watch me perform. I know there are some, probably many, who will feel that to report my uneasiness is to sound unfilial. I can't help it. The truth is that except for the single occasion when she took me to be registered in kindergarten class at P.S. 188, my mother had never accompanied me anywhere in public. I had no trouble imagining how she would look. She would probably wear her good dress, the one with the beaded flowers on the sleeves that she wore to synagogue during the

High Holidays. But would she look the same in it while seated in the auditorium of Washington Irving High School, where the contest was to be held, as she looked behind the white curtain that shielded the women from the eyes of the men in the synagogue? She certainly would not understand what she was hearing from the platform. For the first time in my life I realized I was ashamed of her illiteracy. How could I introduce her to Miss Bongiorno, the woman I loved? Worse than that, how would her presence affect my performance? Already, just thinking about it uneasily, I felt she had thrown me off my stride.

The following night, immediately after supper, I got back on it. My mother helped me into the piece of chain mail James Jew had made of my shirt and then she went to the sink.

"Don't stay out too late," she said, plunging her hands into the tin basin full of hot water that contained the supper dishes.

My spirits soared. It was her way of telling me I could stop worrying about her coming along. Now, of course, when I think of that moment, my spirits do not soar. It is my sense of shame that rockets upward. My mother obviously knew it would embarrass me to be seen with her in public.

A half hour later, when Miss Bongiorno met me in the lobby of Washington Irving High School on Irving Place, it occurred to me that perhaps she had expected my mother to show up. Coming across the marble floor toward me, the elocution teacher gave me an odd look. And when she reached me, Miss Bongiorno looked across my head as though she expected someone to be following me.

"How do you feel?" she said.

142

"I feel fine," I said.

"Are you alone?" Miss Bongiorno said.

"Yes," I said. Seeing that she looked troubled, I decided to set things right. "My father couldn't come because to-night it's his society meeting," I said. "And my mother, she's sick."

"Oh, I'm sorry to hear that," Miss Bongiorno said.

She sounded genuinely sorry, so I knew I was on the right track. I decided to make it sound better.

"She's so sick she couldn't even wash my shirt," I said. "My mother had to send it to the Chinks."

Miss Bongiorno's troubled glance rested for the first time on the strip of ceramic tile in which my neck was encased.

"It looks very nice," she said, and then Miss Bongiorno gave it a closer look. "Are you sure it won't interfere with your breathing?"

It had been interfering with my breathing all during the half-hour walk from East Fourth Street to Irving Place, but I had licked it by tipping my head back and keeping my eyes fixed on the sky.

"No, ma'am," I said, "I'm fine."

"Well, then I suppose we'd better go," Miss Bongiorno said.

We went across the lobby, past the big double doors that opened into the auditorium, toward a smaller door at one side. This led to a short flight of descending stairs that ended in what I later learned was known as a dressing room. When I was led into it by Miss Bongiorno, I did not at first notice the small tables spaced evenly around the walls, and the mirrors hanging over them, but I noticed the boys.

143

There were eight of them, all about my age, and standing next to each one, bent over slightly in a protective attitude, was a woman. These women were of different sizes, shapes, and ages, but I knew at once they were elocution teachers like Miss Bongiorno, and that the boys were the contestants they had trained. All the teachers nodded and smiled when we came in, and then I noticed something else. The smiles were directed at Miss Bongiorno, who nodded and smiled back. The eight boys did not smile. They all watched me.

"Over here," Miss Bongiorno said. "Here's a table that's free." She led me to one of the small tables and said, "Sit."

I sat down and found myself staring into the mirror over the table. In it I could see that the other boys were still watching me. I wondered why. Every one of those eight boys had seven other boys to stare at, but I was the one that held their attention. Miss Bongiorno must have noticed it, too.

"Don't mind them," she said to me in a low voice. "Just think about your speech."

I didn't have to do that. So I thought about why those eight boys were staring at me, and I could feel the excitement begin to mount inside me. They had obviously heard about the work Miss Bongiorno and I had been doing. Rumors about the power of my voice had undoubtedly spread. If any of them had kept their windows open during some of my rehearsal sessions with Miss Bongiorno, I'm sure they heard me. These boys were staring at me because they were scared. I was the one to beat.

They didn't even come close. Except for a puzzling incident that took place just before the contest got under way, the issue was never in doubt. What was puzzling about

144

the incident was that none of the other eight boys seemed to be aware it was taking place.

We were all sitting there in a sort of restless, ear-scratching, foot-shifting, throat-clearing silence, with our teachers hovering over us, when a door at the other side of the room opened and a man came in. Before the door swung shut I caught a glimpse of the stage on which we were about to perform and, below it, a section of the auditorium. The seats were filling up. I recognized some faces from J.H.S. 64, a few from my own class, and I had a feeling of surprise. It had never crossed my mind that any of my classmates would walk at night all the way to the Washington Irving High School on Irving Place to listen to me speak in an oratorical contest.

The feeling of surprise gave way to one of pride. I suddenly understood how Babe Ruth and Lou Gehrig felt when they stepped up to the plate to take their cut at the old apple and they saw the faces of all those Yankee fans spread out above them in the stands.

"Miss Bongiorno?"

I turned toward the voice. It had come from the man who had entered through the door from the stage. He had gray hair parted in the middle, and wore rimless glasses, without earpieces, pinched to the top of his nose. And he held a sheet of white paper in one hand and a silver pencil in the other.

"Yes?" Miss Bongiorno said.

"You are Junior High School 64?" the man said.

"Yes," Miss Bongiorno said.

The man smiled down at me. It was one of those "There's-absolutely-nothing-to-worry-about, sonny" smiles that I had learned really meant "Boy-are-you-in-trouble, kid."

145

"And this young man is your contender?" the man said.

"Yes," Miss Bongiorno said.

Very delicately, almost absent-mindedly, the man touched the top of my head with the blunt end of the pencil. The gesture reminded me of Bobby Jones in the newsreels bending over to sink his tee before blasting off at the first hole.

"I wonder, Miss Bongiorno, if you would mind stepping out into the hall with me for a moment?" the man said.

"Not at all," Miss Bongiorno said.

He opened the door through which Miss Bongiorno and I had entered the dressing room, held it wide for Miss Bongiorno to precede him, then followed her out. The door swung shut with a neat little click. I looked up into the mirror. The eyes of all eight boys and the eight elocution teachers were fixed on me. Not with hostility, which is what I would have expected. If there is any way to describe the way they were looking at me, I would say what I read in their glance was pity. This scared me more than the man's "There's-absolutely-nothing-to-worry-about" smile. Fear always makes me lose track of time, so I don't know how long Miss Bongiorno and the man remained out in the hall. When they came back in, however, I knew at once something unpleasant had happened. Miss Bongiorno's beautiful face, set off by her white hair, had become more swarthy. It was not exactly red with anger, but rage had certainly darkened it.

"Very well," said the man to the entire room. He glared down at the sheet of paper. The glasses pinched to his nose shivered. Somehow his anger no longer bothered me. The fact that Miss Bongiorno was furious wiped out in my mind any threat from this man who was apparently the master of ceremonies. I knew she could take care of anything. "Will

146

you please proceed through that door out onto the stage in the following order and sit down in the chairs arranged for you."

He called our names. I was number three. I followed the two boys ahead of me out onto the stage, and the six remaining boys followed me. There was a spatter of applause from the audience as we sat down. I noticed that the boys from J.H.S. 64 were clustered in a group at the right. Chink Alberg, who was in my class, waved and winked. I managed a small smile, but I kept it very small. A modest demeanor, Miss Bongiorno had explained, always made a good impression on the judges. The man who had read off our names in the dressing room now came out on stage. He went to a mahogany lectern set in front of the line of chairs and waited while Miss Bongiorno and the other eight elocution teachers came down the aisle, single file, from the back of the auditorium and took the seats that had been reserved for them in the front row. Miss Bongiorno's eyes caught mine. She smiled, nodded, and sent me a wink. I risked the disapproval of the judges by sending her back a smile somewhat larger than the one I had given Chink Alberg.

"Ladies and gentlemen," said the man with the hair parted in the middle, "I am James Murchison of *The New York Times* staff."

Mr. Murchison uttered a few modestly complimentary paragraphs about the great newspaper for which he worked. He explained that printing "all the news that's fit to print" was more than a proud banner under which decent men rode into battle every day against the forces of evil. It was a priceless heritage that flowed from the form of government under which we were fortunate enough to live, a government that was enshrined in one of the world's great human documents, namely, the Constitution of the United States. It was because *The New York Times* felt the average citizen, the man in the street, should be made more aware of this priceless heritage that the great newspaper had undertaken the sponsorship of this contest. Mr. Murchison then explained the rules, the series of city-wide regional elimination contests, and the conditions under which the finals would be held in Carnegie Hall.

"And so, without further ado," he said, "I will call the first contestant."

The first contestant was a kid with red hair from Cardinal John F.X. Terence High School. After he spoke his first sentence I knew this was one boy who would never get to Carnegie Hall. He had a nice voice but no volume. The second contestant was louder, but it was obvious to me that nobody had done any work with him on gestures. He had only one. Years later it was made famous by Harry Truman. It consisted of raising both cupped palms to chest-height, about six or eight inches apart, as though the speaker's hands were holding an invisible cocktail shaker and emphasizing a point by jerking the invisible cocktail shaker violently back and forth until the point was made. This boy put a lot of energy into his one gesture but he was not as good at it as President Truman later proved to be. Anyway, in retrospect he does not seem to have been. I suppose high office improves everything, including a speaker's gestures. When my name was called and, as the third speaker, I rose from my chair and moved to the lectern, I did it with a degree of confidence I wish I could command in certain quarters today. From the moment I intoned "In the drama of history," and on the word "history" my right hand, palm

148

up, went out in a wide, sweeping arc and rose to the height of my right shoulder, I knew the confidence Miss Bongiorno and I had both placed in me was not misplaced.

There were three judges: a famous Shakespearean actress then playing a repertory of Ibsen, Strindberg, and Beaumont and Fletcher in a former church on West Fourteenth Street; a professor of English from Columbia University, who several years before had caused a stir in literary circles by publishing a rather steam-heated novel about Demosthenes; and a former Congressman from the Sixth Assembly District, who had started his career and come to public attention as a criminal lawyer with a theatrical manner so photogenic and a vocabulary so quotable that he seemed to live in the public prints. According to the rules Mr. Murchison had outlined, the judges could not confer with each other. They were to vote individually, and the majority vote—two out of three—would prevail.

For several minutes after the applause died down for the ninth and last speaker, the sense of tension in the audience came up onto the stage and gave me a few uneasy twinges. Then, from different parts of the auditorium, the judges came down the aisle and, one by one, handed up their sealed envelopes to Mr. Murchison. He tore them open, pulled out slips of paper, and studied them. Then he looked up, and waited until the judges had returned to their seats.

"It gives me great pleasure to announce," he said finally through a smile that I thought later could have been a bit less grudging, "that the winner, by unanimous vote of all three judges, is the representative from Junior High School 64."

Miss Bongiorno had left nothing to chance. When Mr. Murchison turned toward me and called my name, I knew

149

exactly what to do. I stood up, came toward him, uttered a modest "Thank you," turned toward the audience, and bowed gravely into what after all these years it still seems to me accurate to describe as a hurricane of applause.

It was still ringing in or pelting at—depending upon what hurricanes, with which I am unfamiliar, do when imprisoned in a dubious metaphor—my ears out on the sidewalk in front of the Washington Irving High School. I was surrounded by my classmates from J.H.S. 64 and Miss Bongiorno.

"I am very proud of you," she said. "You are an honor to the school. I will say good night now, and see you in the morning."

She bent down, kissed me on the forehead, and walked off toward the bright lights of Fourteenth Street and the subway. I don't remember very much about my own walk back to East Fourth Street, except that I recall clearly being accompanied by my admiring classmates. They had never admired me before. Not to my knowledge, anyway. My first taste of this heady brew sent me up the stairs of our tenement in a state of euphoria. It vanished as soon as I came into our kitchen.

Miss Bongiorno was seated at the table. My mother was standing at the stove. Both women looked upset, as though I had interrupted them in the middle of a fight, and then I grasped what was happening, or rather, what was not happening. My mother did not speak English, and Miss Bongiorno did not speak Yiddish.

"Benjamin, I apologize," Miss Bongiorno said. "I did not mean to lie to you on the sidewalk in front of Washington Irving High School when I said I was going home, but it was very important for me to come here at once and

150

speak to your parents, and I did not want the other boys to know I was doing it. I knew I would get here before you would, but I did not realize there would be a language difficulty."

"What did she say?" my mother said.

"Excuse me," I said to Miss Bongiorno in English, and then, to my mother, I translated into Yiddish what the elocution teacher had said.

"Benjamin," Miss Bongiorno said, "I didn't realize you could speak the language so fluently!"

Why not? I had never spoken anything else until I was in kindergarten.

"What did she say?" my mother said.

Even at that age I could see that this sort of exchange was heading nowhere. Like the Conrad heroes about whom I was just beginning to read, I decided to do what the great Pole said they always did in moments of crisis: take the tiller into my own hands.

"She wants to know," I said to Miss Bongiorno, "my mother wants to know why you came here tonight?"

"Because of what happened in the dressing room before the contest began," Miss Bongiorno said. "You remember when Mr. Murchison asked me to step out into the hall with him?"

"Yes," I said.

I remembered also Mr. Murchison's angry face and the way her own features had grown darker with fury.

"Well, now, Benjamin, I don't want you to be upset," Miss Bongiorno said, "but you were almost not allowed to compete in the contest tonight." The look on my face, which I cannot describe because I did not see it, obviously spoke clearly to Miss Bongiorno. "It's true, Benjamin," she said. "Mr. Murchison wanted to forbid your appearance on the stage."

"Why?" I said.

"Because you were wearing a sweater," the elocution teacher said.

I looked down over the piece of ceramic tile that still circled my neck. I was still wearing that sweater.

"Surely, Benjamin, you noticed that all the other contestants were wearing suits?" Miss Bongiorno said. "Suits with jackets?"

I honestly don't know whether I had or had not noticed it. Probably I had. My vision had always been twenty-twenty. Still is. But the fact that the other contestants were wearing suits with jackets had conveyed to me no meaning of special significance. I had not yet reached the age when the inconsequential becomes important. What had mattered to me on that night in the Washington Irving High School was delivering a speech that was better than the speeches delivered by the other contestants. I saw now, however, that to Mr. Murchison this was secondary.

"Mr. Murchison wanted to disqualify you," Miss Bongiorno said. "Out in the hall, before the contest, he said showing up in a sweater like that, it was a deliberate insult. You were showing contempt for *The New York Times,* he said. Well, you should have heard what I said to him. Never judge a book by its cover, I said. Clothes may make the man, I said, but they don't make the orator. And then I hit him with *Othello.*"

Miss Bongiorno rose from the kitchen table. Her beautiful face was suddenly flushed. In the light of the flickering gas jet that provided the only illumination in our kitchen, her white hair seemed to flash like a jeweled crown. Her eyes were fixed on a moment of glory which, geographically speaking, seemed to be located just back of the black stovepipe at the place where it cut through our kitchen wall to the back yard.

"*Good name in man and woman, dear my lord,*" Miss Bongiorno bellowed, "*Is the immediate jewel of their souls:/ Who steals my purse steals trash; 'tis something, nothing;/ 'Twas mine, 'tis his, and has been slave to thousands;/ But he that filches from me my good name/Robs me of that which not enriches him/And makes me poor indeed.*"

Miss Bongiorno's voice stopped as though the ceiling had collapsed on her head. She sank back into her chair at the kitchen table. She gasped for breath.

"What did she say?" my mother said.

"She said I almost lost tonight because I was wearing a sweater," I answered in Yiddish.

"You mean you won?" my mother said.

"I beat everybody," I said. "All the judges voted for me."

"So what has a sweater got to do with it?" my mother said.

"What did she say?" Miss Bongiorno said.

"My mother wants to know what wearing a sweater has to do with giving a good speech about the Constitution."

Even at that early age I had a fairly well developed editorial sense.

"Tell her it has absolutely nothing to do with it," Miss Bongiorno said. "But at the second elimination contest, where you will compete against the winner of the northern Manhattan eliminations, there may be another Mr. Murchison. Or somebody worse. I mean somebody I may not be able to talk down. So I came here tonight to impress on your parents that a month from now, when you compete

153

against the northern Manhattan winner, you must be wearing a suit with a jacket."

"What did she say?" my mother said.

I scowled thoughtfully at the stovepipe as though I wanted to make sure I had the right Yiddish words arranged in my head before I uttered them. Actually, I knew what the words were. Or rather, what the one word was. Impossible. I did not own a suit. I lived in the sweaters my mother knitted for me and the knickerbockers my father sewed for me. We were all aware that soon, when I reached my thirteenth birthday, a suit would have to be purchased for me. No family proud of the right to call itself Jewish would allow a boy to appear in the synagogue to go through his bar mitzvah ceremony in a sweater. In fact, no rabbi dedicated to the rituals that had kept the faith alive through thousands of years of persecution would allow a boy to approach the Torah in a sweater. The purchase of this suit was still, however, more than a year away. To move up this event for an oratorical contest would not change the word "impossible" no matter how meticulously I translated it. Money in our house at that time was not tight. It was almost nonexistent.

"Miss Bongiorno says," I said to my mother in Yiddish, "at the next eliminations, when I speak against the winner from northern Manhattan, I must wear a suit with a jacket."

"How can you wear what you don't have?" my mother said.

"What did she say?" Miss Bongiorno said.

Even my fairly well developed editorial sense could not cope with the ineluctable laws of economics. A literal translation seemed the only solution. I made it.

"I do not own a suit," I said in English.

"Oh," Miss Bongiorno said. I could tell from the expression on her beautiful face that my simple statement had injected into her mind a totally new and conceivably complicated thought. She was a wonderful woman, and I loved her, but she came from uptown. There were things she did not understand. She tried, however, and her attempt emerged as a question. "Benjamin," Miss Bongiorno said, "the next elimination contest takes place a month from tonight. Surely your parents could buy a suit for you in a month?"

I didn't bother to translate for my mother. I knew what she would say. Unlike Adam Smith she had learned her economics the hard way.

"It's the slack season," I said to Miss Bongiorno.

"The what?" she said.

"There's no work in the shop," I said. "My father isn't bringing home any money. The slack season will be another two months at least. Maybe three."

"What are you telling her?" my mother said.

"That we have no money," I said. "It's the slack season. You and Papa can't afford to buy me a suit."

My mother turned and went to the window. She stared out into the yard. I cannot prove my next observation because I never asked her to corroborate it. Even if I had, I don't think she would have told me the truth. Not because my mother was a liar, but because she had no education. She had nothing to guide her except rules she had made up herself. One of these, roughly speaking, was: If people want to do something, and you want them to do it, don't make suggestions; just get out of the way.

Miss Bongiorno cleared her throat. "Benjamin," she said. "Ask your mother this. If I advanced the money for your suit, would that be all right?"

"Ma," I said. She turned from the window. I translated Miss Bongiorno's offer.

"Advance?" my mother said. "What's that?"

"A loan," I said. "She'll lend us the money."

"Lend?" my mother said. "That means we have to pay back, doesn't it?"

"Yes," I said.

"Where are we going to get the money to pay back," my mother said. "From where?"

Chancellors of the Exchequer have asked the same question. None, I feel certain, ever received the reply my mother got.

"From me."

I turned toward the new voice. So did my mother and Miss Bongiorno. My father was standing in the doorway that led to the bedroom. He had obviously been asleep. Or at least in bed. His hair was tumbled forward and he was wearing the heavy khaki greatcoat, part of his uniform when he had been a conscript in the Austrian army, that he had brought with him to America and had since then used as a bathrobe.

"What do you know about this?" my mother said.

"What I heard in the bedroom," my father said.

"This must be your father," Miss Bongiorno said.

"Yes," I said. In Yiddish I added, "Pa, this is my teacher, Miss Bongiorno."

"I know," he said. "I heard in the bedroom. Tell her I want to thank her for training my son so good that he won the contest tonight."

156

I translated for Miss Bongiorno. She smiled, stood up, and held out her hand. She did not have to walk toward my father. He did not have to walk toward her. Our kitchen was very small. They made contact without moving their feet.

"It was a pleasure," Miss Bongiorno said as they shook hands. "You have a brilliant son."

My editorial sense told me that a bit of toning down in the translation would not have been amiss. But the praise of my classmates on the walk back from Washington Irving High School was still ringing in my ears. Or pelting at them. I wanted to hear some more. I translated literally.

"I am ashamed that I do not have the money to buy a suit for my brilliant son," my father said. "If he could not go on in this contest and win again because he did not have the suit, I would never again be able to consider myself a father. I am grateful to you, therefore, for your offer. I accept, and I assure you I will pay back. I don't know how, but I will. I thank you very much. You have returned to me my pride."

Anybody who feels he can improve on a literal translation of this speech is welcome to try. Having done it once, on that night when I won the first round of *The New York Times* oratorical contest, I don't ever want to go near it again. It hurt.

"Then we will consider the matter settled," Miss Bongiorno said. "I will go over to the bank tomorrow during lunch hour to get the money and then give it to Benjamin."

"Thank you," my father said. "I will take him to buy the suit on Sunday."

It was the only day on which clothes were purchased by the inhabitants of East Fourth Street. Buying a suit or a dress was a family enterprise of major dimensions not un-

like the decision of a family of Forty-Niners to sell the
farm in Pennsylvania, invest the proceeds in a Conestoga
wagon, and head west toward Sutter's Mill. There were
stores on Avenue B and Avenue A that were open for
business at night. Most men, however, did not come home
from work before seven. By the time they had put away the
evening meal, known as "sopper," it was time to go to bed
so that they could get up at five-thirty or earlier to get to
the Allen Street sweatshops on time. And a man would
no more think of going to buy a suit unaccompanied by his
wife than a woman would even contemplate buying a dress
without her husband at her side. On East Fourth Street, at
that time, the male or female outer garment was the equivalent of the automobile in today's TV commercial. The family
that shopped together stayed together long enough to eliminate at least one reason for screaming fights: color, style,
shape, and price had all been agreed upon before the combatants arrived at home and examined the purchase.

With all five weekdays eliminated, only the weekend remained. Or one half of it, anyway. Saturday, being the
Sabbath, was out. This left only Sunday, but it was enough
to buy a suit on Stanton Street. It was the Savile Row of
the Lower East Side.

Perhaps it would be more accurate to say it was the
Standard Oil Company of the men's retail clothing business
south of Fourteenth Street. It certainly was my first experi-
ence with what the architects of the Sherman Anti-Trust
Act must have meant by the word "monopoly." Nobody on
Stanton Street said you had to come there to buy a suit.
You could go uptown. To Wanamaker's, for example, on
Eighth Street. To Siegel, Cooper on Eighteenth. To Macy's

158

on Thirty-fourth Street, for God's sake. Who was stopping you?

Well, to begin with, it wasn't who. It was what. And what was stopping you, if you were my father, was the fact that to shop in Wanamaker's you had to know how to talk English, which my father did not. To shop in Siegel, Cooper you had to pay what it said on the price tag, which was an impossibility for people like my father, who were incapable of purchasing a slice of lox or a spool of thread without "hondling," the Yiddish word for the combination boxing match, vaudeville act, and exercise in advanced billingsgate that was as much a part of the act of purchase as the Preamble is a part of the Constitution. And to shop in Macy's, which to the residents of East Fourth Street could have been located anywhere between Bering Strait and the Grand Caymans, you needed a visa. So it was Stanton Street all the way, and on the Sunday following my triumph at Washington Irving High School, that's where my father and I went. On foot, of course.

As I look back on those days, it occurs to me that it was in the area of transportation that the civilization of East Fourth Street most closely resembled that of Rome in the Age of the Antonines.

There were no chariots, of course, but we did have the Avenue B trolley car, which was known as the *Puvullyeh* Line. The Yiddish word "*puvullyeh*" finds its nearest Romance language equivalent in the French *doucement*. In English I can think of no equivalent other than a slang expression, popular in my youth, that has vanished from our culture: Take it easy; you'll last longer. The Avenue B trolley certainly took it easy. The cars operated on storage batteries which were never recharged until they ran out of juice. They rarely ran out of juice at convenient times or places.

As in Rome, therefore, so on East Fourth Street. Forward movement—whether by a legion setting out to pacify an unruly Thracian province or a father setting out to buy his son a suit on Stanton Street—was usually accomplished by hiking. And just as a Roman legion heading for truculent Thrace would not enter the rebellious country with trumpets blaring, so my father and I did not enter Stanton Street in a manner that might be described as attention-grabbing. We eased in gently, nervously, out of Avenue B, and turned south. It was like trying to ease gently, nervously into Niagara Falls.

The long street was lined on both sides with men's clothing shops the way the Via Veneto is lined on both sides by prostitutes. I don't suppose the phrase "cheek by jowl" has ever worried too much about its origins. If it ever should, and a prize were offered for the correct answer, I think I would walk away with the award by suggesting Stanton Street in 1924. It wasn't merely that every inch of space on both sides of the street was filled by the windows of a Bernstein's Men's & Boys' Clothing, Inc., or a Yanowitz's Apparel Shop, Inc. It was as though every inch of space on both sides of the street was in endless contest, a battlefield the possession of which kept changing hands from minute to minute. The troops of Bernstein, victorious just a moment ago, now retreating under the onslaught of the armies of Yanowitz, who, even as they were planting the flag of triumph in the disputed terrain, were already being buffeted and driven back by the revivified Bernsteins. This impression of a see-sawing battle was caused by an institution then known as the "puller-in." Every store had one.

The relation of a "puller-in" to a Yanowitz's Apparel Shop, Inc., on Stanton Street was not unlike that of a barker to a carnival. He stood on the sidewalk in front of the shop door, and he pleaded, cajoled, sweet-talked, threatened, and ultimately seized the passer-by and dragged him into the store.

"What a good-looking boychick you got there! A regular shining doll! Mister, you haven't got a son, you've got *eppis* but a real *tzaddik!*"

Even under the most congenial conditions the word "*tzaddik*" defies literal translation. And, of course, in the realm of commercial fantasy, where conditions are rarely congenial, semantic precision takes a beating. Nevertheless, I will try. As employed by the pullers-in who worked the sidewalks of Stanton Street in 1924 the word "*tzaddik*" meant:

"Words are inadequate to express my admiration and awe for the incredible boy, this glowing vision, who is clearly your son, because anybody can see you're just as handsome as he is, this golden medal you have brought to Stanton Street this beautiful Sunday morning in the hope of finding a suit that will even remotely approach the sort of garment that this marvelous young man should rightfully wear to his bar mitzvah ceremony, or perhaps merely to the synagogue for the High Holidays, or even maybe there's a wedding in the family and you want him to look the way a boy like that should look, and what a stroke of luck it is for all of us that here at Yanowitz's Apparel Shop we happen to have precisely the suit that will show the world how extraordinary this boy is, and if you don't like it, which is ridiculous, because how can any man as brilliant as you are fail to like a suit so beautiful as this, we have a dozen other suits just as good and just as beautiful, did I say a dozen, what am I talking about, I must have lost my mind, carried away by the gleaming brilliance of this extraordinary boy, we have a hundred other suits, every one of them just as beautiful, even more beautiful, step in please and take a look."

We didn't exactly step in, because we were being dragged, my father and I, but we managed to stay on our feet and sort of stagger in. I forget how many stores we staggered into, and I forget in which one we finally made our purchase, because all the stores seemed alike, and the procedure we went through, or were put through, in each one was exactly the same as all the others.

Puller-in, having dragged us through door from street, addresses waiting salesman: "A suit for this handsome *tzaddik*."

Shove. I stagger across store and land in the arms of salesman. My father staggers and manages to regain his balance a moment before crashing into salesman.

Puller-in, moving back out to street: "Don't worry. You're in good hands. Monty Geschwind is the best salesman on Stanton Street. The best and the most honest. Take good care of them, Monty. You have in your hands, Monty, two absolutely and completely personal friends of mine."

He exits to street. Monty circles my father. Monty's lips are pursed. His eyes are crinkled in thought. His thumb and forefinger are tugging at a chin for which in all fairness the word "receding" must give way to "nonexistent." Monty speaks: "You're like maybe let's say a thirty-nine short. No?"

162

My father: "It's not for me. It's we're here for a suit for my son."

Monty Geschwind roars with laughter. "I see you're not a man to be fooled with a joke," he says. "Naturally it's for your son. A good-looking man you are, nobody can deny that, but in your family, you lucky man, nobody has to go around asking which one is the *tzaddik*."

Monty goes to rack. He brings down a suit made of material not unlike that used by the tailor who made the uniform worn by General Robert E. Lee at Appomattox.

"Take off the sweater, take off," Monty says.

"It's for at night," my father says. "Something like a little maybe darker, please."

"Here, hold," Monty says. He shoves the suit at my father and seizes the bottom of my sweater. He yanks it up my torso and over my head as though he is skinning a snake. Both my ears get caught in the neckband. I scream. Monty Geschwind roars with laughter.

"You got not only a *tzaddik*," he says to my father. "You got a *vitzler*."

Vitzler means joker. Anyway, it used to in 1924 on Stanton Street.

"Something like maybe a little darker," my father says.

Monty Geschwind punches my pipestem arms into the gray jacket as though he were stuffing a couple of sausage casings and he fastens the buttons of the double-breasted wings. He wheels me to the triple mirror, shoves me in front of it, and steps back. I survey myself in the mirror. So does my father.

"Perfect," says Monty Geschwind. "It was made for him."

"Something darker," my father says.

163

He says it several times. In several stores. In every one of which, my ears smarting from being peeled in and out of my sweater, I end up in something darker. Something that seems to have been cut, not with precision but with approximate accuracy, for a skinny, knock-kneed boy of eleven. Then comes the moment.

"How much?" my father says.

"A suit like this, who can say?" says Monty Geschwind. There is, or was, a Monty Geschwind in every men's clothing store on Stanton Street. "How can a person set a price on something so perfect like this?" all the Monty Geschwinds of this world say at this moment to my father. "How much? Who knows how much?"

"If you don't," my father says, "who does?"

A meek man. Shy. Not given under ordinary circumstances to the tart riposte. But all my father's ordinary circumstances were lived in the shadow of my mother. Here on Stanton Street nobody was peering over his shoulder. Here he had his moments. If he had been able to earn the money with which to buy for me an extensive wardrobe he might have had more such moments.

"So all right," says Monty. "You ask me how much, I'll tell you how much. Fourteen dollars."

My father takes my hand. "Come," he says. "We'll go find a store that it's not run by bloodsuckers."

He leads me to the door. Fortunately, I have managed to skin back into my sweater. Monty races around and heads us off at the door. He spreads his arms wide from jamb to jamb, barring our way out to the street.

"Fourteen dollars for a piece of merchandise like that?" he screams. "And you call me a bloodsucker?"

"What else should I call you?" my father says.

164

"A fool," says Monty. "A man who gives away to charity. That's what you should call me for asking only fourteen dollars for a piece of merchandise like this."

He darts to the rack, snatches up the suit, and dashes back to the door. My father has had ample time to open it. But he has not. So he is in a position to have the suit waved under his nose.

"Look!" Monty shouts. "Feel!"

"Not for fourteen dollars," my father says.

He reaches around Monty for the doorknob. Monty, using his hip, shoves my father's hand away.

"So how much is it worth to you?" he demands furiously. "A suit like this? Tell a person! How much?"

My father shrugs. He looks down at the suit as though he were examining a sample of sputum coughed up by a terminal patient in a tuberculosis ward.

"If I was a fool," he says finally, "but a really big fool, I could hear myself say maybe ten dollars."

The effect of my father's words on Monty Geschwind is not unlike the effect of the iceberg on the *Titanic*. Monty's knees buckle. His body sinks back against the door. His free hand comes up to his forehead. His eyes turn to heaven with a look of accusation that would have made St. Peter turn shamefacedly from the gate.

"For this," Monty says bitterly, "I hired the best *schneiders*. For this I bought the best cloth. For this I chose buttons like they were diamonds. For this I made a suit only a *tzaddik* should wear. So his father should stand there in front of me and say ten dollars."

"I won't say it again," my father says.

He reaches behind Monty. This time he seizes the doorknob. He pulls open the door. He drags me through it.

Monty stares with disbelief. My father and I take a step down to the sidewalk. The puller-in comes rushing across the sidewalk.

"Where are you going?" he cries.

"To buy a suit from a man he doesn't tear the skin off a customer's back," my father said.

The puller-in puts his hand on my father's chest and speaks across his shoulder. "Monty," he says. "What have you done to this marvelous man? This father of this wonderful *tzaddik?*"

"What have I done?" Monty says, his voice throbbing. "I made him a present, that's what I did. I said here, take this suit it's worth twenty dollars, here, take it for fourteen."

The puller-in staggers back. "Monty!" His voice adds a dimension to the word "consternation" from which in all probability it has not yet recovered. "How can you do such a thing?" the puller-in says. "For a *tzaddik* like this you ask fourteen dollars?" He seizes my father by the shoulders. His voice drops to a seductive whisper. "Take it for thirteen," he murmurs.

My father shrugs himself free from the grasp of the puller-in. "Maybe eleven," my father says.

"Eleven?"

It is Monty's scream. And as screams go, he has set a mark to shoot at.

"Shut up," the puller-in hisses. To my father he says, "Twelve, with both pairs of pants."

"Even a *tzaddik* can wear only one pair at a time," my father says.

Monty's head reappears across my father's shoulder. The veins stand out on his throat like blue hawsers.

166

"When he wears out the first pair," Monty says, choking out the syllables in a voice that seems to be coming up out of a bed of bubbling lava, "the jacket will still be as new as the second pair!"

"He'll be too big then to wear the second pair," my father says.

Monty falls back against the black iron railing. His face disintegrates. Piteously he says to the puller-in, "What are we going to do with this man?"

"Give it to him for eleven dollars," the puller-in says.

They did, and the next day I could hardly wait to report to Miss Bongiorno. There was no elocution class on Monday, so the waiting period lasted until the three-o'clock bell. When I came into her classroom Miss Bongiorno was seated behind her desk. A short, not exactly fat but very thick around the middle sort of man was standing in front of the desk. At least that was my first impression. I was surprised to find Miss Bongiorno was not alone, so I had stopped in the doorway. Neither she nor the man saw me. While I was wondering if I should back out of the room, and wondering why I should be wondering about such a thing, a number of impressions etched themselves into my mind.

The man, I saw, was not really standing in front of Miss Bongiorno's desk. He was moving back and forth in front of it. Not exactly pacing. Sauntering, I would say now that I have learned the meaning of this word that I did not then know. As though he had just put away a rather large dinner and he was stretching his legs in a room of his own house or, as I learned years later in London, what the Cockney describes as "walkin' around the 'ouses." Then I saw that the man was holding a cigar. It was not lighted. In fact, it had never been lighted. There was no ash. Yet the fact that the man was holding a cigar was shocking.

This was a time when the attitude of teachers in the public school system toward tobacco was not unlike what their attitude today is toward marijuana, LSD, and heroin. In private a great many teachers probably smoked. By private I mean away, and probably far away, from the school premises. But the official point of view was so clear and inflexible that the sight of a cigar in a classroom rocked me back, almost literally, on my heels. I think I would have felt the same way if the cigar had been lying down. On a desk, for instance. But this one wasn't. It was held between the fingers of this short, thick man's hand, and as he moved the cigar to his lips, I noticed three things: he wore a large diamond ring on his pinky, his hair was black and slicked straight back but the sideburns were white, and his complexion was almost exactly like Miss Bongiorno's—swarthy.

"It's not something for you to argue about," were the first words I heard him utter. "It's something for you to do."

"I'm sorry," Miss Bongiorno said. "I'm not going to do it."

It was the tone of her voice that completed the act of recognition. Miss Bongiorno and this stranger looked exactly the way she and Mr. James Murchison of *The New York Times* had looked when they came in from their private talk in the corridor outside the dressing room at the Washington Irving High School just before the other contestants and I had walked out onto the stage.

"You know something?" the man said. "For a teacher here in a school, a woman that's supposed to teach kids, you got a great big fat stupid mouth hung on you."

"And you've got a dirty one," Miss Bongiorno said. "This

is my classroom. I belong here legally. You don't. Now get out of here before I ask the principal of this school to call the police and have you thrown out."

The unlighted cigar went up to the mouth, which I now saw was lipless. A razor nick in the swarthy skin. A set of the straightest, strongest, whitest teeth I had ever seen clamped down on the pulpily chewed end of the cigar.

"You know who you're talking to?" the man said through the teeth clamped down on the cigar.

"I certainly do," Miss Bongiorno said. "And I'm not going to talk any more to your kind. You can scare a lot of people, I know that, but you better know this. You can't scare me. So just get out of here right now."

"Okay, sister," the man said. "You asked for what you're gonna get. Remember that when you get it. Remember you asked for it."

"This is not Sicily," Miss Bongiorno said. "This is America. A lot of stupid immigrants don't know that, so you can frighten them, but you can't frighten me." She turned and saw me. So did the man. "Benjamin," she said.

The thick hand decorated with the diamond ring went up and removed the unlighted cigar from the lipless mouth. I now saw that the eyes in the swarthy face were a dark nut-brown. They seemed to shine, as though the pupils were marbles that had been rubbed down with some sort of oil. The polished marbles rested on me steadily as their owner came slowly up the aisle of the classroom, tapping the desks as he moved with the two fingers that held the unlighted cigar. He stopped in front of me, paused for a moment or two, then tapped my head delicately with the unlighted end of the cigar.

"So this is him, huh?" the man said. He did not sound at

all the way he had sounded when he was talking to Miss Bongiorno. The gravel was gone from his voice. He now sounded friendly. Bemused. Contemplative. Almost gentle. I was not surprised when he chuckled. It made his face crinkle pleasantly. "Nice-looking boy," he said. "Very nice-looking boy."

"And the best orator in the southern part of Manhattan," Miss Bongiorno said sharply.

The man turned back to face her. "Not so good like Frankie Lizotto," he said. The gravel was back in his voice.

"I don't know Frankie Lizotto," Miss Bongiorno said. "I never heard of him."

"That's why I came here today," the man said. "To educate you about Frankie Lizotto. I been here. Now you heard of him."

"I don't want to hear about him," Miss Bongiorno said. "He does not attend this school."

"Your trouble, you don't listen," the man said. "I told you where he attends. Mangin Junior High. On Goereck Street."

"I happen to know that Mangin Junior High has a very fine elocution teacher in its English department," Miss Bongiorno said. "Frankie Lizotto is her responsibility."

The man with the diamond ring shook his head. Slowly. From side to side.

"Not any more," he said. "Because four days ago, over at Washington Irving, your boy won. So your boy, this boy here, he's supposed to show up three weeks from now up at this Town Hall, they call it, for the all-Manhattan finals." The man again tapped my head with the unlighted cigar. "This boy."

Miss Bongiorno placed both hands on her green desk

blotter, pushed herself up out of her chair, and came around the desk into the aisle.

"And this boy will show up at Town Hall," she said.

The massive head of gleaming black hair began to shake again. Slowly. From side to side.

"No," the man said. "Frankie Lizotto will show up."

I was unaware of any change in his tone, his manner, or even his stance. Yet change there must have been, because there was a noticeable change in Miss Bongiorno. Her defiance vanished.

"You've got to be reasonable," she said. I wondered what had caused the defiance to vanish. She seemed to be pleading. I found the change very confusing. Confusing and distressing. "I can't do what can't be done," Miss Bongiorno said. She came up the aisle and put her hand on my head. "This boy won at Washington Irving," she said. "His name is on the records. This is the boy they'll be expecting to compete with the winner from north Manhattan. How can I substitute for this boy a boy named Frankie Lizotto?"

"You can call Frankie Lizotto by this boy's name," the man said.

Miss Bongiorno looked as shocked as I must have looked when I came in and saw a cigar in a J.H.S. 64 classroom.

"That's lying," she said.

"It's family," the man said. "We want a family boy should be up on that platform in Town Hall. Frankie Lizotto is a family boy." The man turned and smiled down at me. Again he tapped my head with the unlighted cigar. "You're a nice boy," he said. "But you're not in the family."

And he walked out of the classroom.

I have never been quite sure about what happened during the next few minutes. I did not know, of course, who the man was, or why he was in a position to threaten Miss Bongiorno, but I was intensely aware that the threat, though directed at her, was actually designed to affect me. I did not like that. I liked the feeling of victory I had achieved on the stage of the Washington Irving High School auditorium, and I liked the prospect of repeating it on the stage of this place I had never seen but I knew was more important than Washington Irving High School: Town Hall. I remember thinking there must be something I could say to stiffen Miss Bongiorno's backbone, and I remember the way, after the man left, she turned away from me, and walked slowly back to her desk. She did not sit down. I think she walked around the desk two or three times, and I have a feeling she kept her head down because I did not see her face until she suddenly turned back to me and looked up. All my worries fled. Miss Bongiorno's face was creased in a smile of determination.

"Did you get the suit?" she said.

"Yes, ma'am," I said. "Yesterday. That's what I came to tell you."

"With a jacket?" Miss Bongiorno said.

It seems, in retrospect, a foolish question. A suit without a jacket is not a suit. Nor was it in 1924. But Miss Bongiorno was not a foolish woman. Mr. Murchison of *The New York Times* had tried to eliminate me from the oratorical contest because I had not been wearing a jacket.

"Double-breasted," I said.

"Good," Miss Bongiorno said. "Now to work, to work, to work. I've been worried about the opening two minutes of our speech. It could use a bit of lift right after the reference to Philadelphia. I've thought up a couple of ways to strengthen the third paragraph. Where for the first time

172

you mention the names of George Washington and Benjamin Franklin? Go to the back of the room and start from the beginning. Loud and clear, please."

I went to the back of the room and—loud and clear—started from the beginning. I did it every afternoon for three weeks. Three days before I was scheduled to meet the champion of north Manhattan at Town Hall, I saw for the second time the man with the diamond ring and the unlighted cigar. Again it was after the three-o'clock bell. I was coming down the hall for my after-school-hours rehearsal session with Miss Bongiorno. The man was coming out of her room. He stopped and smiled at me as I approached. I stopped in front of him. I had to. He was standing in my way. I don't think I was frightened. There was something relaxed and pleasant about him. Nothing to be upset about. But I could not forget the angry words that had passed between him and Miss Bongiorno at our first meeting. So, while I was not frightened, I was not comfortable, either. The man took the unlighted cigar out of his mouth. I thought he was going to tap my head with it, the way he had tapped my head three weeks ago, but he didn't. He tapped my shoulder.

"That's a very nice sweater," he said. "Where do you get such a nice sweater?"

"My mother," I said. "She knits them for me."

"Very nice," the man said. "Beautiful work. Only a mother could make a sweater like that. You should always wear them. Nothing else."

Again he tapped me on the shoulder with the unlighted cigar. Then he circled me in a wide arc, as though I were a fire hydrant and he didn't want to scrape the fenders of the invisible car he was driving. When he disappeared around the bend of the corridor, I turned and went into Miss Bongiorno's room. She was sitting at her desk, staring across the room at the door with a troubled frown.

"What did he say to you?" she said.

I told her. What strikes me as odd today, so many years after it happened, was that I did not think there was anything odd about my encounter outside Miss Bongiorno's room or her question about it. I suppose children are so accustomed to expecting the behavior of adults to be odd that they accept the oddity as normal. It even seemed normal to me that Miss Bongiorno now said an absolutely abnormal thing.

"I never saw your suit," she said.

A pretty silly thing to say, of course. How could she have seen my suit? Since my father and I had brought it home from Stanton Street it had been hanging in the closet of the bedroom on East Fourth Street.

"No," I said.

"I would like to see it," she said. "Do you think your mother would mind?"

I didn't understand the question. Did she expect my mother to bar our door? Or throw my elocution teacher down the stairs? So I said, "No."

"Let's go to your house and look at it," Miss Bongiorno said.

Now that I did understand the question I regretted my answer. My mother did not like visitors. Miss Bongiorno, however, had risen from her desk, crossed the classroom to her closet, and was getting into her coat. There was nothing I could say. More accurately, there was nothing I could think of saying that might have aborted a visit I sensed was a mistake. I was relieved, therefore, when Miss Bongiorno

174

and I arrived at our flat, to find that my mother was merely surprised, not angry. She brought out the suit. Miss Bongiorno admired it. She asked me to slip into the jacket. I did. Her beautiful face spread in a smile of delight.

"It was made just for your speech," she said. "It's perfect."

I translated this for my mother, who seemed pleased, and asked me to ask Miss Bongiorno if she would have a glass of tea and a piece of honey cake. It was just baked fresh.

"No, thank you," Miss Bongiorno said, "but would you ask your mother if she'd do me a favor? I'd like to take this suit with me and keep it in the school closet until the night of the contest."

This, it seemed to me, was carrying oddity a bit far. Even for an adult. When I translated Miss Bongiorno's request, my mother obviously shared my view. A look of suspicion crossed her face.

"What is she afraid of?" my mother said. "We won't pay her back for the suit?"

I did not, of course, translate this for Miss Bongiorno. Instead, I said, "My mother asked why do you want to take the suit and keep it in the school closet?"

Miss Bongiorno's smile changed slightly, in a way that distressed me. Ordinarily her smiles were like sunshine. This one seemed fake. I had a feeling that she was worried about something but did not want me and my mother to know she was worried.

"Somebody might steal it," she said.

"The suit?" I said.

"Yes," Miss Bongiorno said. "Somebody could break in here during the night. Somebody who doesn't want you to appear on the stage at Town Hall this Saturday." She must have seen the look on my face, because Miss Bongiorno said hastily, "But don't tell that to your mother. She might worry. Just tell her that the man from *The New York Times* made such a fuss last time about how you were dressed," Miss Bongiorno said, "I want to make sure it won't happen again. Three nights from now, when we go to Town Hall, I want to supervise the way you are dressed. Tell your mother you will meet me in my classroom at seven o'clock, and I will help you get dressed. Tell her I hope she doesn't mind."

In actual fact my mother did mind, and she said so, but I had even then all the instincts of a Jewish Henry Clay. I did not want my mother and Miss Bongiorno to fight. I wanted to win *The New York Times* oratorical contest. So I compromised. Not in a manner that Henry Clay would have approved, I'm afraid. But it worked. I juggled the translations back and forth. My mother was not mollified, then she was mollified, then she seemed undecided, but a half hour after Miss Bongiorno and I arrived from school my elocution teacher departed with my brand-new suit.

This proved to be a mistake. Sometime during that night a fire broke out on the second floor of J.H.S. 64. Four classrooms were gutted. One of them was Miss Bongiorno's. Among the things that were destroyed: her carefully annotated Lamb's *Tales from Shakespeare* and my brand-new sharkskin suit. The police suspected arson, and Miss Bongiorno suspected the man with the gleaming black hair, white sideburns, brown marble eyes, and unlighted cigar.

"If he thinks this is the way he's going to keep you from appearing on the stage at Town Hall this Saturday," she said to me grimly when we were examining the wreckage after class, "he's got another think coming."

"Who?" I said.

I didn't really expect or even want an answer. What I was worried about was the suit that had gone up in smoke. Miss Bongiorno had advanced the money for the suit. My father had pledged to repay the cost. Now I was faced by an upsetting question: the cost for what? The suit had vanished. As I saw it, this meant I would not only be barred from appearing on the stage at Town Hall but my father owed Miss Bongiorno the money for a suit that had been destroyed. Who cared about the name of the man responsible for this mess? What I cared about was the mess.

"That gangster," Miss Bongiorno said.

It was not, at that time, as definitive a word as it became after Warner Brothers invented the kind of movie that starred Edward G. Robinson, James Cagney, and Lew Ayres. In those days, hearing a man described as a gangster aroused in a boy approximately the same emotional response as hearing a man today described as an arboreal designer. I didn't know what Miss Bongiorno was talking about.

"You come with me," she said.

She led me out of the school. We walked down to Eighth Street and then headed west. It was not familiar terrain, but neither was it terra incognita. This uncertainty added to the uneasiness I already felt about the fire that had destroyed my brand-new suit and the comments my mother would have to make about the event. As it happened, my mother never got a chance to say a word.

When we reached Astor Place, Miss Bongiorno led me past the asphalt island in the middle of the street that housed the subway entrance, across Fourth Avenue, and into Wanamaker's. I had never before been inside a department store. I don't know to this day if I was more

177

dazzled by walking into this display of seemingly endless artifacts that did not exist on East Fourth Street, or by the authoritative familiarity with which Miss Bongiorno made her way through these massed, puzzling splendors. Without asking any questions she led me across the ground floor, into an elevator, and out into what I later realized was the boys' clothing department. In view of my recent experience with my father on Stanton Street, what happened that afternoon in Wanamaker's has always lingered in my mind as A Study in Contrasts.

Miss Bongiorno marched up to a man of, I would guess, middle years. This man in the Boys' Clothing Department at Wanamaker's was to the puller-in at Yanowitz's Apparel Shop, Inc., on Stanton Street as a dripping faucet is to the Yangtze at flood time. I was, of course, partial to Miss Bongiorno. After all, I loved her. Even if I hadn't, however, I don't understand how anybody could have been indifferent to her dramatic presence. Nonetheless, this man was. He managed to acknowledge her appearance in front of him by lifting his eyelids a fraction of an inch. He obviously poured into the effort all the energy at his command. Directed into other channels it might have rearranged the dusting on the wings of an ailing butterfly.

"Yes?" he said.

"I want a dark blue double-breasted suit for this boy," Miss Bongiorno said.

Again the leaden lids lifted. Their owner stared at me for a disinterested moment, then went to a rack against the wall. He took down a suit that was undeniably dark blue, brought it to me, and indicated by an expression of weariness dismaying in its totality that unless I removed my sweater at once he would fade into the woodwork. I removed my sweater. He helped me into the jacket and stepped back.

"How much?" Miss Bongiorno said.

"Eleven-fifty," the man said.

Miss Bongiorno opened her purse, counted out the money, and said, "We'll take it with us."

We did. When we had entered the store I had noticed the clock over the door of the hot-dog stand across the street. I took a look at it as we left. The entire transaction had consumed eighteen minutes. It took Miss Bongiorno and me another twenty-two minutes to walk back to East Fourth Street. My mother was, of course, surprised to see her. Or perhaps she was surprised to see the new suit.

"What happened to the old one?" she asked.

It had never been given the chance to become old.

"Tell your mother I made a mistake," Miss Bongiorno said. "Ask her please not to show this suit to anybody. Tomorrow night I'll come and get you myself and we'll go to Town Hall together."

"What did she say?" my mother said.

"She said in this suit I can't lose," I said.

It was not what Miss Bongiorno had said, of course, but it was less taxing than a complete translation of the day's events. And anyway, it proved to be true.

Town Hall was somewhat different from Washington Irving High School, but the difference was a matter of numbers. At Town Hall, I competed against only one boy, the finalist from northern Manhattan. He was very good, better than any of the eight boys I had faced at Washington Irving, but he was no match for Miss Bongiorno. She had sandpapered my every phrase and polished my every gesture. I did not even have to think of the rise and fall of my voice. All I had to do was face the audience, open my mouth, start the magic sentence "In the drama of history," and what emerged for the ears of the audience was not unlike a beautifully edited phonograph recording. The judges were not the two men and the woman who had handed me the laurel at Washington Irving, but the result was the same. The only difference between my triumph at Town Hall and my victory at Washington Irving High School took place after the event.

None of my classmates had come to Town Hall. I am not sure of the reason. Forty-third Street west of Sixth Avenue was certainly a longer walk from East Fourth Street than Irving Place. The subway fare may have had something to do with it. It was a nickel each way, and a dime was a large coin in those days. It is also possible that I was having my first taste of public fickleness. The boys who had walked me home from my first victory in Washington Irving may well have become bored with an orator who recited the same speech, with the same gestures, every time he came out on a platform. If they had turned to another hero, I can say honestly it did not bother me. Not at the moment, anyway. I came out onto the sidewalk of Forty-third Street with Miss Bongiorno's arm across my shoulders and the applause of the audience still making a nice noise inside my head.

"We'll go home in a taxi," she said. "I don't want you to catch cold."

I had never been inside a taxi, but like every boy on East Fourth Street, I gave them a great deal of attention. Yellows and Checkers were a waste of time. Luxors were the ones to watch for. Luxor cabs were all white and had fat chrome pipes that snaked in and out of the motor hood on both sides. I'm pretty sure these pipes were purely decorative, or so I was told years later, but they were very dashing to the eye and very important to your fate. When you sighted a Luxor cab, if you spit into your palm and then punched the blob of saliva home with your fist before the taxi reached the corner, you were guaranteed twenty-four hours of good luck. I was thrilled, therefore, when Miss Bongiorno raised her hand as we reached the corner of Sixth Avenue and Forty-third Street, to see a Luxor cab cut out of the traffic toward us. When it stopped, I was surprised by two things: the door opened from the inside, and Miss Bongiorno tried to pull me away. She was too late. An arm had reached out and dragged me into the taxi. I fell onto the back seat and turned. Miss Bongiorno was standing on the sidewalk, hesitating. It was only after I saw the look on her face that I realized I was frightened. Miss Bongiorno looked scared stiff.

"You better get in," a voice said above my head. I looked up. It was the man with the shiny black hair and the unlighted cigar. Miss Bongiorno's hesitation seemed to annoy him. He reached out, grabbed her hand, and tried to pull her into the taxi. She held back, not exactly struggling, but clearly not cooperating, and then a strange thing happened. A man came out of the passers-by moving along the sidewalk and gave Miss Bongiorno a violent shove. She came sprawling into the taxi on top of me. The man on the sidewalk shoved the door shut and the driver gunned his motor. The taxi lurched away from the curb, into the traffic. Miss Bongiorno and I helped each other to straighten up on the back seat. The man with the shiny black hair just sat there, holding his unlighted cigar and looking sad.

"You didn't listen to me," he said.

"I couldn't," Miss Bongiorno said. "This boy won the lower Manhattan. His name is in the records. *The New York Times* has his name. He was the winner. I had to bring him here tonight."

"I told you names mean nothing," the man said. "I told you to bring Frankie Lizotto and forget the records. I told you we would fix the records. But you wouldn't listen. No, you wouldn't listen. So now you better."

The expression of sadness on his face did not change as he put the cigar into his mouth. He set the wet end firmly between his beautiful white teeth, as though he did not want the cigar to be damaged by what was going to happen next. What happened next made Miss Bongiorno scream. The man had punched her cheek with the side of his fist. The old lady fell against me. The man reached over, grabbed a handful of her beautiful white hair, pulled her toward him, and with a hard downward chopping motion, smashed his fist on the back of Miss Bongiorno's neck. She screamed again, just once, then lay still.

"Hey!" I said.

"You shut up," the man said, and then he made it impossible for me to do otherwise. He smashed his open hand across my mouth. The hand went up for a second blow. I covered my face.

"Leave the boy alone."

I spread my hands and peered through the fingers. Not to see who had spoken. Even in a series of strangled gasps I recognized Miss Bongiorno's voice. I felt I couldn't duck the second blow unless I saw where it was coming from. It came, curiously enough, from her. The old lady put up her hand to shield me. The man's fist, coming down as though he were driving an ice pick, caught her on the elbow and

182

drove her hand against my head. It was the first time I realized Miss Bongiorno wore a ring. The small diamond tore down the side of my face.

"Leave the boy alone," she gasped again.

"It's up to you," the man said.

"All right," the old lady said.

The man reached into his breast pocket, pulled out a large, immaculate, neatly folded white handkerchief, and handed it to Miss Bongiorno. Her breath kept coming in gasping sobs as she wiped my face. When the taxi passed under a lamppost I saw the blood. It looked black.

"It's not deep," Miss Bongiorno said to me through her sobs. "It's just a scratch."

It was more than a scratch, of course, but I didn't know that until later. At that moment the taxi stopped at the corner of Avenue D and Fourth Street. Again the man with the shiny hair reached into his breast pocket. This time he pulled out a knife. One of those large, ugly affairs that you see in the windows of stores that sell hunting equipment. He pressed something in the side of the bone handle. There was a click. A long, shining blade leaped to ugly life. I screamed again.

"Shut up," the man said again.

Then, with clean, methodical, and surprisingly graceful movements, as though he were peeling an apple, he proceeded to cut the brand-new Wanamaker's suit from my body. He left just enough of the pants to make it look, when he opened the taxi door and shoved me out on the sidewalk, as though I were wearing a pair of torn swimming trunks.

"Don't do any more public speaking," he said. "It could be bad for your throat."

He threw the pieces of sliced suit out at my feet and

183

pulled the taxi door shut. Miss Bongiorno looked out at me through the window. I have never been able to understand the expression on her face. What confuses me to this day is the recollection that she looked out at me not only with bitterness, but also with contempt. In some way I had not measured up. It was clear from the look on her face that I had failed her. The cab pulled away from the curb.

The next day Mr. McLaughlin, our school principal, announced at morning assembly that the Board of Education had transferred Miss Bongiorno to a junior high school in Brooklyn. Perhaps they had. I don't know. I never saw her again.

She was replaced by a Miss Carney, who was a very good teacher, but did not care much for volume. She said I shouted. I lost interest in public speaking.

I don't know how the man with the cigar tampered with the records of the oratorical contest, but apparently he did nothing that had a retroactive effect. For having reached the city semi-finals at Town Hall, I was given by *The New York Times* a bronze medal, which I still carry as a good luck piece, and a check for fifty dollars, with which my father started an account for me in the Bowery Savings Bank. When he learned that Miss Bongiorno had disappeared, my father insisted on placing the cost of the Stanton Street suit into my bank account, fifty cents at a time. Some day she might show up, he said, and we owed her the money. Since he did not have a bank account of his own, he might as well put the money into mine. It took my father a little over a year to reach the amount Miss Bongiorno had advanced.

The *Jewish Daily Forward* did not cover *The New York Times* oratorical contest, so all these years I did not know how it came out. Last week I ran into Chink Alberg on Madison Avenue. He is today a highly successful certified public accountant. We talked about the old days on East Fourth Street. He remembered the walk back from Washington Irving High School on the night of my first triumph. The next day Chink called me on the phone.

"I couldn't stand not knowing what happened," he said. "So this morning I sent my secretary over to the *Times*. She looked it up. They've got everything on microfilm. Guess who represented Manhattan in the finals at Carnegie Hall?"

"Frankie Lizotto," I said.

"Jesus," Chink said. "How did you know that?"

"It figured," I said. "Frankie had a lot going for him."

"Not enough," Chink said. "Frankie didn't win."

He would have, if he'd had Miss Bongiorno in his corner.

6

In Memoriam

One thing about the obituary page. It starts people talking. Men and women who for years have been afraid to open their traps, they read a four-line item on the obituary page, and suddenly they become garrulous. I'm no exception.

Yesterday, if you had mentioned the name Jazz L. McCabe to me, I would have given you an innocent look and said, "Who?" Today, try and shut me up. This morning's *Times* reports that McCabe died last night at Mt. Sinai. A coronary at the age of sixty-three. High time.

His name was James, but down on East Fourth Street we called him Jazz because that's the way he signed his name: "Jas. L. McCabe." Nobody on East Fourth Street had ever seen that before. The first time I saw it, "Jas. L. McCabe" was written at the bottom of a letter. The letter was typed. That, too, was something new on East Fourth Street. It threw my mother into a panic. She thought it was a *moof tzettle,* which is Yiddish for eviction notice or, if you took French at Thomas Jefferson High School as I did, a *cadeaux de conger.* These were just about the only communications written on a typewriter that arrived on East Fourth Street. They arrived often.

"It's not from the court," I said after studying the letter. "It has nothing to do with our rent."

"What is it, then?" my mother said.

"It's for Natie Farkas," I said.

"Then why did the letter carrier put it in our box?"

"Well, it's for Natie and me," I said. "The both of us."

This was not strictly true, but things went on in this country that my mother did not understand, and at the age of twelve I had not yet developed any great desire to waste my time enlightening her. I had other fish to fry.

This one had been hooked by my friend Natie Farkas. His father owned the grocery store at the corner of Lewis and Fourth Streets, and the Farkases lived two floors above us in the huge, dirty gray tenement that faced the store. Natie was a great reader. Most kids on East Fourth Street were. Borrower's cards to the Hamilton Fish Park Branch of the New York Public Library were standard equipment for every kid on the block. The reason was simple. Art Acord in *The Oregon Trail* at the American Theatre on Second Street cost a dime. *David Copperfield* cost nothing. That is, if you got to the front door of the library at nine o'clock on Saturday morning before the next guy. Dickens was big stuff on East Fourth Street.

What got me involved with Jazz L. McCabe was Natie Farkas' laziness. He was a tough kid to get out of bed in the morning. Natie was late for *Nicholas Nickleby.* Some other kid got it. What Natie got was a book called *The Boy Scouts of Bob's Hill.*

My wife doesn't believe me. But I swear. There once was

188

a book called *The Boy Scouts of Bob's Hill,* and it changed
my life.

"I want you to read this," Natie said to me the day after
he missed out on *Nicholas Nickleby,* and he handed me a
book.

"Why?" I said. I was working my way through *Great
Expectations.* I hated to be deflected.

"You wait and see," Natie said.

I didn't have to wait long. *The Boy Scouts of Bob's Hill*
was a short book. It told the story of a group of boys about
the same age as Natie and I who formed a boy scout troop
with headquarters in a cave at a place called Bob's Hill.
Don't ask me where Bob's Hill was. Probably somewhere
in New England or out West or maybe even in California.
Wherever it was, it was about as different from East Fourth
Street as I imagine Addis Ababa is from Radio City.
Furthermore, until I read this book I had never even heard
of boy scouts. But I had never heard of London, either,
until I read *Martin Chuzzlewit.* The effect was the same.
It was immediate, and it has lasted. I still feel about London the way Troilus felt about Cressida, and even though
I have sons who are draft age, when anybody mentions the
Boy Scouts of America in my presence, my heart starts to
go like Man o' War breaking away from the barrier. The
moment I finished reading *The Boy Scouts of Bob's Hill*
I ran down to the grocery store to find Natie Farkas. He was
stacking empties out in back, a chore for which his father
paid him twenty-five cents a week.

"I know what you're going to say," he said, "and I'm
way ahead of you. Let's start a scout troop."

It was not what I was going to say. I was going to say I
liked *The Boy Scouts of Boy's Hill* and I intended to hotfoot

189

it right over to the library and see if maybe it was part of a series, because if it was, I wanted to read them all. But as Natie had said, he was way ahead of me, and not for the first time, either.

"How can we do that?" I said.

"We write to the National Headquarters," Natie said. "I looked it up in the telephone book. It's right here in New York."

Natie wrote the letter, but I helped with the phrasing, and we chipped in for the stamp. It cost two cents, and no nonsense about zones or zip codes. Two cents, no matter where you were writing to, Seattle or the Bronx. Actually, Natie and I were writing to Two Park Avenue, but the answer came from New Rochelle.

It was a short, handwritten letter, not unlike the letter Natie and I had written, and it was signed "Lester Osterweil." The letter said that the National Council of the Boy Scouts of America had advised Mr. Osterweil that Master Nathan Farkas and a friend, both of East Fourth Street in New York City, had made inquiries about organizing a boy scout troop in their neighborhood, and Mr. Osterweil had been asked to pursue the matter because he, Mr. Osterweil, worked not too far from East Fourth Street. Mr. Osterweil asked if we knew the location of the Hamilton Fish Park Branch of the New York Public Library, which was like asking Gertrude Ederle if she knew the location of the English Channel, and if we didn't he hoped we could find it, because that was where he would like to meet us the following Tuesday night at eight P.M., a time that was convenient for him, and he hoped it was convenient for us, too, but if it wasn't he would be pleased to make a more convenient arrangement. In the meantime he begged to remain

yours for more and better scouting, sincerely, Lester Osterweil.

In those days, when life was still uncomplicated, anything
was convenient for me that I didn't have to explain to my
mother, and to make things convenient for himself, all Natie
had to do was steer clear of the grocery store in which his
father and mother were trapped until close to midnight
every day except Friday, when they shut up shop at sundown.

The following Tuesday night Natie and I were on the
front steps of the library by seven-thirty, and a half hour
later a tall, thin, hatless man with a sad face, wearing a
dirty raincoat, came down the block and introduced himself
to us.

Looking back on it now, I would guess that Mr. Osterweil at that time was a young man around thirty, give or
take a couple of years, but to me and Natie, who had just
turned twelve, he looked as old as Calvin Coolidge. He
talked like Coolidge, too. Not that I ever heard Coolidge
talk, but there were a lot of jokes in those days about how
rarely our President opened his mouth, and when he did,
how little came out.

One of the first things that came out of Mr. Osterweil
was an explanation of what he'd meant in his letter when
he wrote that he worked not too far from East Fourth
Street. He made his living as the manager of the F. W.
Woolworth store on Avenue B between Fourth and Fifth
Streets, which was like maybe a five-minute walk from the
Hamilton Fish Park Branch of the New York Public Li-
brary. The next words Mr. Osterweil uttered put me and
Natie Farkas in his pocket forever. He asked us how we'd
like a couple of ice cream sodas.

191

Between that first night, when he came into my life, and another night, almost two years later, when he left, I learned a lot about Mr. Osterweil, but I no longer remember how I learned it. For example, I don't know how I learned he was a bachelor and lived with his mother in a house in New Rochelle in which both of them had been born. Not that at twelve I was what you would call shy, exactly, but I can't believe I ever asked Mr. Osterweil for this piece of information.

I have a theory, which I can't prove but which I will never stop defending, that if you feel strongly about anybody, if you really love or really hate, you pick up information about them without trying, the way a blue serge suit picks up lint, because all your pores are always open, so to speak. Or maybe I don't mean pores. Maybe I mean antennae.

Whatever I mean, this much I know: what I remember about Lester Osterweil, I remember because I was crazy about him; and what I remember about Jazz L. McCabe, I remember because for years, from the time I won the hiking merit badge, until this morning when I read his obituary in the *Times,* I have not lived through a day during which at least a few moments have not been spent on hating the bastard. Even now that he has finally gone to what I used to think only hypocrites call his just reward, I won't take odds that getting this off my chest will free those terrible moments for more useful and more worthy thoughts. He was something, Jazz L. McCabe was. Something rotten.

Not Lester Osterweil. He was just the opposite. Goodness came out of him the way hot air comes out of politicians. He didn't even have to try. To my knowledge, he never did. Maybe that's what drew him to the boy scout movement. There is something simple-minded about it.

192

Like the Golden Rule. If you want boys to be decent, if you care about helping them grow up to be good men, why, just get them out into the open, take them on hikes, teach them to tie knots, make fire with flint and steel, and believe that the kingdom of heaven is not a bull market but a scrap of embroidered khaki the boy has won by proving he has accepted the ludicrous belief that it is admirable to be trustworthy, loyal, helpful, friendly, courteous, kind, obedient, cheerful, thrifty, brave, clean, and reverent. Silly stuff, of course. I shudder to think what a fool I must have been at the age of twelve to believe such nonsense. I have, however, a good excuse. I was corrupted by Lester Osterweil.

Not only did he believe this nonsense. Mr. Osterweil built his life around the belief. He had very little money. This is no reflection on F. W. Woolworth and Company. I'm sure they paid their store managers a fair wage, and I'm sure Lester Osterweil was paid as much as he deserved. If the money didn't go as far as he wanted it to go, that was his fault, not Barbara Hutton's. Where Lester Osterweil wanted it to go was to the boys of East Fourth Street, and he didn't have enough to go around because his mother lived in a wheel chair and she earned very little herself by sewing for her New Rochelle neighbors. Mr. Osterweil did pretty good, though.

He helped me and Natie Farkas and a dozen other kids to buy our first scout uniforms. Troop 224, which met every Saturday night in the downstairs reading room of the Hamilton Fish Park Branch of the Public Library, always met as a troop should meet. Every member properly dressed. Every member wearing the insignia to which he was entitled. I still get a kick out of remembering the day I gave Mr. Osterweil four quarters, a dime, and a nickel, the last \$1.15 I owed him for the \$3.50 he had advanced so I could buy and wear a merit-badge sash at the troop ceremony when I was inducted as senior patrol leader. I earned the money by taking over Natie Farkas' job of stacking empties for his father. Natie hated the job. Not me. I wore that merit-badge sash the way Arthur wore Excalibur. For the man who made it possible for me to wear it, I would have killed. I very nearly did.

Before that happened, though, there were the good times. Pretty damn near a year and a half of them.

The weekly meetings. The new skills. The shiny badges. The useless knowledge picked up for the fun of it. I don't know why, but I still enjoy knowing that the large-toothed poplar can also be identified as the trembling aspen. Or that the square knot is used for tying ropes of equal thickness. If they are of unequal thickness, you've got to use a sheet bend, and I still do. Morse Code? I can wig-wag ten words a minute to the marines with a single flag. Assuming there are still any marines around who can read wig-wagged Morse. If there aren't, I can send it electronically, with a bug, or vibroplex, faster than the AP bulletins come in on a news ticker. I haven't had occasion to call on my knowledge of the proper pressure points to stop much arterial bleeding lately, but once not too long ago, when on our lawn a neighbor's son went back for a long fly and instead came through our kitchen window on his back, the ambulance interne later complimented me on the neatness of the spiral reverse bandage I'd put around the kid's forearm. Just a few of the things I learned from Mr. Osterweil.

But the best things were the Sunday hikes. That's what I remember. The Sunday hikes.

Getting out of the bed I shared with my kid brother, and

out of the house without waking him or my mother. She thought Mr. Osterweil was an American militarist working to turn me and Natie and the other boys of Troop 224 into "pogromniks," her word for all people who wore uniforms, whether they worked for the New York Sanitation Department or Czar Nicholas II. Meeting Natie in the grocery store, which would not open officially for another hour. We sneaked in with a key Natie was not supposed to have. Stuffing our knapsacks with stale rolls, a scoop of butter out of the big wooden tub in the icebox, a block of silver-wrapped cream cheese, a can of baked beans. No, let's take two. Baked beans were the best. But what about your old man? Aah, I'll push the other cans to the front of the shelf. He won't notice we took two. I think Mr. Farkas did notice. But I also think he didn't mind. If we thought we were fooling him, he let us continue to think so. He was proud of the way Natie's merit badges kept piling up. Mr. Farkas had come to America when he was still a young man. He was not as scared as my mother.

Knapsacks loaded, there was the long walk across town to the Astor Place subway station. Except that it never seemed long. Mornings at seven. Especially Sunday mornings. Browning knew. The streets empty and quiet, except for the sparrows screaming their heads off, and with their screaming somehow making it all seem quieter. The sun coming in across the First Avenue El, putting golden covers on the garbage cans. On Seventh Street, beyond Second Avenue, the young priest, his skirts hiked up to avoid the dust, sweeping the steps of the church, getting ready for early Mass. On Third Avenue, in the slatted shade from the El, the sleeping drunks looking friendly and curiously clean in their insensibility. And the sky, like a long wedding

195

canopy over the tenements, smooth and blue as Waterman's ink all the way to Wanamaker's. Yes, Robert Browning knew. Robert Browning, and Natie Farkas, and I.

Then the troop gathering slowly outside the subway kiosk. The comparison of knapsack contents. The arrival of Mr. Osterweil. The long ride in the almost empty subway car up to Dyckman Street. The ferry crossing, standing at the gate up front, catching the spray in your face when she hit a big one. On the other side, the briefing by Mr. Osterweil. Tall, skinny, his Adam's apple bobbing in and out of his khaki collar, his yellow hair blowing in the wind, his sad face looking sadder with the seriousness of his instructions: we needed flint for our fire sets; he'd heard there was quite a lot of it lying around as a result of the blasting they were doing for this new bridge, so would we keep our eyes open?

We kept our eyes open. By the time we arrived at our camp site, we were loaded down with so much flint, I've often wondered how they managed to get the George Washington Bridge finished without it.

Then the fires. And the cooking. And the smell of roasting hot dogs. And lying around on the grass, digesting the baked beans, while Mr. Osterweil read aloud from the *Handbook*. Watching the traffic on the river. Skipping stones out toward the sailboats. The sinking sun. And finally, as Mr. O'Neill once put it, the long voyage home.

I never realized I was doing anything more than having the time of my then still very short life, until we won the annual all-Manhattan rally. Then, all of a sudden, I was famous. Well, Troop 224 was famous. The morning after I won eight of our winning forty-nine points for speed knot-tying, and Natie Farkas rolled up sixteen for flint and steel

196

and two-flag semaphore, a picture of Troop 224 appeared in *The New York Graphic.* All thirty-three of us, standing around Mr. Osterweil, who looked as though the camera-man were pointing a gun at him. The *Jewish Daily Forward* ran a somewhat smaller picture, but my face and Natie's were clearly visible, and they called Mr. Osterweil, in Yiddish of course, "a fine influence on the young people of the Sixth Assembly District."

All this was very surprising and very pleasant. None of it was a preparation for the appearance in our lives of Jazz L. McCabe. The typewritten letter over his signature that scared my mother, because she thought it was a *moof tzettle,* was in our mailbox the morning after the pictures appeared in the *Graphic* and the *Forward.* The letter was addressed to me, as the troop's senior patrol leader. I stared at it for a while, then took it across the street, where Natie stared at it for a while.

"There's something fishy about this," he said finally.

It was the *mot juste,* all right. The letter advised me that Mr. Lester Osterweil had resigned as scoutmaster of Troop 224, and the National Council had appointed as our new scoutmaster the man whose name appeared at the bottom of the letter and who looked forward eagerly to meeting me and my colleagues at our next weekly meet-ing: "Jas. L. McCabe."

"Why should Mr. Osterweil resign?" I said.

"I don't know," Natie said. "Who is this Jazz L. Mc-Cabe?"

"I don't know," I said.

"Let's go over to Avenue B and find out," Natie said.

Mr. Osterweil had asked us long ago never to visit him during working hours. He did not think it was fair to his

197

employers to devote to scouting any of the time for which they paid him to serve the customers of the F. W. Woolworth Company. We had always obeyed Mr. Osterweil's wishes, but Natie and I agreed that Jazz L. McCabe's letter was important enough to justify breaking this rule. We did not, however, get the chance to do it. Mr. Osterweil, we learned when we got to the store, had not shown up for work that day.

He did, however, show up at our next troop meeting, which took place the following night. When Natie and I came into the meeting room, the scoutmaster was standing at the table up front, talking to a man I had never seen before.

Mr. Osterweil called us over. "This is Mr. McCabe," he said. "He says he wrote you a letter."

"Yes, sir," I said.

I pulled the letter from my pocket and handed it over. While Mr. Osterweil read it, Natie and I studied Mr. Jazz L. McCabe.

I have always had a tendency, which I'm sure is fairly common, to form mental pictures of people I have not yet met from the sound or appearance of their names. From seeing the syllables Jas. L. McCabe at the bottom of his letter, my mind had at once constructed the image of a large, bluff, hearty Irishman. I was wrong.

Jas. L. McCabe, when I saw him for the first time that Saturday night, reminded me at once of the man pictured on the bottle of Ed. Pinaud's Eau De Cologne that stood on the marble shelf in Mr. Raffti's barber shop on Lewis Street.

Jas. L. McCabe was small, neat, and dapper. He wore a tight double-breasted sharkskin suit and highly polished

198

black shoes with sharply pointed toes. A diamond stick-pin in the form of a fleur-de-lis supported his tightly knotted black tie in an elegant little fop's bulge that arched out under his stiff white collar. His face was round, and either plump or seemed plump, because his collar was so tight that the flesh of his neck bulged out in sagging little dewlaps. His black hair was parted in the middle and slicked back with some sort of ointment that gleamed in the glaring electric light. Under his tiny button nose the two sharp points of a waxed mustache gave Mr. McCabe something to do with his nervously darting hands, and he kept them both constantly busy doing it, so that he seemed to be swatting flies that were trying to settle on his greasy skin.

He didn't look as though he had ever heard of a sheet bend, much less knew how to tie one. Jas. L. McCabe looked as though he was ready at any moment to whip a towel around your neck and give you a haircut. What he gave me and Natie Farkas that night was the willies. When Mr. Osterweil looked up from the letter, the scoutmaster's face was pale.

"This letter is a lie," he said to me and Natie. "I have not resigned as scoutmaster of this troop."

What happened next was, to me at any rate, startling. The man who looked like a foolish barber suddenly looked like one of those men handcuffed to policemen on the front page of the *Daily News*.

"Okay, you son of a bitch," he said in a cold, hard voice to Mr. Lester Osterweil. "You asked for it."

He stalked—no, he sort of hopped—furiously out of the meeting room, and slammed the door.

"Do you want this back?" Mr. Osterweil said.

A couple of moments went by before I realized he was talking about the letter.

"No, sir," I said.

Slowly, deliberately, as though he wanted me and Natie to realize his movements held a message for us, Mr. Osterweil tore Jazz L. McCabe's letter into small pieces, and dropped them into the wastebasket.

"All right, senior patrol leader," he said. "You may call the meeting to order."

I did, but it was not a successful meeting. Neither was the next day's hike. Everything was the same, and yet everything was different. Even the sky, on the long walk across town to the Astor Place subway station, did not look smooth and blue as Waterman's ink all the way to Wanamaker's. The unexpected, troubling appearance of Jazz L. McCabe in our lives had spoiled everything, even the feel and smell of those mornings at seven.

I did not realize how upset we were until the next day, in the back of the Farkas grocery store, where I was helping Natie stack the empties, when his father asked what we were making so much noise about. We told him about the letter we had received from Jazz L. McCabe, and the scene that had taken place at the troop meeting.

"What kind of a name this is, a man should call himself Jazz, this I don't know," Mr. Farkas said. "But what it means, what he wants, this anybody with a head on his shoulders can see."

"What does it mean?" Natie said.

"You boys won the rally, so you got Mr. Osterweil's picture in the papers," Mr. Farkas said. "This Jazz L. McCabe, he's the new Democratic leader here in the Sixth Assembly District. What a district leader wants is votes.

You don't get votes if nobody knows who you are. But if you get your picture in the papers, that's how people learn who you are. So this Jazz L. McCabe, he figures if he gets rid of Mr. Osterweil, and he becomes the scoutmaster, the next time you and the troop you win something, the *Jewish Daily Forward* it'll be saying about this Jazz L. McCabe, not about Mr. Osterweil, they'll be saying it's Jazz L. McCabe who he's a fine influence on the young people of the Sixth Assembly District."

They never got around to saying it. Not in my presence, anyway. Or Natie's, either. Two days later, there was another typewritten letter in our mailbox.

This one was from the National Council of the Boy Scouts of America. Over a dramatically illegible signature, Natie Farkas and I were asked if we would be good enough to appear in the offices of the National Council at Two Park Avenue on the following day at four P.M. It was a matter of the utmost urgency.

I was impressed. Not because this was a typewritten letter. After all, I had seen one before on East Fourth Street. I was impressed because this was the first time I had ever seen the word "utmost" on anything but a page written by Charles Dickens.

"We better get over to Woolworth's and ask Mr. Osterweil what the hell this is all about," Natie said.

We got over to Woolworth's, and for the second time in a week, we learned that Mr. Osterweil had not shown up for work. The next day, when Natie and I came into the offices of the National Council of the Boy Scouts of America, we found Mr. Osterweil waiting on a bench in the anteroom. He did not look good.

Under ordinary circumstances this would not have mattered. Or even made an impression on me. Mr. Osterweil never looked good. He always looked sad. But sad in a nice way. As though the cause of Mr. Osterweil's sadness was not something bad that had happened to him, but his troubled concern because he was afraid something bad might happen to you. These were not, however, ordinary circumstances.

This was a man who had changed my life. He had brought something into it that I had never known existed. And I don't mean only the knowledge that the large-toothed poplar can also be properly called the trembling aspen. He had broken down the walls that until his arrival had always surrounded East Fourth Street. He had let in the sunlit world outside the ghetto. I did not, at the time, understand all that. But I felt it. And I did not want to lose it.

"Mr. Osterweil," I said. "What are we all doing here?"

"Well," he said slowly, "I'm not sure, but I think it's because Mr. McCabe wants to take over Troop 224."

Natie, as always, struck nearer to the point. "But why did they ask us to come here?" he said. "Not you, Mr. Osterweil. Us."

The scoutmaster's Adam's apple bobbed a couple of times, as though he were revving up the motor in his throat before he could speak, and then he said, "If the boys in the troop want me to stay on as scoutmaster, the Council will have to let me stay on."

"You mean," Natie said, "if we say the word, it's nuts to this Jazz L. McCabe?"

"Pretty much, yes," Mr. Osterweil said.

"Okay," Natie Farkas said grimly. "You got nothing to worry about, sir."

202

All these years, during all those minutes of every day when I have found myself hating Jazz L. McCabe, I have also found myself hearing again the sound of Natie's voice as he uttered those words: "*You got nothing to worry about, sir.*" If it's confidence you want to feel in the power of decency and justice to direct the movement of the forces that rule the world, the best time to take a shot at it is when you're thirteen going on fourteen. After that, it's an uphill fight.

I didn't realize that, of course, when a door opened at the far side of the anteroom and a secretary said, "Mr. Osterweil, please?"

He stood up, and followed her out of the room, and the door closed behind him.

"When he comes out," Natie said, "I think it would be a good idea if we talked to him for a couple of minutes before we go in."

It was an excellent idea, but we did not get an opportunity to try it because, about a half hour later, when the door opened again, the secretary was alone.

"Scout Farkas, please?" she said. Natie and I stood up, and she said, "One at a time, please. Scout Farkas first."

Natie followed her out of the room, and I wondered what had happened to Mr. Osterweil. Ten minutes after that, when the door opened once more, and the girl said to me, "All right, please," I wondered what had happened to Natie. I followed the girl into a corridor with doors on both sides. All were closed. At the far end she opened a door on the right and smiled encouragingly at me. I stepped through. She pulled the door shut, and I looked around.

I was in a room that reminded me of the "closed shelf section" in the Hamilton Fish Park Public Library, except that the walls were lined not with books but with pictures of men like Dan Beard and Sir Arthur Baden-Powell. Also, the windows looked out on Park Avenue instead of on East Second Street. But there was that same feeling of a room in which nobody lived but people came to visit for a special purpose.

At a long table between the windows sat three men. I had never seen men like these in real life, but I had seen hundreds of their pictures in the newspapers. These were the faces, photographed by Underwood & Underwood, that appeared in the financial section of the *Times* when the corporations for which they worked announced their appointment to new vice-presidencies and old board chairmanships. They looked prosperous and well scrubbed and what my mother called clean-cut. They were all smiling kindly at me. They all had good teeth.

"Please don't be afraid," said the man in the middle. "We just want to ask you a few questions."

"Yes, sir," I said.

"Why don't you sit down," said the man on the left, pointing to a chair facing the table.

"Thank you, sir," I said.

"It was you and Scout Farkas who were responsible for the founding of Troop 224, were you not?" said the man on the left.

"Yes, sir," I said.

"May we congratulate you on your fine showing at the recent all-Manhattan rally," said the man on the right.

"Thank you, sir."

I don't think, looking back on it, I was all that polite at that time. But there was that Fifth Scout Law, which came

204

out squarely in favor of courtesy, and I was at that moment seated in the heartland of the American scout movement.

"Now, then," said the man in the middle, and even if he had not hiked himself forward in his chair and leaned a little further across the table, I would have known the preliminaries were over. There was a main-bout sound to that "Now, then."

"We have asked you and Scout Farkas to come here today because we are faced with a very painful problem," said the man in the middle. "We gather from Scout Farkas that you and the other members of Troop 224 are very fond of Mr. Osterweil. Is that true?"

"Yes, sir."

"And you think he is a good scoutmaster, do you not?"

"Yes, sir."

"Good," said the man in the middle. "Because we assigned him to your troop in the first place, and we would feel derelict in the performance of our duty if we had assigned someone who is not a good scoutmaster. What's that?"

I jumped slightly in my chair before I realized that the last two words had not been addressed to me. The man on the left had leaned forward and was whispering into the ear of the man in the middle.

"Right," the man in the middle said finally. The man on the left leaned back. "You understand, of course, that to be a good scoutmaster requires more than a knowledge of the various skills in which scouts are trained. He must also be a good man in the moral sense. Do you understand what I mean?"

"Yes, sir," I said, and it is possible that I did, but I

205

think my main interest was in not causing any trouble by appearing to be stupid. If I'd had a minute with Natie before I was brought into that room, I would have been more sure of myself. As it was, feeling my way without advice, so to speak, I felt the best thing I could do for Mr. Osterweil, as well as for myself and Natie, of course, was to appear calm and act as though nothing unusual had ever happened during all the time Mr. Osterweil had been our scoutmaster, because with a man like that in charge, how could anything unusual happen?

"When we assigned Mr. Osterweil to Troop 224," the man in the middle said, "we had every reason to believe he was a morally upright person. Otherwise, of course, we would never have admitted him to the scout movement. A couple of weeks ago, however, we received a communication from a man named McCabe. Do you know him?"

"Yes, sir," I said. "Jazz."

"What?"

I sensed I had made a mistake, so I said quickly, "It's the way he spells his name, sir."

Again the man on the left leaned forward, but this time he was holding out a sheet of paper and pointing to something at the bottom. The man in the middle leaned over the sheet, adjusted the glasses on his nose, peered for a couple of moments, then nodded and leaned back.

"I see," he said to the man on the left. Then, to me, he said, "Mr. McCabe wrote to us that he had only recently assumed certain political duties in your neighborhood, and in his efforts to learn as much as he could about the people he would now be serving, he had made a thorough investigation of the area. He wrote that he had discovered a number of parents were worried about the relationship

206

between the scoutmaster of Troop 224 and the boys in the troop. Are you aware of this?"

Of course I was aware of this. But I wasn't going to tell a man with an Underwood & Underwood face that my mother believed Mr. Osterweil was training us all to be "pogromniks" because we wore uniforms, so I said, "No, sir."

The man on the right leaned over and whispered in the ear of the man in the middle.

"Good point," he said to the man on the right, and turned back to me. "What about your relationship with Mr. Osterweil? Is it a friendly one?"

"Yes, sir."

"How friendly, may I ask?"

I thought about what it was like, lying around the campfire on Sundays, watching the boats on the river and digesting roasted hot dogs and baked beans and listening to the sound of Mr. Osterweil's voice as he read aloud from the *Handbook,* but I didn't know how to put that into words. Not for those faces out of *The New York Times* financial section at the other side of the table. I tried for something I felt they would understand.

"Well," I said, "Mr. Osterweil lent me the three and a half dollars to buy my merit-badge sash so I could wear it when I was inducted as senior patrol leader."

"You say he lent you the money?"

"Yes, sir."

"You're sure he didn't give it to you as a present?"

"No, sir," I said. "I paid him back by stacking empties."

"By doing what?"

I explained about Natie's father's grocery store, and how Natie felt about empties.

207

"Oh, I see," said the man in the middle, but I wondered if he did. He seemed disappointed in my answer. "Just a moment, please."

Now both the man on the right and the man on the left leaned forward. There was a whispered conference.

"Good point," the man in the middle said finally. All three men leaned back. "I'm now going to ask you something very important," the man in the middle said. "Please think carefully before you answer, and please answer with complete honesty, on your honor as a scout. Will you do that?"

"Yes, sir," I said.

"On your honor as a scout, remember?"

"Yes, sir."

"Has Mr. Osterweil ever made any attempt to molest you?"

I thought that over. Not because I didn't understand the question. I knew what the word molest meant. Miss Marine, my English teacher, had said more than once that I had the best vocabulary in her class. But I was here for a purpose, and that was to keep Mr. Osterweil as our scoutmaster. Just saying no, he had never molested me, was not enough. I had to do better than that.

"No, sir, he never did," I said. "Just the opposite."

"How do you mean, just the opposite?"

"Mr. Osterweil is very friendly."

"In what way?"

I knew it sounded a little silly, but I wanted to counteract that crack about molesting, which I knew had come out of that bastard McCabe's letter, so I said, "Mr. Osterweil puts his arms around us."

"He does, does he?"

208

"Yes, sir."

Again the heads on the left and on the right joined the one in the middle for a hurried conference, but this time I wasn't worried. I could tell from the excitement in the unintelligible whispers that I had given them the right answer. The heads separated.

"Could you . . ." the man in the middle said, then paused and cleared his throat. "On your word of honor now, as a scout," he said, "could you tell us under what circumstances, how often, for example, is what I mean, and yes, with whom, any particular boys, does Mr. Osterweil, as you put it, put his arms around you?"

"All of us," I said. "Any time you do something good. Like when we won the rally. Or like when I was inducted senior patrol leader. Mr. Osterweil put his arm on my shoulder and he said he's proud of me."

That was the end of the interview. It was also the end of Mr. Osterweil, but I didn't know that at the moment. Even when I found out, three days later, I didn't put it all together. I merely thought—through the pain that later turned into years of hatred for Jazz L. McCabe—I merely thought stupidly: What a funny way to become a part of history. The Department of the Interior had just opened to the public the upper section of the Statue of Liberty, which for several years had been under repair. Lester Osterweil was the first person who ever jumped from the aperture over her left eye.

7

Rowboats and Canoes

You never know you've been living in history until somebody comes along later and writes it. Then you realize that not all history is written by historians. Back in 1930, when I last saw Pinny Slater, I certainly never thought that one day he would turn out the best history I have yet seen about the time when I grew up.

You would think anybody with brains would have realized, in 1930, that he was living in history. It wasn't one of those periods, like the Mauve Decade or the Era of Good Feeling, that had to wait for a historian to come along years later and give it a name. Everybody in 1930 knew he was living through The Great Depression, all in upper case. And if I didn't have any brains, why had Dean Foote made me valedictorian of my graduating class at Thomas Jefferson High School?

I think my lack of awareness of what I was living through was probably due to my total immersion in it. When you get dropped into an ocean, you don't have much time to think about being wet. Most of your thoughts and efforts are devoted to the problem of how to stay afloat. I managed it by sheer luck.

In my last year at Jefferson I had, like all seniors, one free period every day. It was the custom to spend this time doing some sort of volunteer work that would indicate to the faculty you were endowed with enough of the right school spirit to make them give you a couple of second thoughts when they were handing out recommendations for college scholarships. One day, while I was helping Mr. Pullman's drama group splash paint on some flats they intended to use for a mid-term production of *The Pirates of Penzance,* I got a poke in the ribs from Natie Farkas.

"Now, what's that for?" I said.

"You enjoying this?" Natie said.

"The only other thing open today is kitchen monitor," I said. "At least with paint you know what you're smelling. Why do you ask?"

"I been thinking," Natie said. "Here I am, knocking myself out painting this crap, for what? So some jerk like Pullman or Dean Foote or somebody else will think I'm a great guy and recommend me for a scholarship. Suppose they do? What have I got?"

"You've got some of your college tuition paid somewhere," I said. "Maybe all of it, if you're lucky."

"Suppose I'm lucky, okay. I get a full scholarship," Natie said. "*Then* what have I got?"

Natie and I had been together all through P.S. 188 and J.H.S. 64 as well as Jefferson. I thought I knew him pretty well. Yet there were times, like now, when I couldn't follow his thinking.

"If you've got a full scholarship, you've got your college

212

tuition paid for," I said. "Four years. What more do you want?"

"Food," Natie said.

"Oh, you mean living expenses," I said. "I hear they have all sorts of jobs for scholarship students, stuff you can do between classes to earn your keep. Like waiting on table."

"I've got to do better than that," Natie said. "My old man's got to close the grocery store. Business is lousy. I'm just going to be able to make it through to graduation. I almost had to quit at the end of last term and look for a job. I mean it's just a break I'll be getting a high school diploma at all. The point is what I'll be needing is not a job that'll support me, but a job that'll bring money into the house. I don't think there's any jobs like that on a college campus. Jobs where I mean between classes a guy can earn enough to keep himself going, and also send money home to his folks. So if that's the situation, I ask myself what am I doing on my free period every day polishing Pullman's you know what?"

"What else can you do?" I said.

"I could stop wasting this free period every day and start doing something that will help me get a job after graduation," Natie said. "That's the way my thinking is going, kid, and that's just what I'm going to do."

We did it together, because my thinking, which was not always as good as I would have liked it to be, had the benefit of this assist from Natie.

If business was so bad that Natie's father had to close the grocery store, what was to prevent my father from being fired from the pants shop? As I soon learned, nothing. My father did not have to ask the permission of his

213

boss to attend the graduation exercises, which were held in the afternoon. When he sat in the Jefferson High auditorium, listening to his son deliver the valedictory, my father no longer had a job.

Two weeks later, however, I did. Because what Natie Farkas and I had done with our daily free period during our last three months at Jefferson High was sit in on Mr. Tully's typing and shorthand class.

When I saw the ad in the *Times* that said "Male secretary wanted," I could type ninety words a minute, touch system, and I could take down almost the same number of words per minute in Pitman shorthand. The first thing I did when I read the ad was run over to Natie's house.

"He's not home," Mrs. Farkas said. "He went out a little while ago."

This surprised me. I had bought the *Times* in Mr. Gordon's candy store a few minutes before seven o'clock. Job hunting in 1930 was an early-morning business. It was now not quite a quarter after seven. Where could Natie have gone so early?

"I don't know," Mrs. Farkas said. "What did you want to see him about?"

"There's a job in the paper," I said. "Male secretary. I wanted to tell him about it. I thought we could go uptown together."

"You mean there's two jobs?" Mrs. Farkas said.

"No, just one," I said. "They want a male secretary. I thought Natie and I, we'd go and apply together."

"But what good would that do?" Mrs. Farkas said. "If there's only one job?"

I hadn't thought of that. As I've already pointed out, my thinking was not always as good as I would have liked

214

it to be. Natie and I had been friends for a long time. It was because of Natie that I was now able to type and write shorthand. We had learned together. My first thought, when I saw the ad, was that Natie and I would apply for the job together. Anything else would have been—well, I didn't know what anything else would have been, because anything else had not occurred to me.

It did, on the way uptown. I had plenty of time to let things occur to me, because I walked. In 1930 a subway ride cost only a nickel, but that word "only" is relative. One Sunday not too long ago I heard my mother talking to one of her young neighbors about The Great Depression.

"It's hard to explain," my mother said. "How can I tell you that in 1930 a nickel looked so big, most of the time you couldn't see around the edges?"

I didn't have many nickels, but my shoes were still good, because my father had bought me a new pair for graduation, and doing boy scout pace—fifty steps running, fifty steps walking—I could get up to Seventh Avenue and Thirty-fourth Street from where we lived on Lewis corner Fourth in a little less than an hour. The ad said "Call for interview at 8:30." Even if I didn't rush, I could get there in plenty of time, but I did rush: sixty steps running and forty steps walking. This made me sweat a little, but it didn't stop me from thinking, and what I was thinking was that going uptown by myself to apply for this job made me a rat. No doubt about that. But it made me a rat only technically.

After all, I had gone to Natie's house first. It wasn't my fault that Natie had not been home. And I was in the clear on another count: I had given Natie's mother the address from the ad. In case he came home, she could tell him to follow me.

As it turned out, she didn't have to. When I came into the outer office of Maurice Saltzman & Company, my friend Natie was crossing to the door on his way out.

"Don't waste your time," he said. "These bastards want a real shark. A hundred twenty words a minute."

He was gone before I could answer, and that was just as well, because the answer that had taken shape instantly in my mind was: "Why, you son of a bitch!"

Friendships died fast in 1930, and that was bad. Far worse, however, was the way they were buried. Natie Farkas and I never again spoke a word to each other. Not because he had seen the ad in the *Times* before I had, and he had hot-footed it uptown without telling me. That was bad enough, but that could have been repaired with almost any sort of lie, because I would have accepted any sort of lie, and so would Natie. What killed the friendship was something that, in 1930, nobody on God's green earth could have repaired. Not in New York City in that strange year when Natie Farkas and I were growing up: I got the job.

Not because I could take a hundred and twenty words a minute. I think I got the job for the same reason a lot of people get jobs: the man who had the power to give me the job had obviously reached the point where he was sick and tired of interviewing people for it. Also, I think, because I was tall for my age, and I've always looked stronger than I am.

What Maurice Saltzman wanted was not a male secretary. He wanted an office boy, a valet, a bodyguard, a chauffeur, a receptionist, a janitor, and an apprentice accountant who could also, when it became necessary, take a letter in shorthand and type it neatly. I don't know how Mr. Saltzman knew I could perform any of these duties. He put me through no tests. All he did, after staring at me with a small frown for several minutes, was ask how much I expected to be paid. I took a long chance, hoping my greed would not cause him to throw me out of the office, and said, "Twelve dollars a week, sir."

"We'll see," said Mr. Saltzman. He meant, I learned six days later when I opened my first pay envelope, eleven dollars a week.

This was more than I expected. It was almost more than I needed. The funny thing about growing up in The Great Depression was that while money was the most important factor in your life, because without money you didn't eat, it wasn't really money you worried about. What you worried about was what you were going to be, what you were going to do with your life, and whether, by doing what you were doing now, you were on the right track.

Speaking for myself, I had grave doubts. My guess is that I wouldn't be far wrong if I spoke for any young man of seventeen who had started work at that time in the offices of Maurice Saltzman & Company. The company dealt in disaster.

Mr. Saltzman and his "Company," a man named Ira Bern, had a number of clients whose books their staff audited for a fee every month. The main income of the firm, however, came from its bankruptcy work.

When it became clear in those days that a businessman was foundering, the people to whom he owed money would get together, form a creditors' committee, and hire a firm of accountants to audit the unfortunate man's books. If the audit indicated that there were enough assets to pay the creditors a respectable fraction of their debts—in 1930, thirty cents on the dollar was considered very respectable —the creditors' committee would liquidate the business and divide up the proceeds. If the audit revealed even a hint of fraud on the part of the unfortunate businessman, or merely that there were not enough cents on the dollar worth distributing, the creditors' committee would resort to the law and throw him into bankruptcy. The entire process of hunting down assets would then be repeated by a government receiver, with one significant exception: if there actually was fraud, and if it violated a federal law— let's say the poor sap had sent his financial statement through the mails, for instance—he could be prosecuted, he usually was, and he went to jail.

There was, in all this, a great deal of work for accountants. The size of their fees depended on the number of men assigned to perform the audit. I cannot remember ever hearing a member of a creditors' committee or a receiver's staff question the skill or experience of a man working on an audit. I don't think they cared. All they wanted was a finished report, and they wanted it fast. Maurice Saltzman & Company was noted for its speed. This was undoubtedly the reason why they got so much of this work.

It was also the reason why Mr. Saltzman and Mr. Bern —when I was not out having rubber heels put on their shoes, sweeping their offices, bringing them hot pastrami sandwiches, or typing their letters—sent me along on so many of these bankruptcy audits. It didn't matter that when I went to work for them I did not know a debit from a credit. The more men they put on the job, the bigger the bill they could send the referee. Besides, a boy who had been valedictorian of his class couldn't be totally hopeless. The chances are I would learn. I did.

The first thing I learned is that "bankruptcy" is one of those words, like "war," that you have heard all your life and think you understand until you actually become involved with the process the word is intended to identify. When the shock begins to recede, you begin to wonder about the value of the dictionary as a preparation for life.

Before I went to work for Maurice Saltzman & Company, in my circle—which in those days did not extend very far beyond my schoolyard, the Troop 224 meeting room, and a couple of street corners—the word "bankruptcy" had always had humorous overtones. It was always used in connection with some sharp character out of the tabloids—a spendthrift movie actress, a notorious gigolo—who had run up enormous bills, usually for immoral purposes, and then thrown himself on the mercy of the foolishly merciful government to escape paying them. How this was done I didn't know, and neither did the person who was telling the story about the sharp character. It never occurred to me to ask. What I was interested in were the details of the debaucheries that had cost so much money, and that's what the narrator was interested in, too. In all these stories, the word bankruptcy was no more than a punch line. Get ready, now: this is where you laugh. I always did.

Why not? There was always in these stories of the shrewd manipulator who managed in the end to thumb his nose at the law-abiding world some element—perverted, it is true—of the last coming out first. You had to admire a man who could do that. You had to chuckle at the discomfiture of those who had so much money that they were foolish enough to lend some of it. Even the euphemism for bankruptcy sounded funny. It was known as "taking the bath."

So many people were doing it in 1930 that I must have had a lot of laughs during those early days with Maurice Saltzman & Company. If I did, I don't remember them. What I remember is my first bankruptcy audit. Associated Leather Arts Corporation, somewhere down on Leonard Street. Manufacturers of wallets, handbags, belts, and briefcases. "A big one," was the word in the offices of Maurice Saltzman & Company. "A big one" meant liabilities of over a hundred thousand. The receiver was in a hurry. To do the audit Mr. Saltzman sent six men, led by our best senior, Mr. Jablow. I had finished my chores in the office, so Mr. Saltzman sent me along as a junior.

Juniors went down on the bill to the receiver at thirty-five dollars a day. At a salary of eleven dollars a week for a six-day week, Mr. Saltzman was paying me $1.83 a day. For anybody who has trouble with simple arithmetic, I will do the subtraction. A dollar eighty-three from thirty-five dollars leaves $32.17 profit to Mr. Saltzman on my mere physical presence in the Leather Arts Corporation loft on Leonard Street. No wonder I was excited. I had never before realized how valuable I was. I couldn't wait for the custodian to unlock the door and admit us to the otherwise deserted premises.

Mr. Jablow and the more seasoned members of the staff went directly to the bookkeeper's office to sort out the books and records. But I had never before been in a manufacturer's loft. Disregarded by Mr. Jablow and the others, I moved on across the salesroom into the factory. It was a huge room, dotted with sewing machines and cutting tables. Not surprisingly, it smelled strongly of leather. I was staring about, trying to imagine what the room looked like when people were working at the machines and tables, when Mr. Jablow came up behind me.

"What are you looking for?"

"Nothing," I said. Then, because even to me that sounded foolish, I said, "I mean I was looking for the can."

"Then what are you standing around in the middle of the room for?" Mr. Jablow said irritably. "You're old enough to know they always build those things up against a wall."

The premises of the Associated Arts Leather Corporation were no exception. Except in one respect. When I opened the door, I did something that still makes me blush. I let out a scream. Just like a frightened girl. Not because the man hunched up in a crooked squatting posture on the tiled floor was sitting in a pool of his own blood. I had seen blood before. I had seen dead people, too. On East Fourth Street privacy was a difficult enough state even for the living to achieve. What I had never seen before was a slit throat. The accounts of suicides and murders I had read in newspapers and books all seemed to indicate that the process was neat. Why shouldn't it be? The word "slit" sounds neat. On my first bankruptcy audit in 1930 I learned it isn't. Things stick out.

I learned a great many other things, among them that bankrupts don't always solve their personal problems with a razor, and I learned fast. By the time the DuValle's Men's and Boys' Pants Corporation took the bath, I had been working for Maurice Saltzman & Company for less than four months, but I had picked up enough to make my boss feel he could get away with listing me on the bill to the receiver as a semi-senior, fifty dollars a day. This was not quite as crooked as it sounds.

The DuValle Men's and Boys' Pants Corporation had been inconsiderate enough to attract the annoyed attention of its creditors when the staff of Maurice Saltzman & Company was already spread dangerously thin on three other audits. But Mr. Saltzman could not turn down a job that promised a nice fat fee. The DuValle Men's and Boys' Pants Corporation was a "real big one." Real big ones meant liabilities of over two hundred thousand.

"We'll do like this," Mr. Saltzman said to his partner, Ira Bern. "You take the kid, here, and you go down and get started. I'll try to skin off some men from the other audits."

This was a common practice, and when I first heard Mr. Saltzman use the phrase, I thought he meant "skim off." But I was wrong. The verb "to skin," in 1930, meant "to cheat." Perhaps it still does. Anyway, Mr. Bern and I took a taxi to the DuValle quarters on Lafayette Street, near Astor Place. In 1930, as I recall, the only people who took taxis were Howard Hughes and accountants who were ordered not to lose a minute in completing a bankruptcy audit.

The DuValle loft was a dreary place, cramped, poorly lighted, and dirty. It was difficult for me to imagine creditors trusting to the tune of more than two hundred thousand dollars anybody who functioned in such disreputable quarters. The creditors had done just that, however, and as Mr. Bern and I worked away at the books in the deserted office, it soon became apparent that they had done more. The DuValle liabilities were probably closer to three hundred thousand.

"Boy, oh, boy," Mr. Bern said in mid-afternoon. "I wish we could skin off some of the other guys for this job. Looks like we're on a sockdologer, kid."

Mr. Bern's wish was not granted. On the contrary. Shortly before four o'clock he was himself skinned off, by a phone call from Mr. Saltzman. Before he hurried off uptown, Mr. Bern said, "Keep going till you got the cash payments schedule wrapped up, then you can knock off for the day. Don't forget to lock up, and I'll meet you here in the morning."

I had the cash payments schedule wrapped up by five o'clock. I got out the ring of keys left in our charge by the referee's custodian and started trying to figure out how to use them. It seems to me everything was complicated in 1930, even locking up a loft on Lafayette Street. I was just getting the hang of the two steel crossbars, which one of the keys released on a heavy spring, when a fist hammered on the outside of the door.

"Anybody in there?"

The voice sounded familiar. I pulled open the heavy door, and saw why. Facing me was Pinny Slater, who had been in my and Natie Farkas' class at Jefferson High. He was clearly just as surprised to see me as I was to see him.

"What the hell you doing here?" he said.

I pointed to the referee's notice the custodian had pasted on the door. "This place is bankrupt," I said.

"I know that," Pinny said impatiently. "Don't you think I can read? What I'm asking, what's that got to do with you?"

"I'm doing the audit," I said. "For the receiver."

223

This was not strictly true, of course. But I had never liked Pinny Slater, and this was the first time I had ever had a chance to say anything to him that would cut through the snooty attitude that had made me not the only guy at Jefferson High who hated his guts. It worked. Pinny's good-looking features, always arranged in a pattern of supercilious elegance that made you want to punch it off his face, rearranged themselves in a commonplace, even a proletarian, look of astonishment.

"You're doing what?" he said.

"I work for a firm of accountants," I said. "Maurice Saltzman & Company, up on Thirty-fourth Street. They got hired by the Receiver in Bankruptcy to audit the books of this firm."

"And you're doing it?" Pinny said. "Alone?"

"No, of course not," I said. "Nobody can do an audit this size by himself. My boss sent down a whole staff, the way he always does on a big audit, but they got called off on some other emergency job, so the boss left me down here to finish up on my own."

Without asking permission, Pinny came in across the threshold. That, too, was typical. He was the sort of cocky bastard to whom the word please was a one-way street: a syllable other people used to him, never the other way around. I think it's only fair to say at this point that my reasons for disliking Pinny were many, but they all grew out of a single, hard economic fact: Pinny Slater was a rich kid. There were quite a few at Jefferson High.

It was one of the oldest public high schools in the city. As a result, it had accumulated the sort of scraps of reputation that often are the result of nothing more than longevity but are frequently interpreted as traditions. One of these was that you couldn't get a better secondary school education in New York City no matter how much money your father was willing to pay for it. Frankly, I had always believed this. In 1930 I certainly felt as well educated as any kid who had attended an expensive prep school. This conviction may have been based on the fact that I had never known a prep school kid. But I had known Pinny Slater and a few others at Jefferson High who, according to locker room gossip, sat down every night to meals served by servants. I never quite believed this about the others, but I believed it about Pinny Slater.

He was delivered at the front door of Jefferson High every morning in a long black car driven by a man in uniform. I think what impressed us most was not the uniformed chauffeur, but the glass window that separated the driver on the front seat from Pinny on the back. I seem to recall an explanation for the manner in which Pinny came to school. His family lived at Seventy-second Street and Central Park West, and Jefferson High was located at Fifty-ninth Street and Tenth Avenue. There was, the explanation went, no form of public transportation between these two points, and Pinny was too lazy to get out of bed in time to walk. The chauffeur and the car were on hand anyway, waiting to deliver Pinny's father to his office downtown, around nine-thirty, so why not run Pinny over to school an hour earlier? The only person to whom this could make any difference was the chauffeur, and all you had to do was watch Pinny in action for a while to realize that nobody in the Slater family was going to lose any sleep over that chauffeur's extra hour of work. What I mean is this: while I don't remember how the other rich kids at Jefferson High handled being rich, you could never forget how Pinny Slater handled it. He rubbed it in.

Watching him wander around the deserted loft of the DuValle Men's and Boys' Pants Corporation, peering at things as though he owned the joint, a pain that was still fresh nudged me into a bitter summation of my feelings: Pinny Slater would never lose a friend the way I had lost Natie Farkas.

"I didn't know you were an accountant," Pinny said.

"I guess there are a lot of things you don't know."

My attempt at sarcasm went over his head. Either that, or Pinny hadn't heard it. That irritatingly handsome face was creased in a puzzled scowl so deep that I suddenly had the feeling Pinny was surrounded by an invisible fence, something he had put up to keep away outside noises while he concentrated on working out a difficult problem inside his head.

"Listen," he said abruptly. "What makes a man go bankrupt?"

"What?" I said.

Pinny flipped out his hand irritably in a large scooping gesture, as though he were gathering up the entire loft to support his question.

"A place like this," he said. "It goes along for years, grinding out money for the man who owns it. Then one day, boom. It stops. How come?"

At once I forgot that I hated his guts. Indeed, I had a sudden feeling of affection for him. By asking a question I could answer, Pinny had handed me a small piece of something he'd had all his life: the gift of superiority.

226

"There's all kinds of reasons," I said. "A guy overexpands, and his sales don't keep up with what he laid out. Or the thing he's been selling goes out of style. People stop buying it."

"Don't tell me people have stopped buying pants," Pinny said.

"No, those two reasons, they don't apply in this case," I said. "This outfit, DuValle, what knocked this firm out of the box was rowboats and canoes."

"Rowboats and what?" Pinny said.

I liked the quick interest in his voice. I enjoyed the way he was looking at me, as though he was seeing me for the first time.

"A man's got a business," I said. "Say like this one, DuValle. He draws a certain amount of money out of it regularly. Enough to live a certain way, let's say. Then the way he lives, that changes suddenly. He needs more money."

"What do you mean changes?" Pinny said. "How?"

"Say he starts gambling heavily," I said. "Maybe in the market. Maybe at the track. Or he starts keeping a chorus girl. Or he goes into some other racket on the side. A secret venture, sort of. Like maybe he's backing a night club for his chorus girl and he doesn't want anybody to know about it. Like his wife, for instance. Whichever one it is, all these things cost more money than our man has been drawing out of his business up to now, so he starts drawing out more. Naturally, he doesn't want anybody to know he's drawing out more, especially if he has partners, so he covers it up by having the checks drawn to phony names or phony things. After a while he's drawn off more than the

227

business can stand, and the business can't pay its bills, so his creditors throw him into bankruptcy."

"But what's that got to do with rowboats and canoes?" Pinny said.

"It's a joke," I said. "A funny name accountants give to this milking the business secretly. Here, look." I pointed to the yellow sheets of analysis paper on which I had just wrapped up the DuValle cash payments schedule. "For the last two years the guy who owns DuValle has been drawing big fat checks every week to someone called D. G. Crystal. On the stubs, in the checkbooks we've been auditing, the explanation for what the money is for, he's written in things like, look." I ran my finger down the left-hand column on the top yellow sheet. "*Forecast analysis,*" I read aloud. "*Chandeliers. Luggage racks. Statistical study.* And so on." I looked up. "You get the point?"

"Chandeliers," Pinny said slowly, sending his glance around the dirty loft. "Luggage racks. You mean how come they're spending all that money on chandeliers and luggage racks?"

"*And* forecast analysis," I said, nodding. "*And* statistical study, whatever those things are. To us, to an accountant, it looks suspicious. These things are just words used to cover up what the money was really being used for. Like suppose, instead of saying chandeliers and luggage racks, he'd written on the check stubs the money was going out to buy rowboats and canoes. It makes just as much sense. Why should a company that manufactures pants spend all that money to buy a lot of rowboats and canoes? Get the joke?"

Pinny didn't answer. He was scowling down at the yellow sheets.

228

"You mean you make a list of all these checks?" he said finally. "The money that went out for all these suspicious things? And you do what with it?"

"We turn it over to the receiver," I said. "It's part of our audit. Our report says here, from such and such a date to such and such a date, the owners of this business deflected so much and so much of the company's funds into channels we can't explain. The receiver then drags the guy into court and makes him explain. What did you do with the money? they want to know—and he better tell them."

"But you guys?" Pinny said. "The accountants. You don't know?"

I laughed and said, "What do you think we are? Dumb? Of course we know. We just don't put it in the written report. We can't say a man is a crook even though we're damn sure he is. Not in writing, anyway. What we do, we give the receiver our opinion, where we believe the money went, and the receiver tells the lawyers, and they get it out of the guy when they get him into court."

"This firm," Pinny said. "DuValle. The guy that owns it. This outfit's rowboats and canoes. The money he milked out of the business so it went bankrupt. What did this man spend the stolen money on?"

There was something in Pinny's voice, a the-kidding-is-finished note, that brought me back to earth. I had the feeling that he had been treating me like an equal because he'd wanted to get something out of me. Now that he had it, or most of it, his impatient arrogance would not allow him to continue the pretense. The man for whom I'd had a sudden feeling of affection was gone. I was back with the kid whose guts I'd hated at Jefferson High. He might have addressed

229

his question to the chauffeur who used to deliver him to school every morning.

"Who wants to know?" I said and, in my anger, I realized there was a lot more I wanted to say. "What the hell are you doing here, anyway?" I said. "What gives you the right to follow me down here from my office and come busting in here and ask a lot of questions? In fact, what are you doing in New York? Why aren't you up at Yale or Harvard or Princeton? Cramming away at your courses in how to clip bond coupons without soiling the lifted pinky?"

"It happens to be N.Y.U.," Pinny said coldly. "And what right I've got to come busting in here, who the hell do you think owns the DuValle Men's and Boys' Pants Corporation, you stupid little son of a bitch?"

He shouldn't have said that. I am not stupid. Anyway, in 1930 I didn't think I was. And I am not a son of a bitch. More accurately, I hadn't yet learned how to be one. It was Pinny Slater who helped me take my first big stride toward that achievement, and he did it on that day in 1930, at that particular moment. Because at that particular moment a scrap of information that had been lying around in the back of my mind all day now stood up and started to scream inside my head: the major stockholder of the DuValle Men's and Boys' Pants Corporation, the bankrupt whose books Mr. Bern and I had been auditing, the man who had signed all those nice fat rowboats and canoes checks made out to D. G. Crystal was named Ernest Slater.

"You mean this is your father's firm?" I said. "Ernest Slater is your old man?"

"You're not as dumb as you look," Pinny said. "At least you're able to put two and two together. I guess you have to be able to do at least that much, to get a job with an

230

accountant. Now let's see what else your big brain is able to do. This D. G. Crystal. The one all those checks were made out to. What's that?"

Suppose Pinny had been a nice guy? Or suppose he had been like the other rich kids at Jefferson High? Someone you were jealous of, but did not actively resent? Or suppose, being what he was, Pinny had merely been a little more self-controlled at that particular moment on that particular day in that particular year of The Great Depression?

What I mean is this: if Pinny hadn't called me a stupid little son of a bitch, would I have answered his question as I now answered it? Truthfully?

I like to think I wouldn't have. But I'm not sure. A number of things that you always considered absolutes, things about which it never crossed your mind there could be two points of view, vanish once you master the not too difficult skill of being a son of a bitch.

"D. G. Crystal," I said, speaking just as coldly as he had spoken to me, aware of why I was uttering every single word, "is a female. Girl or woman, I don't know. I can only judge from the indorsement on the checks made out to her. My boss and I agree it does not look like a man's handwriting. For two years D. G. Crystal has been receiving checks from the chief stockholder of the DuValle Men's and Boys' Pants Corporation. He may have been giving her money in other forms for longer than that. I don't know. All I know as an accountant is what the audit shows. It shows that for two years large sums of money have been milked out of the DuValle corporation by its president into the hands of this female. Is there anything else you'd like to know?"

"Yes," Pinny said icily. "Since when has keeping a dame

231

become so expensive it can bankrupt a firm as big as this?"

"I didn't say the president of DuValle was keeping her," I said. "That's only one of many possible interpretations. Assuming your interpretation is correct, though, I don't know why this dame should be so expensive. I'm just an accountant. Accountants can learn a lot from studying a man's books and records. One thing an accountant can't learn from a ledger is the kind of mistress a guy has got."

"I'll bet a good accountant could," Pinny said.

I didn't need that extra prod. But it helped. This guy had asked for it. Okay. I'd give it to him. In spades.

"You happen to be talking to a good one," I said. "As a matter of fact, there are a few things along that line that I have learned." Actually, it was Mr. Berns who had learned them. As we had worked away, piling up the figures, he had given me his experienced guesses. I now passed them on as my own. "Our examination of the canceled checks made out to this D. G. Crystal," I said, "indicate that the biggest ones she indorsed over to Parke, Turner, and Rhodes, the Wall Street brokers. In plain English, which I don't know that you ever managed to learn at Jefferson High and maybe they don't teach at N.Y.U., the DuValle corporation was not only paying her rent. It was paying her gambling debts in the market, and she seems to have been a lousy gambler. Anything else?"

"Yes, one more thing," Pinny said. "Where can I find this—this whatever her name is?"

"Why don't you ask your father?" I said.

"I can't," Pinny said. "Since he disappeared from home on Thursday, the day this bankruptcy petition was filed against him. But I want to see him. I've got some questions to ask him."

"Like what?" I said.

"Like how come my tuition at N.Y.U. hasn't been paid, and why our rent, my mother's and mine, it's so far behind, the landlord is evicting us. We're broke, my mother and I. Flat. I want to ask my father how come. Since my mother and I don't know where he is, I thought I'd come down here and see if I couldn't find out where he's hiding out. It looks like I've run into somebody who knows."

In actual fact, I didn't. Any more than I knew that D. G. Crystal was a chorus girl. As far as my actual first-hand knowledge went, she could have been the Queen of Sheba, or even a he. What I knew were not really facts. What I knew was how to make certain guesses that almost always turned out to be right. I had learned this from working with Mr. Berns and Mr. Jablow and the rest of the staff of Maurice Saltzman & Company. Some of these guesses I had already, in my anger, passed on to Pinny Slater. Now, all at once, anger gave way to uneasiness.

I had passed on these guesses to a rich kid I hated because he had advantages I'd never known. Now, all at once, I grasped that he was no longer a rich kid. When you got right down to it, Pinny now had less advantages than I had. At least I had a job. It occurred to me that now, for the first time in his life, Pinny Slater was in a position to suffer the pain of losing a friend the way I had lost Natie Farkas. It gave me a funny little feeling in my heart.

"Listen," I said. "I don't really know where this D. G. Crystal lives."

Perhaps he sensed a change in my voice. At any rate, Pinny sounded quite different, too, as he said, "You know everything else."

"Not really," I said. "All those things I told you, they're

233

just guesses. They're guesses based on facts and figures turned up by the audit, and they may prove to be right, but they could also prove to be wrong. They're just guesses."

"All I'm asking is make a guess about where this girl lives," Pinny said. "It might prove to be right, like your other guesses." He hesitated. It didn't occur to me until a couple of moments later that he was pulling himself together to make a special effort. "I really want to see my father," Pinny said. "Please."

The single syllable did the trick. The word that had always been a one-way street, a word other people used to him, never the other way around, had become a thoroughfare on which Pinny Slater had no more privileges than I had.

"Look," I said. "I'm sorry about all those things I told you. I mean about your father. They may not be true. I don't want you to be sore at him because of my guesses."

"I'm not sore at him," Pinny said. "I'm sore at the guys who hired your boss to do this audit. I'm sore at the creditors. It was those bastards put my father into bankruptcy."

"Wait a minute," I said. "They couldn't do anything else. Your father owes them almost three hundred thousand bucks."

"That's nothing compared to what they're going to owe me," Pinny said. The look on my face must have been something to see. Pinny laughed. "I know it sounds crazy," he said. "But I'm going to get those guys. To hell with college. I'm going into my old man's business."

"The pants business?" I said in astonishment.

"You bet the pants business," Pinny said. "I'm going to start a new firm. Men's and boys' pants. It's going to be the biggest pants manufacturing firm this town ever saw. I'm going to buy all my piece goods from these same bastards who just threw my old man into the bath, and when I've run up bills for half a million, maybe even a million, as much credit as I can get, instead of paying them, I'm going to milk off the cash. Rowboats and canoes, boy, rowboats and canoes. And then they can throw me into the bath, too, the way they did my father, and they can whistle for their million bucks, the rotten bastards."

It sounded exactly as he had said it sounded: crazy. Pinny Slater was my age. The notion that a seventeen-year-old boy could start a million-dollar corporation to manufacture pants was a joke. Maybe that's why there was laughter in Pinny's eyes.

"You don't believe me," he said.

Curiously enough, I wasn't sure. It wasn't laughing laughter in his eyes. It was mean laughter. It made me feel that someone who could laugh like that was capable of doing anything.

"It's not that," I said. "It's just that, well, what you just said you're going to do, it'll take years and years."

"I know," Pinny said. "But it'll make my father feel good to hear it. Wherever he is now, he must be feeling the whole world is against him. I'd like to go see him, and tell him what I have in mind. A man hearing a plan like that from his own son, at a time like this, it'll make him feel good. Come on, where does this girl live?"

"Well," I said, "it's only a guess, but here, look at these checks." I picked up the batch of canceled checks Mr. Bern and I had accumulated in our hunt through the Du-Valle records. "You'll notice every one of them is marked on the back with the rubber stamp of the bank where she

235

deposited them. The Northeastern Trade Bank & Trust. It's a small bank. No branches. We run into it on a lot of these audits. Just one office on the street floor of the Saranac Hotel on Seventy-second and Broadway."

"I know the Saranac," Pinny said, his voice lifting in surprise. "It's practically around the corner from where we live at Seventy-second and Central Park West. Just up the block, anyway."

It occurred to me with equal surprise that it was just up the block from his mother, too. I had always assumed that men who kept mistresses kept them as far from their legal homes as they could without creating an inconvenience that took the fun out of the whole expensive enterprise. Apparently Pinny's father, however, had not worried about the fact that on his way into the Saranac to visit D. G. Crystal, he might run into his wife on the street.

"Well," I said, "on these audits, these rowboats and canoes accounts, we find a lot of these kept women live at the Saranac, I don't know why, and they use the Northeastern Trade & Trust because it's convenient, I guess. Right there in the building. So, as I said, while it's only a guess, it seems a pretty good one that you'll find your father at the Saranac Hotel."

"Thanks," Pinny said. He touched my arm briefly, in a curiously inept gesture that puzzled me until I thought about it later: he had apparently never made it before. Certainly not to somebody like me. "Don't look so worried," he said. "I won't tell anybody how I found out. Your job is safe."

"I'm not worrying about that," I said. This was only partially true. "I was thinking about your father," I said. "You're going up there to make him feel good, you say,

236

but I wonder if what you're going to tell him will do the trick."

"Why shouldn't it?"

"What you have in mind, sticking his creditors for a million bucks," I said. "He'll see right away that a thing like that takes years, even assuming it can work. What I mean is, you're going up there to tell him you're planning revenge on the guys who threw him into bankruptcy, but this thing you've got planned, it's an awful slow kind of revenge."

"Maybe on the way uptown I'll think of something quicker," Pinny said.

Apparently he did. The next morning every newspaper in New York reported on its front page that moments after he walked in on his father and his father's mistress at the Hotel Saranac, a seventeen-year-old boy named Pinny Slater shot them both dead.

Years later, after he was paroled, I received a letter from Pinny. It came from Caracas in Venezuela, where, his engraved letterhead indicated, he was in the wine business. My wife, who over the years has heard the story of my life in The Great Depression, thought Pinny could have said a little more. I thought he said enough.

"Pants are slow," he wrote. "Liquor is quicker."

Besides, the printed letterhead answered a question that had puzzled me for years. Pinny was called Pinny because his given name was Pinero. I still wonder who thought that up.

8

"The great business of life is to be, to do, to do without, and to depart."

John, Viscount Morley

On Columbus Day of 1930, Maurice Saltzman & Company enjoyed its most successful day since Mr. Saltzman and Ira Bern founded the firm. On that day the Receiver in Bankruptcy for the Southern District of New York retained the partners to do four bankruptcy audits. Two big ones, one real big one, and one sockdologer. The staff had to go on a seven-day week, and the firm had to do something about it. One of the things they did was raise the salary of Benny Kramer from eleven to thirteen dollars a week. As a result the Kramer family moved from 390 East Fourth Street on the Lower East Side of Manhattan to 1075 Tiffany Street in the Bronx. Mr. and Mrs. Kramer were pleased with their new surroundings. For a while Benny didn't have time to think about it.

About
The Author

JEROME WEIDMAN, who won the Pulitzer Prize for *Fiorello!*, has long been a distinguished novelist, short-story writer, essayist, and playwright. Among Mr. Weidman's seventeen novels are *I Can Get It for You Wholesale, The Enemy Camp, The Sound of Bow Bells,* and this evocation of his youth, *Fourth Street East.* His successes in the theater include *Tenderloin* and *I Can Get It for You Wholesale,* which he adapted for the stage from his own novel of the same name. His courtroom drama, *Ivory Tower,* written in collaboration with James Yaffe, was the American Playwrights Theater selection for 1968 and won the National Council of the Arts Award for that year. He has also won the Drama Critics' Circle Award and the Antoinette Perry ("Tony") Award. His short stories—which have appeared in *The New Yorker,* the *Saturday Evening Post, Harper's, Esquire,* and every other major magazine in this country, England, Canada, Australia, Europe, and Asia—have been collected in six volumes, including *The Horse That Could Whistle "Dixie,"* *The Captain's Tiger,* and *My Father Sits in the Dark.* His best-known travel books and collections of essays are *Letter of Credit, Traveler's Cheque,* and *Back Talk.* His books and plays have been translated into ten languages.

Mr. Weidman and his wife live in New York City—where he was born—and their hope is that their two grown sons will drop in more frequently than they do.

W418f c.4

Weidman, Jerome, 1913–

Fourth Street East.

W418f   c.4

Weidman, Jerome, 1913–

Fourth Street East.
$5.95

NO RENEWALS!

PLEASE RETURN BOOK AND REQUEST AGAIN.